Some love me for what I do. Others hate me, some fear me. Even more will never know that I live this life, a life I chose as much as it chose me, because I believe, delusional or not, that it's my purpose to help those who feel they have nowhere else to turn, on-realm or off.

And to do it as well as I can, as often as I can, for as long as I can. Because one day, maybe soon, maybe today, maybe even right here, right now, my time in this life will end. The story of Angela Hardwicke will have closed its final chapter.

So yeah. As much as I don't like to talk about it, as much as I bury that love, don't say the words out loud because once you can't ever take them back... I live the life I do and take the cases I choose, absorb the pain, navigate the madness, so others don't have to.

I know I'm damaged and imperfect and on the edge of my own demise. But for however much longer my tenure will last, I'm going to keep being this Angela Hardwicke. This is who I am. I'm not gonna stop.

I0664400

— AN ANGELA HARDWICKE SCI-FI THRILLER —

TRIGGER POINT

RUSS COLCHAMIRO

CRAZY 8 PRESS

To Hildy... for all the reasons.

PART I:
THE
PIMP'S CREDO

CHAPTER 1

Another shitty night's sleep.

It ain't easy muddling through life when I can still hear the screams. The way she calls to me from that dark, cold place. Gut shot. Freezing. Alone.

Don't leave me, she says to me in my dreams. My nightmares. *Not like this.*

Then I wake up. I'm paralyzed. I can barely breath, barely even blink. I panic, terrified this is it for me. My forever state. Conscious but immovable. I can't feel my form. Can't wriggle my fingers or shift my eyes side to side.

Have I been roofied? Anesthetized? Magnetized? Hypnotized?

Maybe I've stroked out, my mind active, but unable to speak. Maybe I'm surrounded by everyone I know, yet they can't hear me. Can't even see me. I don't know where I am or what's happening to me. I'm vulnerable. Helpless. Alone.

It's bleeding. I'm bleeding.

I call out in horror, my voice screeching from inside my mind. Or maybe that's someone else. Maybe it's her.

In my mind, or possibly in my waking nightmare, if I'm actually awake, I see—no, not see, I sense—bioluminescent flutters in the darkness, like glowing tips of a moth's wing. Then nothing.

My heart thunders, but I don't know if it's my own heart. Or even my own chest, because I can't move my arms, not even my finger, to check if I'm physically whole. If I exist at all.

It's just me, my consciousness, locked in a box. Or is it a coffin? Am I trapped in a tomb, concealed far enough beneath the soil that no one will ever find me? Buried alive?

No. I see shadows on the wall. Black, morphing figures.

Which means there's light. And if there's light, there's a source—a way out. Which means it's not a box, not a coffin. It's worse.

It's me.

Slowly I regain some visual acuity. I'm able to shift my gaze downward, the outline of my nose on the edge of my visual spectrum. I still can't move my neck or head. But I can see there's nothing physically holding my body down—no ropes, chains, force fields, or power dampeners—except my legs twirled up in the blanket.

I'm in *my* bed, in *my* room.

And my black lab, Page, perched at the foot of the bed, down on her belly, ready to strike. Staring at me. Her black eyes narrow. My throat cinches, my heartbeat detonating in harrowing beats. There's a knot in my gut. Page senses the fear. Staring at me, like she doesn't know me. Seeing a stranger. An invader.

She offers a low, guttural snarl, bares her teeth. The posture of fear. Of violence. My short breaths accelerate, the vibrations traveling to her sensitive paws. She arches her back, her eyes wide with bloodshot rage. Her jaw opens wider, wild saliva dripping from the tips of her flesh-tearing fangs, growing longer. Sharper. Deadlier.

Here it comes. Fuck fuck fuck.

Page, I say although my lips don't move. *Please. Don't. It's me.*

It's too late. She doesn't believe me. My own dog lunges at me, pouncing like an uncoiled rattlesnake. My chest fills with tormented air. I scream.

Until Page licks my face, wags her tail.

I exhale, my breaths now sharp and tight. As if hoisted by a pully system, I'm upright. I'm awake. I check my phone. 6:12 a.m.

Time to meet my pimp.

The last year's been an adjustment.

As a private detective—essentially, a private spy for hire—I work the kinds of cases you might expect. Missing persons, kidnapping, homicide, blackmail, burglary, forgery, arson. But I also take on cases dealing with time travel, shapeshifters, alien races, folds in spacetime, and other entanglements throughout the Cosmos.

I spent fifteen years building up my practice, taking the cases I want to take. But not lately. Ever since I got early release from prison—and the reason I got out early—I've been working for Lionel Tarrish. He's a Lieutenant with the Intergalactic Crime Division.

He's also my mentor. Ish.

He's not quite a friend, but he's not *not* a friend. Although it's difficult to see him these days as anything less than what he is—my warden, parole officer, and for now, my authoritarian boss, all rolled into one. The controller of my fate.

As per the terms of my release, I work the cases he wants, when he wants, until my record is expunged and I'm free and clear. The end date of my term is a bit hazy. Because he hasn't given me one.

But after nearly a year being a good soldier—well, as good as I can muster, given that he's him and I'm me—I got him to agree to let me work some cases on my own again. I still gotta earn. We're now in a kind of one-for-him, one-for-me situation. Today, it's one for me.

Except I don't want to take the case. Not because of the kind of case, but the kind of client. This client.

"Damn, girl." Dante tears at his slab of yolk-slathered meat. He slurps the breakfast food against the edge of his yellow teeth. "You still lookin fine. Mm!"

Dante wanted to meet here at Junebug's Diner. They serve breakfast all day, including their special, steak and eggs with toast, coffee, and two strips of bacon for less than it costs to buy a gourmet latte across the street. It smells... hell, it smells greasy and delicious. But I don't want to eat around him. I don't want to *be* around him. For any reason. So I stick with coffee. Hot. Black. Bitter.

"I don't want to rush you through this heart healthy breakfast," I say, "but I'm on the clock. What do you need?"

Several customers are scattered about, a few at the counter, the others at tables or in booths. A silver bell pings. A plate of cottage cheese, cantaloupe slice, poached egg, and wheat toast slides along the high counter between the kitchen and counter. Order up.

"Don't be tellin me what time it is, girl. I know *exactly* what time it is."

Bald, with a wide forehead and a roadmap of acne pock-marks and divots etched into his pale white face, Dante is dressed in a wrinkled maroon, paisley shirt, purple slacks, black zip boots. Diamond-encrusted rings sparkle on every finger on both hands, except for the thumbs. Each ring is the face of a functioning clock.

Sunlight beams in through the slatted shades, lowered against the long storefront windows to keep from blinding us all.

"You got any idea what a Top Slot earns me? You got *any* idea?"

Most pimps call them the Bottom Bitch. I'll give Dante that. But not much else.

"No. But your best earner's gotta be worth something extra."

Ripping apart a long bacon strip with his incisors, he looks up at me with brown eyes as dead and pitiless as a vampire bat. His bling rings sparkle from the slatted sunlight. Beneath his chin are three healed scars. At first I thought they were from fingernail scratches, but they're so deep, ugly, and jagged, I think they might've been from a three-clawed rake. A garden tool nearly tore out his throat.

"Somethin? Bitch... she *every*thing."

Still twitchy from the nightmare I had, I've got a low-grade headache, and my heart jumps. I don't show it. At least I hope I don't. Inherent stalkers, pimps have a primal sense of weakness in others. I can see his mind at work, compartmentalized. He's talking to me while actively listening to everything around him.

Plotting. Looking for an angle. An edge. To manipulate me, undermine my confidence. To poison my soul with self-doubt, self-loathing. Self-destruction. Searching for a desire he believes is buried just below the surface—that I want to be used, debased. Punished. For all my sins. And for my pleasure.

He's also been eyeing me up and down. It's like I can see inside his mind, him envisioning me in compromising outfits and positions, calculating how much money he could make off me if he had me hooking in his stable.

As a private detective, and a woman, being subjected to leers, gestures, and licking lips are an occupational hazard. I've trained myself to deflect the lurid and unsubtle attempts to sub-jugate me, preventing predators from getting under my skin.

But Dante does. It's as if he can taste the thick puddles of sweat pooling in the small of my back, in my armpits, and behind my knees. Even though I make a living keeping my cool, my body naturally runs hot. I sweat a lot. Layers of deodorant help, but it can only do so much.

However Dante got to be who he is, it didn't come from finishing school. He's a product of the streets. The streets are a product of him. Always keep your guard up. Every situation tee-ters on the precipice of prison, beatings, death, and addiction. Everyone's an enemy or a mark; no one's a friend. So if he's call-ing me, a private investigator, to poke around in his business, there's a story behind it. I don't want to know that story. We have history. It ain't good.

"Why me? You must have people who can look into this."

Dante runs a thick, pink tongue over his teeth, slurps a clump of eggs with tabasco sauce.

"People. *Pss.* Who you shittin? For this? I don't *think* so. Kimmie was a champ, no doubt, no doubt. She could out-earn, out-think, and outhustle any of them other bitches. And she was high-class, too. Nah, man, she didn't work no streets. She was all *concierge*. Five-star hotels and executive *conferences*, if you knowadda mean? And yeah, she kept my other bitches in line. Kept 'em from thinkin they know more 'bout my business than I do. But Kimmie..."

I never thought I'd live to see the day, but he almost looks... sad. Heartbroken. For a flash of time, a microsecond, it's almost as if he isn't a cold-blooded beast who beats and demoralizes women into trading their bodies for money, most of which he keeps for himself.

"All I know is that Kimmie was the best Top Slot I ever ran. Ever. I know I ain't the finest kind, but me and Kimmie... we had somethin special, ya know? She had this way of makin me more... I dunno... human. Found a tiny corner'a my soul that ain't pure poison. Let it breathe a little. Gave it some love, gave it some life. And some mutha!"

He slams an open palm on the table, rattling the plates

and utensils, drawing stares. He lowers his voice, leans in close enough that I can smell the funk on his breath. His open mouth exposes unchewed clumps of food, shredded and dangling from his back teeth like the souls of the girls he turns out.

"And some muthafucka bashed her beautiful brains in. So, nah, Hardwicke. I ain't got people. Not for this one. Losin Kimmie ain't just 'bout business. Oh, it's about that. It's *always* 'bout that. She ain't gonna be easy to replace. But with Kimmie"—his face puckers, lips pursed, nostrils flared—"this one hit me where I *live*."

Tough solve, few reliable witnesses. Unless you get a string of them close enough together to establish a pattern, missing sex worker cases tend to get tossed in a pile so high they topple over. But if there's no one there to hear the files spill onto the floor, do they really make a sound?

"I'd need to talk to your other girls. How many in your stable?"

"Five." He stiffens, closes his eyes, opens them. "Four. Fuck. Them other bitches don't know yet, but soon as they do, they're gonna freak the fuck out. I gotta keep 'em chill. I think one's gonna bounce on me. She's too green. Kimmie ain't got her locked down yet. It's a fragile ecosystem. I don't wantchu pokin around in places I don't wantchu pokin around in."

There's my out. "If I can't do my job... I can't do my job."

Dante digs that big pink tongue of his deep into his gums, thinking on what to do. He makes sure to squish the saliva so it gurgles like a peptic ulcer. Another way to make me feel disgusted.

"You gonna talk to my girls, we gotta have some muthafuckin ground rules. About whatchu ask, what they say, and whatchu hear."

"How's that gonna work?"

"Easy. You hear shit, but you don't *hear* shit. You feel me?"

I manage to crack his code, but I make him work for it. "Not really."

He's clearly exasperated. "You ask them bitches what you gotta ask. But the only person in the *whole fuckin universe* you tell... is me. And if you hear shit 'bout my business ain't got shit to do with Kimmie, you don't hear it, don't know it, can't remember it. Or it's the last muthafuckin thing you hear. Ever."

I stare at him wordlessly, watching him stew. I want to see how he handles himself. The longer I hold out, the more I see the tension lines rise in his face. Like most pimps who know what they're doing, he rules his little fiefdom with draconian fire. He needs to be in control. Always.

"*Ohh,*" I say finally, as if I've suddenly come to an important realization. "Yeah. I feel you. I can hear shit, but I can't *hear* shit."

Dante exhales. His shoulders relax. "Ex*zactly.*"

But control is an illusion. A parlor game. I see how he plays it. And countermoves.

"Sorry, Dante. I'm working other cases. I don't know how deep I can chase this."

With weary pimp eyes, Dante leans back in the booth. A man who's been up all night, he chuckles, a disturbing combination of amusement and threat. Shorter than I'd remembered but thick as a bull, he stretches his arms at the shoulders and cups his clock-ringed hands behind the backrest.

With his thick left hand, he uses the edge of a matchbook like a toothpick, prying a lump of bacon fat from between his two large front teeth. He makes a smacking sound, spits the gristle and saliva flecks on the table. They land in front of me. A droplet of his saliva hits my cheek. I wipe it off.

"You gonna work this muthafucka the rest of your life, that's what it takes."

Just like a pimp. Always looking to dominate, always on the hustle.

"Why would I do that?"

Dante rolls his neck, surveying the diner, and through the large window, studying the foot traffic. Looking for another angle. Another edge. Just like me. He ignores my inquiry.

"And it better not take that long, you feel me? Or that day's gonna be up your skinny white ass like an early sunrise. Inevitable, and rising from the dark." He leans to one side, pops his hip. From his trouser pocket he produces a star drive with a silver edge, slides it across the table. He smirks, conveying that my choice in taking this case is no choice at all. "Enough credits on there to getcha started, and then some. You on the payroll,

effective right... fuckin... now. Hit me soon as you know shit.
Make me *one* on speed dial."

Dante doesn't know this about me, but I'm hurting for credits. With Tarrish making me work off my debt at barely subsis-
tence level, I need the gig. Any gig. Badly. I can't let Dante sense
that about me. So I leave the drive on the table, all that money.

I haven't been this desperate for a payday since I first got
started in this racket. Me holding out is a power play. Not a
strong or good one, but a play, nonetheless. I take the money
too quickly, he knows he's got me. That happens, if I let him
stick his hooks in my soul like that, he might actually have me.
I leave it too long, he knows I'm trapped in my head, indecisive,
unsure what to do. In which case, he's also got me.

I take a sip of my coffee, study the diner. It's circular, win-
dowfront along most of the circumference, except to my left.
The counter, and behind it, the double swinging doors into the
kitchen. I don't recall being here before, and yet, it feels familiar
somehow.

Did I bring Owen here for pancakes once? I have a vague
recollection. Doesn't matter. I can't stall any longer. I take the
star drive, plug it into my phone. Confirmed. Credits are there.

"Besides," Dante says, getting up from the booth. He leans
over to intimidate me, curls his thick right hand into a closed
fist. Each of the diamond-encrusted clock rings sparkle in my
eyes. "You owe me. I been waiting to collect that muthafuckin
chit for *years*. I ain't sure when or where it would happen or how
long it would take. But you listen here, woman, and you listen
good. It's the Pimp's Credo—every debt gets paid, one way or
another. We both knew that bill was comin due. And that day,
Angela Hardwicke, is today."

He holds his icy stare, then eases back and smiles like we're
old friends. I notice a few patrons noticing us, but they know
better than to get involved. With a hop in his gait so practiced
it's become muscle memory, Dante nods to the waitress, directs
her to give me the check. He struts toward the door.

"I expect an update. On the regular. I gotta come looking for
you, it ain't gonna be me that comes knockin. *That's* what my
people are for."

CHAPTER 2

The problem is, I really do owe Dante.

Once upon a time he did me a kindness, at a time when I wouldn't accept kindness from anyone, no matter who offered, and when I most needed it. And let me be clear. Dante doesn't do *kindness*. He makes investments, sees angles, plays the moment. Like he played me.

It makes me want to vomit, wakes me up in a cold sweat, knowing that Dante Maurice Browning kept me from making the biggest mistake of my life. Probably *saving* my life. Owing him makes my skin crawl. But like he said, all debts need to be paid.

One way or another.

I work the case. Nóirín Alton-Hughes. Top Slot. Bottom Bitch. Street name, Kimmie. Thirty-seven-years-old. Five-foot-seven, 128 pounds give or take, dirty blonde hair, green eyes. Single, no kids. High-class sex worker. Deceased. Found in her apartment, skull bashed in. Last seen alive at the Fiasco, the second-floor bar at the Pointe Class hotel.

Dante gave me a set of keys to her apartment. The police had already been through there, but they almost always forget something. On the books, for tax purposes, Kimmie is a self-employed escort. Nothing illegal about it. Unless there's a proffer of sex for money, but that's not part of her business model. Not officially.

The detective assigned to her murder, Joanna Olin, is smart. Smart enough to know Nóirín was a prostitute named Kimmie, and that, more likely than not, that's why she was killed. Detective Olin is also on Dante's payroll. So I'm working this case with Olin whether we want to or not. I'm supposed to head over to Kimmie's apartment to do a secondary walk-through with her, but Olin got called to work a double homicide involving an elementary school teacher and her wife. For now, I'm on my own.

Even with a rush order, the tox screen won't be back for a week or so, depending on how backed up the lab is. Olin's report notes a broken bottle of white wine on the floor next to Kimmie, as well as a half-smoked joint, and the broken heel on her left shoe. According to the forensic tech who worked the scene, with Kimmie's position and angle on the floor, blood pooling, type, and degree of wound, and with no defensive wounds, everything points to a single blow to the back of the head. A slip-and-fall.

Olin said as much. But Dante insists it's murder. He's almost certainly holding out, keeping key details away from me until I prove I'm working the case for real. But I've taken his money, so it's the case I'm working.

I should've eaten something, my headache lightly *whumming* in my left temple. But after sitting with Dante, my stomach's too tight. Can't keep anything down. I buy a bottle of water from a street vendor, and before I can think about it, I've guzzled the whole thing. Pushing past the wave of nausea, I'm panting like after a five-mile run. I was more dehydrated than I realized.

A light autumn breeze washes over me, the streetscape a cacophony of urban activity in the heart of E-Town, the core city in Eternity. The cosmic realm whose fundamental purpose is to serve the ongoing needs of the physical Universe—designing galaxies, building planets, reorganizing asteroid fields, stitching up critical tears in the fabric of spacetime.

The realm's infrastructure and ecosystem changes for us down at street level, with advanced technology being integrated into everyday life faster than we can keep up. And all at the discretion of the Minders of the Universe.

The ones with the real power.

Speaking of discretion, I text Tarrish about my new case. Normally he takes his sweet ole time getting back to me, if at all. Because when you're one of the top cops on-realm, there's rarely a moment when someone, somewhere, isn't vying for your attention. But this time he responds within seconds. Reminding me, again, of our arrangement. As if I need reminding.

This is a one-for-you. Cuz I LET you. If I need you working a one-for-me, you drop yours ASAP and do mine. No bullshit. Don't fuck around.

I text him back, *"aww"* with a fluttering eyelash heart and kissy face emoji. For some reason, he doesn't text back.

Though I hate having Tarrish's boot on my neck, it beats prison. Being back on the street, walking the city, neighborhood by neighborhood, avenue by avenue, block by block, soaking up the smells, the sounds, the frenetic energy, absorbing the relentless rattle and hum through pure osmosis, is what makes me feel alive.

Cool breeze at my back, I walk through the urban carnival and past the monorail's sloping concrete legs and platforms supporting the chrome tube whisking passengers from one end of E-Town to the other.

It's difficult to remember the days without them, but the city's become overrun with 3-D billboards, augmentation centers, the metaverse, and security drones, the digital realm bleeding into the physical one to a point where I can't always tell them apart.

It's progress, though. Progress. That's what they say. Challenging the impossible until it becomes possible. Yet in our quest to move forward, to advance our technologies, I often wonder if the actual goal is to drive us the other way. Maybe that's just my delightful brand of cynicism. Or maybe that's the realm we actually live in now.

I call Whistler, just to check in. Our relationship has got ten... sidetracked.

It's my own damn fault. Whistler and I worked a case last year on a galaxy cruise ship. It went to hell. Fast. I ended up killing a woman—if anyone deserved it, she did—but I did it in front of Tarrish. That I also helped save hundreds of lives is the reason he arranged for my release into his custody, with the chance to clear my record.

But until I'm no longer Tarrish's indentured servant, my agency—the agency I founded, built, and grew—was placed into quasi-receivership. In the name of Eric Whistler. My former protégé, ten years my junior. My current partner. My—I choke on the word just thinking about it—boss. Temporarily.

Truth is, Whistler and I don't work many cases together these days. He pretty much runs the agency on his own, taking whichever cases he wants, while Tarrish has had me infiltrating a criminal intergalactic Guild. Whistler's been working the Guild, too, from another angle—he's the one who cracked the case open to begin with—but it's been his choice.

An over-eager beaver with no experience who I found and trained and who until a year ago was my employee, Whistler is, as an outside consultant, getting paid by the ICD five times what I am to work the same case. How do you like that shit casserole? I think Tarrish is overpaying Whistler on purpose, another way to stick it to me.

I guess I'm working for two pimps.

In Tarrish-like fashion, Whistler doesn't answer my call. I leave a voicemail and text him. I used to know where he was 24/7. But lately, he's been elusive, as if he's avoiding me. Or I'm avoiding him.

I head over to Kimmie's apartment. Third-floor walkup in a cute 10-unit brownstone in West Kartlan, only five blocks from where I live. That's a little too close for comfort, but everybody lives somewhere. I wonder if I've seen her around.

With the spare keys Dante gave me I access the building, then unlock the deadbolt to her apartment. I slip beneath the yellow police tape stretched diagonally across the doorway, enter the unit, and close the door behind me.

Large studio with a compact kitchen, high ceilings, bathroom, loft bed with a desk beneath it. There's also a wall-mounted flatscreen TV opposite a love seat, coffee table, and a soft-glide rocking chair, the kind pregnant or nursing mothers use. Interesting.

Long, multi-paned windows, camouflaged in cream-colored drapes overlook the side street. A black, metal-framed door leads out to a quaint, brick balcony with a metal table and two chairs. Lots of greenery in here, potted plants including a ficus tree with fully bloomed leaves the size of a toddler.

The place is neat and tidy, except for the pool of dried blood on the throw rug and hardwood floor where Kimmie's body fell. I did notice tiny scratches on the lock plate, as if someone picked it. The scratches could also be from wear and tear, or when she'd drunkenly jiggled the key while it was in the lock.

Forensics teams are good about preserving crime scenes. That tells me whoever broke in or was let in, wanted to talk to Kimmie, maybe had a beef with her, or was there during her slip-and-fall.

The medical examiner ruled this an accidental death, so there's no police investigation. But if she was murdered, as Dante insists, the list of suspects could be enormous. Her killer could be one of her johns, although that seems less likely since sex workers like Kimmie rarely, if ever, allow their clients to know where they live. But it does happen. I need to know her better.

The best way for me to do that is to sit quietly in her home, let it speak to me. You can learn a lot about a person, being in their space, letting the entirety of their environment wash over you. I take a seat in the glider. It's been years since I sat in one, when my son, Owen, who's eight now, was just a little guy, feeding him from my breast.

I dreamt about possibilities and tomorrows, and wonder what kind of life he would have, given that he was my son, and I—Angela Hardwicke, private investigator—was his mother.

Staring at the drapes along the windows, flowing subtly from a breeze blowing through the pores in the window frame, my mind drifts.

One of my friends, Lanie, paid for her entire college education and a two-bedroom condo working as a dancer at a gentleman's club. She was only nineteen when she started, so she had the normal reservations at first. But the club management, staff, and other performers all looked out for each other. In five years she banked more than I did in twice that long as an investigator.

After that she switched to a private webcam model, where from her apartment bedroom she dressed in lingerie and used new sex toys on herself. She rated them from one to five in red lipstick kiss prints. She said the gig was empowering and exciting. And the commute was great. Plus she made another cool million. Now she does whatever she wants.

But not all sex workers go that route. Some are your traditional prostitutes—sex for money. If it were up to me, prostitution would be legal, with a union, health benefits, and a pension. They damn sure deserve it. But that's not the law.

That leaves the girls to run their own businesses, or work for a service, which comes with its own risks. Especially when it's for a charmer like Dante.

He institutes the give-the-johns-whatever-they-want-and-shut-your-face-if-you-don't-like-it business model. Some girls who go that way don't know any better, and others think they don't have a choice. Which is really no choice at all.

So when I think about Nóirín coming home after meeting a john, or many johns, I envision her kicking her heels off, pouring herself a much-needed cocktail. Then unzipping her dress, peeling off her uniform—her Kimmie uniform—and letting the alcohol slide down her throat. Feeling it anesthetize her trachea and all the semen she may have swallowed that night, cauterizing the physical and psychic wounds inevitable under those conditions.

Then turning on the shower, letting the water get so hot it burns off the sexual grime. The water cascading over her desecrated body, washing her sore and punished vagina, and her anus, if that's what she permits with her johns. Scrubbing the dead cells and sexual stink off her until Kimmie could fall away and Nóirín could re-emerge. Then sitting in this very glider, the alcohol soothing what's left of her soul.

Did she take prophylactic antibiotics to prevent various infection from sexually transmitted diseases her johns might have introduced into her body? Did she insist they wear condoms? Did she allow her clients to penetrate her bareback for an extra fee?

Many sex workers enjoy the life. Lanie sure did. There are far worse ways to spend your time than with orgasms and pillow-talk. Some participants experience a deeper sense of intimacy and trust than in any other type of relationship.

But the experiences aren't always pretty or glamorous. Depending on the situation, it can be dirty and dangerous. As I sink into the glider, studying Nóirín's bookshelves and mounted artwork, I don't see the apartment of a *sex worker*, but of a fully formed woman, who's created a home for herself. With friends and neighbors, maybe a family, and even a child who lives... elsewhere.

And now, in the recess of my mind, I hear those muffled cries again. At first, I think it's Owen. But no. It's her. It's Dolores. One of my best friends.

Dead. Because of me. From that case on the cruise ship. Because she chose to put the lives of everyone on board— including mine—ahead of her own.

I wake up with another swamp of sweat puddled under my neck. My heart's pounding, my throat dry. I stand up, achy, my mind caught in a drowsy post-nap haze. It's dark outside. I was out for—I check the time—almost six hours. With the pads of my wrists, I rub my eyes, go to the kitchen sink, splash water on my face.

I need to get out of here.

Back on the street I turn the collar up on my olive-green utility jacket to block the breeze, bringing with it a nip in the air. I wrap a beige and maroon scarf around my neck and thread it down into my jacket, keeping my chest warm.

My pace brisk, within minutes I'm halfway south through West Karltan and then Nosha Village. Cabs, cars, delivery trucks, and buses—some traditional, some hover vehicles— hiss through the late end of rush hour. Streetlamps, headlights, brake lights, and storefront window displays shimmer in the haze of dusk as the sky slowly fades to its nighttime black.

Pedestrians whisk along the sidewalks, heading home, to dinner, for cocktails, dates, sex, shopping, drugs, movies, plays, concerts, violence, and every other kink and distraction money can and cannot buy.

Yet we're all unsure when E-Town transmuted into less of a thriving urban landscape and more of a police state, with hordes of security drones spying on us from overhead with a constant low buzz.

Always there. Always watching.

The change happened so quickly the city feels palpably different than even just a few years ago. Yet it's difficult to pinpoint an isolated event—a declaration from the mayor, chief of police, or even the Minders themselves—no official moment that set us down a new path. One where AI, cloud computing, robotics, androids, and cybernetics became the unofficial rule of law and our quasi-overlords, rather than digital tools and playthings to make our lives easier and more joyful.

No drug, implant, computer algorithm, or holographic program helps me work through my anxiety and confusion like being on the street. Feeling the sway of my arms and the night air on my skin. Whether in shouts or whispers or a constant chatter, the city talks to me. I just need to listen.

The roar of sirens, the hiss of steam. A shrieking baby, a drunken brawl. Friends laughing. A sobbing lover. A blitzkrieg of neon signs and enormous holographic advograms tempting us all to embrace one sin or another. The city speaks a thousand languages.

Whether I'm drawn by some external force or pure muscle memory from decades of walks just like this one, I find myself passing beyond canyons of skyscrapers, hotels, and apartment buildings and into familiar territory.

I'm back in the center of E-Town, cutting through Half Moon Garden overlooking the former Anaya Pavilion, a public space separating Midtown East and Midtown West.

I was here on the regular when the Anaya Pavilion was my outdoor sanctuary, a winding path of cobblestone steps leading from the top of the tree-lined hill down to the pavilion itself. I'd run alongside the Anaya Reflecting Pool, a marble monolith stretching more than two thousand feet long, mesmerized by the shimmering water and the city's soul reflected on its dark surface.

That's all gone now. About five years ago an accountant hired me to track down a middle-aged intern who absconded with sensitive files, only to discover he was a madman from Earth. In a blaze of deranged glory, he incinerated nearly every ounce of marble and anyone who was here, rendering the site a steaming wasteland of toxic soot and ash, and charred flesh and bones.

He didn't just kill this site. He flayed off a protective layer of our individual and collective souls, striking at the heart of E-Town, whether we knew it or not. Maybe that was the turning point, the moment where the city we *were* became the city we *are*.

To overcome the trauma of that awful night, of death and madness and nightmares, we've since ignored the reality that we've been grieving all this time. That an elemental component of our humanity died that night, and watched those parts in each other die, the pain and shock of it all just too much to confront.

So we did what we usually do when we don't have the capacity, perspective, or vocabulary to express that pain and shock. We kept on keeping on, pretending we're resilient, that we've been through worse, and that we're all okay, when we are very much not okay.

Yet we are resilient, aren't we? Yeah, maybe we gave up an illusion of control, and no longer had the energy or will to fight against the inevitability of this new digital age that consumes our every moment. But look what we did.

Renamed Breoniki Park, the old pavilion has been reborn. In the place of marble pillars and an extensive promenade are communal arcs. Gently sloping pathways and greenspaces shaped like sand traps on a golf course, some longer and more subtle, others with more obvious curves and gradations.

Moreso than merely reinvent the space, the structural engineers and design architects had a different vision in mind. Not unlike flexible office space where walls and doors can shift and fold to accommodate various shapes, sizes, and configurations, these new communal arcs glide and rotate, set atop a complex mechanism below ground, such that they mimic the ebb and flow of lily pads on a pond.

New greenspaces were landscaped, with polished marble walkways and various gazebos. Trees were planted. Some are already more than fifty feet tall. White, sanded boulders were placed throughout for balance. To admire, to sit on. To feel grounded.

And the new centerpiece. The Eye of Time. An eyeball the

size of a small moon. The Eye of Time crackles with energy, its iris changing in color much like the gradations of the sky. The black pupil, with a golden hue behind it, is a viewscreen. But it is not a collective experience.

Gaze into the Eye and revealed to you and you alone—even if a hundred thousand people surround you—is a unique moment in space, time, and dimension. Even standing side-by-side I would experience one moment, you another. Like clouds and snowflakes, what the Eye reveals to you will never again be revealed to anyone, ever, in precisely the same manner. It's unique. And it's yours.

To stand beneath this behemoth Eye is mesmerizing and terrifying. Yet once you've caught its attention, or it's caught yours, it's difficult to look away. I feel drawn to it, a force far greater than myself. One that will reveal mysteries of the Cosmos. Or of me.

"Mayzhhhh!" I hear, the word buzzing as if being spoken with lips secured tightly against wax paper. *"Mayzhhhh!"*

My heart jumps. It sounds like... nah. No way. I squint, as if that will somehow fine tune what my hearing can discern. "Whistler? Is that you?"

"Mayzhhhh!" the buzzing repeats, until I see what looks like my partner, but I'm not sure. Like his voice, his image is buzzing... vibrating... such that he's almost entirely out of focus. Yet I get intermittent glimpses of him. *"Mayzhhhh!"* He's speaking frantically. *"Heeeeelpppzzz meeeeee... find... gonnazzz happenzzz."*

"Whistler! What's happening? Where are you? What—?"

"... dee... ive."

"What?! I can't hear you! *What's* gonna happen? Help how?"

Whistler's phasing slows to the point where I can nearly make him out.

"Mache. I can't coontrollzzz thizzz. Don't... ave... timezzz... to.... Eddie... Eddie..."

"Eddie? What do you mean Eddie? Time for what?"

Whistler fades again, vibrating so fast and hard he's a complete blur to me. *"Eddie... zzhive!"* he yells out. *"Help me... Eddie... fffzine... findzz.... Eddie... Eddie hzzive!"*

Whistler's gone. No fade, no phase out. Just gone. In the blink of an eye.

Leaving me here, alone, in the dark. I'm shaking, my gut tight, blood rushing to my ears.

I feel more buzzing. I spin around, look for Whistler. But he's nowhere. It's not him. It's me. My phone. I fish it out of my pocket and answer, although I'm not sure what I say, if I say anything at all.

Dante shouts at me. "Hardwicke!" A question and a command. "What's the four-one-one? Whadaya got for me? Whatcha learn?"

Unsure what's just happened, I gaze dumbfounded, beyond the replanted tree line, at the lights from skyscrapers, police drones, and galaxy cruisers soaring in the near distance. Then I turn back to the Eye of Time, this giant orb with its iris and cornea and blood vessels, peering down on me. Revealing secrets of the Cosmos, as if it's gazing directly into my soul.

"Sorry, Dante. I'm gonna have to call you back."

CHAPTER 3

Before I know it, I find myself in the only place I can be right now. I don't remember how I got here or what I saw along the way.

I don't typically experience overwhelming recall, but being back at the old pavilion, where I was almost incinerated along with everyone else, and failed to stop it, retraumatizes me.

I'm reliving that horrible event as if it's happening right now—the terror, the anxiety, the shock. It's dualistically brutal, because while I'm yanked back to that scenario of psychotic madness, I'm incapable of preventing or neutralizing its progress, knowing how violent and torturous the individual moments and outcome will be for me and so many others.

I can see those demented orange flames and plumes of black smoke, smell the chemical accelerant and toxic fumes wafting off the graveyard of charred bodies, blackened bones melted into permanent shrieks of terror. I can feel the heat warbling on my skin.

In the hallway entrance to Bernice's warehouse bunker, I put my right eye up to the retinal scanner. A horizontal beam reads my optic nerve. The light whirs. After a short delay, the scanner readout says: *ACCESS DENIED*

That's never happened before. I'm shaking so hard the scan doesn't take. I breathe in then out, in then out. My heartbeat accelerates like after a horror movie jump scare. The bitter taste of adrenaline coats my tongue. My face goes flush, but it passes, my fingers trembling as the last of the wave jitters its way through me.

I try the scanner again:

ANGELA HARDWICKE – AUTHENTICATED

Gears unlock. The chrome-plated door, thicker than a bank vault, heaves open.

Bernice's bunker is its customary beehive of wires, tools, hydraulic arms, video screens, computer terminals, workbenches, wire-cage server racks, coolant systems, diagnostic portals, and experimental gadgets. Reconfigured from an old printing press, it has soundproofed walls and flooring with reinforced Diradium alloy plates, and a laser-grid security system tracking every inch of her property. The vault door closes, sealing us in.

Bernice is set back in a hoverchair she controls by way of a chrome-plated implant fused to her right temple with cybernetic interface. Her gray hair is twisted into a rope braid running down her back, her arms amputated at the shoulders, legs below the knees.

"Angela," says my tech ninja, who, for a considerable retainer, supplies me with all manner of devices and lab work in service of my business. "Come come."

The armrest panels on Bernice's hoverchair slide back. Like hissing chrome asps, synthetic arms rise from each side, then rotate. With a *thop*, the artificial ball-and-stem configurations insert into her shoulder-socket interfaces, completing the limb syncs. Her arms now fully attached and functional, she reaches for me, takes my hand.

This also never happens. I must be more fucked up than I thought.

Bernice directs me to a rolling chair at one of her workstations. Without noticing where it comes from, I've got a cup of hot tea in my hands.

She stares at me intently, her eyes widening. The artificially enhanced corneas, a crystalline blue, draw me in, as if she's overly empathetic and sensitive to my aching distress. Her personality has, historically, demonstrated the opposite. But it seems the women in my life these days are not the women I thought I knew. Or, more than likely, I'm the one who's changed—and they notice.

She wants me to taste. That's the Bernice I know, somehow able to control the environment by controlling me. I put the cup to my mouth, take a sip. As the hot liquid hits my lips, I'm instantly wide awake and hyper-focused.

"Whoa." I hold the cup away from me, examining it. I'm more alert than if I just did five tight lines of cocaine. "What's in this?"

"Purified honey. A sweet little kick."

I raise an eyebrow. "Honey?"

"Stimulant-infused honey, but honey, nonetheless. My own recipe." Her hoverchair rotates so that she's half-facing me, half-facing her computer terminal. Servers hum throughout her dimly lit bunker as various lights flash like in a never-ending game of Whac-A-mole. I assume there's a pattern, though I have no idea what it is or what it might mean. So many secrets in here, so many cyphers. "What, my dear, Angela, happened to you?

My brain fully reactivated, I explain about Whistler.

"The Eye of Time," Bernice says, as if she both marvels and mistrusts the enormous orb. "I've studied the specs, run diagnostics. And my delicious Eric. He phased? Is that accurate?"

"As best I can tell. It's like he was... trapped. Being pulled somewhere."

"The pulling, as you described it. Did you get the sense he was being pulled in time? Space? Dimension? All three? Come now, Angela. For a woman of your vast cunning, experience, and intelligence, I expect more from you. Try to keep up."

Her point is valid. It's easy to forget, but when dealing with the fabric of the Universe, time can speed up or slow down. It can leap ahead or jump back. It can travel in loops. It can bend (but not break). It can twist, flatten, knot, and gyrate, as well as oscillate, pendulate, undulate, and rotate. It can also whirl, purl, revolve, slant, spin, expand, and retract, and—when it really gets going—whiz, shimmy, shake, buckle, tangle, tremble, tread, roll, flip (although not flop), or completely reconfigure. And it can all happen simultaneously or in any combination.

"I'm not sure."

"Working a case?" Bernice inquires. "Eric, that is."

"It's possible. But with Tarrish calling the shots, I don't know what he's up to." That utterance deflates me, leaving an emptiness where my confident sense of self used to reside.

"And what does the good lieutenant have to say about this?"

I take another sip, the stimulant whooshing through my veins. "Radio silence."

"There's a certain comfort in his predictability, is there not?" Bernice's face contorts into a subtle grimace. She has her own issues, not just with Tarrish, but with the entire ICD. Any governmental agency or their representatives, for that matter. Bernice lives in near seclusion for a reason. You know what they say about paranoia. Just because you think someone's out to get you, it doesn't mean they're not. "The spatial-temporal links the Eye forms with our minds is fascinating, but I've heard no reports of an occurrence such as you describe. Which implies to me that Eric's phasing is the result of the Eye functioning properly, only in a different fashion than we've previously understood. Or it's malfunctioning."

"Or it may have nothing to do with the Eye at all," I say.

The look on her face suggests she hadn't considered that, but her ego won't let her admit as much. When it comes to advanced tech, Bernice does not appreciate being corrected by those whose expertise doesn't match her own. Which is pretty much everyone.

From a tray of tools on her workbench, she produces a thin chrome device, with a scanner on the tip. She hoverchairs closer to me and points the device toward my face.

"Let me check your eyes. Are you wearing your lens?"

Bernice custom designed a plasma sensor lens, one that syncs to my phone. It records data, has infrared scanners and signal blockers, and allows me to access most computer terminals and mainframes. She consistently upgrades the lens with new features, including an external signal boost, for one-time use if I'm caught in a heavy distortion field.

With her chrome fingers on her other hand, she plies open my right eye. Her metallic fingertip grazes against my eyelid so she can better scan the lens. My eye twitches.

"It's working. Let's see if it picked up anything useful."

From her mechanical wand she syncs my lens to her computer terminal. "I'm running my most sophisticated audio-visual filtering program and..." A block of red light scrolls horizontally across the center of her monitor, followed by lines of green computer code scrolling down it. "The files are corrupted," she says, almost a question. "That shouldn't be." She types at the keyboard furiously. Her cranial interface blinks yellow-brown-yellow. Brown-yellow-brown. *Curiosity and confusion.* She activates more keystroke commands. "If this program can't recover the remaining bytes, nothing can. It'll take a minute."

We sit wordlessly. Bernice avoids all but minimal direct human contact because emotions are messy, illogical, and unpredictable. Code, on the other hand, is well within her control.

"Are you still having the dreams? About Dolores?"

Bernice is making me nervous. Our interplay almost entirely focuses on whatever case I'm working or the tech she upgrades. She rarely asks me questions like this. Too personal.

"Every night."

"I see. And what about Nini? Has she accepted your invitation?"

I try avoiding Bernice's gaze, instead finding comfort in the sterile, emotionless bunker filled with wires, tools, and humming computer terminals. But the reprieve is temporary. My gaze finds hers. My heart jumps. "I tried a few times, but... she's not ready."

Nini was on the cruise ship when Dolores died trying to save us all. An immense woman, Dolores used to do muscle work for me now and then. Because of her day job as a baggage handler who worked at the galaxy cruise port, she also had a network of eyes and spies, including delivery drivers, mechanics, engineers, and dockworkers who are constantly on the move.

Nini and Dolores bickered like they were angling for points, but they were as loyal to each other as any two people I've ever met. Unlike Dolores, Nini is just a tiny thing, barely four foot ten, her skin as black as night. She got roughed up on the cruise. Badly. And while Nini doesn't blame me, exactly, for what happened to Dolores, she doesn't *not* blame me either. It's hard to go through life without your best friend.

Bernice continues to analyze me. "When you wake up from the nightmares, how do you feel?"

"I don't feel anything. I'm just awake."

"Angela. We have an understanding, do we not? You have entered my sacred space. Or, to be more precise, I have granted you access, permissions rarely afforded to anyone. If you take that to mean you hold a special place in my heart"—with her chrome finger, she taps on her human chest—"I will not entirely dissuade you of that notion." Her eyes side-shift, then refocus on me. "Which is to say, without impunity or interruption, I may insult you as the moment strikes. But you never insult *me*. And in this context, withholding information, then denying that you do so, is an insult of the highest order." She repeats her question, more pointedly. "When you wake from the nightmares... how do you *feel?*"

She's right. I didn't come here just to check on my tech. I need help making sense of what my life has become. Having nightmares is another occupational hazard. But they've rarely, if ever, consumed me like this.

"I'm..." I don't know why it's so hard for me to say. My eyes are open, but all I see now is a black, empty space. "I'm paralyzed. Like I've been bolted to a raft in a dead, lightless galaxy. I can't speak, I can't move. I can't call for help. But I feel everything so intensely, like I'm being smothered by my own fear. And then it passes. But for those first few minutes..."

"You feel the terror of uncertainty."

I dry swallow. It's rough on my throat. "Yes."

"Well, then," Bernice says. "It's time you found out."

My lips part slightly, corrupted air escaping from my lungs. My mouth tries to form words, but they don't come. Until they do. "H-how?"

Her computer terminal pings. "Let's see what we've got." Bernice double clicks on the file. "Video is trashed. But there's a partial section of recoverable audio..." She leans forward, dragging two chrome fingers upward on her screen, raising the volume.

"...*Eddie*..." and then garbled language. "...*ive.*"

"Yes," I acknowledge. "That's it. But Whistler's voice kept

dropping in and out. All I heard were fragments."

Bernice aggressively shushes me. "Let me listen." She types again, clicks the mouse, then turns one dial. The audio plays again.

"Help me... findzz." More garbled audio. "Eddie... hive." She replays the segment. Same again.

"That's the best I can retrieve," Bernice says. "I'll run more diagnostics to determine the source of the distortion. There's a—" Her eyes go wide, nervous.

"A what?"

"It's nothing." A lie. "I thought I recognized the signal patterns. I was mistaken." Another lie.

"Bernie. What is it? Are you sure it's—?"

"Eddie Hive," she says authoritatively, and with finality, pushing past my inquiry.

"Eddie?" I pace around her bunker, studying the workshop as if the answers I need are right here, if only I knew where to look. "Do you think he means Eddie Eddie. My Eddie? Patch?"

With a cold, exacting whir, Bernice pivots her hoverchair so that she's facing her computer terminal, her back to me. Avoiding me. Avoiding her past.

"You heard it yourself. The rest is up to you."

Outside Bernice's bunker I walk into a dense, humid rain, thick droplets cascading down on me as stray light refracts off the slick pavement. I press the snap on my left cuff, activating my jacket's camouflage mode. Thanks to another of Bernice's upgrades, adaptable fabric, I'm concealed in a water-resistant raincoat with hood.

Instinctively I duck my head, shielding my face from the torrent of rain falling from a sky well past midnight, and serpentine through a maze of back alleys and underpasses. I take shelter in a brick alcove, my mind caught in a furious loop of Eddie and Whistler, and whatever he meant by hive.

A beehive? A rash? Or did he mean—

I should have heard it sooner, but the patter of rain and my own confusion drowned out the noise. Footsteps behind me. I reach for my gun, but my jacket's zipped up, so I pivot on the heel of my black sneaker, to protect myself. It's too late. There's a gun in the back of my neck. I'm pushed against the brick wall, my face scraping against the coarse surface. Light from a distant source tosses beams of illumination into this otherwise dark tomb.

"I snuck away from a double homicide. Tell me why."

It's Olin.

"You tell me," I say, my face still flush against the brick wall. "You wanna let me go?"

For someone who's supposed to be working *with* me, she takes what feels like an awfully long time to back off. I hear her switch on the safety. Her hand releases me. I turn around.

An inch taller than me, with jet black hair pulled into a tight ponytail against dark brown skin, Olin secures her weapon. That she pulled her gun on me so early in our relationship tells me something about who she is and how she handles herself. She's been tailing me. But for how long?

"You seem a little edgy," I say, the rain nearly a monsoon.

With side-eye glances, Olin scans the area. "I don't want to be seen with you."

"We're not even dating, but you want me all to yourself."

True to her reputation, Olin cuts through the b.s.

"Let's get something straight. With you working off a murder beef—don't delude yourself, Hardwicke, the details are hard to come by, but everybody knows you did something nasty on that cruise ship—I'm the one with friends in the system. But you? You're nobody's best friend. And with fresh stink on you, as far as the department is concerned… as far as *I'm* concerned… you're not even a PI anymore. You're less than that, and it was already tough to go lower. You are what your rap sheet—marked as classified—says you are. A murderer. A convict. With nowhere left to run."

Olin' making a power move. To keep me in my place. To let me know she's in charge.

We've crossed paths before, but only on the periphery. I've seen her at a few crime scenes over the years. She knows her job, doesn't take crap. But from what I've seen, and the very little chatter I've heard about her, she's solid police. Mostly.

"Maybe," I say. "But I've got more friends than you think. I make one phone call and Internal Affairs will be *real* curious about you and Dante. And you know the IAD. When it comes to a cop's life, they dig into *everything*. No matter where it leads."

Two detectives—a private eye on parole, a tainted murder cop—both on a pimp's payroll, are isolated. With sheets of relentless rain so thick and loud on either side of us we're secluded in this brick, rain-soaked cocoon. She lays it out.

"If I didn't absolutely have to work this case, and I do... I wouldn't. Neither would you. And if given the choice, we'd go our separate ways."

This is either her way of acknowledging we're stuck with each other, or she's playing me, showing me a more humane side of her personality so I'll be less likely to see the monster in her coming next time. Sorry, Olin. Fool me once...

"Yet here we are," I say.

A single stream of rain drips down from the underside of the alcove, trickles between her two brown eyes. She wipes it from her face.

"Yet here we are." Fortyish, trim, with milky white teeth, she takes a step back, giving me some space, as if conceding we're both fucked, so we might as well be fucked together. "Let's review the scene. There are more than three thousand slip-and-fall-related fatalities a year in E-Town alone. It's utterly plausible that Kimmie-slash-Nóirín died just the way it looks. But..."

All I want is to get back to Whistler. But if I try to ditch Olin now, she'll only come back on me later, treating me like the enemies we might very well turn out to be. I let the thoughts linger, deciding if I'm really in this with her or not. But I'm here now. Might as well dive in.

From my phone, I project crime scene photos I took onto the wall.

Accepting my gesture of teamwork, she reluctantly scrolls through the photos on her phone, but doesn't send them to me. "These show up anywhere but here, your life gets awful. Quickly."

It's not a bluff.

"Noted," I say. "It ain't so great now."

Satisfied with my response, Olin sends me official ETPD forensic photos from the initial crime scene investigation. I project them on the wall.

"This doesn't look right." Although I'm not immediately sure why.

It's unclear what happens between us, but we look at each other with shared recognition. No matter which side of the investigation you're on, if you take your job seriously, there's a certain buzz you get when you know you're onto something. Whether through skill, observation, or divine intervention, a mechanism within you clicks.

"Yeah," Olin says, more encouraged than antagonistic. "Yeah, it was... I don't know—"

"The way she fell. It's off."

"Right! Yes. It *is* off. I just can't put my finger on it."

We study the enlarged images, including Kimmie-slash-Nóirín, on the floor, outlined with white tape. Her limbs at angles, her dirty blonde hair mussed, dark blood pooled beneath her head. She's wearing a pumpkin-colored skirt and white satin blouse, diamond stud earrings, and a jade ring on the middle finger of her right hand. The broken wine bottle, the half-smoked joint.

Her eyes are open, up and to the right, as if they'd fallen into the back of her head.

Olin and I shift within the alcove, studying the images from different vantage points. She accidentally brushes against the brick face, dust transferred to her jacket. Olin starts to wipe the dust off and... freezes. She realizes something. Her gaze goes to her hand, near her hip.

"The skirt," I say, craning my head, to study the angle of Kimmie-slash-Nóirín's fall.

Olin agrees. "I've fallen like that. The skirt wedges in the crotch. It bunches."

I continue her line of thought. "It's too smooth. Like someone..."

Our eyes go wide with revelation. We speak in unison: *"Went through her pockets."*

"Holy shit," Olin says. "Slip-and-fall, my ass. This was a murder."

"You might be right."

"Might be? What else?"

I exhale, the release of nervous energy. "I don't get the glider."

"Yeah," Olin concedes, "that's been bugging me."

"She *was* a prostitute. She could have a kid we don't know about. Or even a grandchild."

"A grandmother? At her age?"

I fall back into painful memories. When I was a stupid-in-love teenager, I had an unplanned pregnancy, long before Owen, one that irrevocably altered the trajectory of my life. I lost that baby. I did not handle it well. "Crazier shit has happened."

"True enough. But other than the glider, I didn't find anything baby-related in her apartment. Not sure what to make of it. I'm not convinced there is, but let's assume there's a kid involved. How does that help us?"

"It might not," I say. "The place isn't trashed, and nothing seems to be missing. But maybe someone was there that night, someone she knew. Boyfriend? Girlfriend? Neighbor? A john, possibly. And maybe it *was* a legit slip-and-fall. The john panics. Doesn't want to get caught with a dead hooker in her own apartment, with no good explanation as to what happened, even if it was just an accident. The optics are bad. And maybe the john thinks there's something in her pocket that can implicate him, takes it, and runs."

Olin sighs, I'm assuming, because she didn't think of that herself. And that I thought of it first. "Or maybe it was just a murder."

I concede her point. "More than likely."

"More than."

We study the photos a bit longer but come to no other conclusion.

"You know," she says, "as an investigator, you don't completely scrape the bottom of the barrel."

"It's the agency motto."

Trouble is, we've still got a dead sex worker and an impatient pimp on our hands. And my partner, who would normally work the case with me, has literally vanished into the ether.

"I'll pick this up with you tomorrow," I say. "There's some-place I need to be."

Olin's not having it. If anything, *she* needs to be the one who dismisses *me*. "You can't leave now. We're just getting started."

"Tomorrow." I produce a handheld device that will immedi-ately transport me from where I am to where I need to be.

"No!" Olin bearhugs me as I depress the button. "You're not going"—we reappear inside a secret bunker, miles from the heart of E-Town, deep within the Baldamere Mountains, when she stumbles, before regaining her balance—"without me."

CHAPTER 4

It took some getting used to when I first began to teleport to and from the facility, the immediacy of it. Until I was granted privileges, I had to drive the hour plus it took to get here up and along a byzantine path of windy roads through a snow-capped mountain range miles from the heart of E-Town.

So it's no surprise my parasitic traveling companion is finding it difficult to accept that, whereas we were just outside in the rain, in less time than it took to complete a single breath we're now inside a hangar, staring up at one of several mechanical beasts with various arms, scrapers, and blowtorches.

"Hey, Eddie," I say sheepishly.

"Hey," he says, with a raised eyebrow. "Who's your friend?"

"Eddie... Detective Olin, Homicide, ETPD. Detective Olin... Eddie."

Eddie "Patch" Azarante is a member of a specialized team of construction workers and engineers. They're summoned when the fabric of the Cosmos suffers a significant tear or other injury across time, space, or dimension, requiring a cosmic patch. Thus the name.

Patches are a rare breed. Children of the Universe. I have no idea how, when, or where the first Patches arrived, but their essence is beyond that of any standard citizen. Patches are part Eternitarian and part cosmologic, in organic form. Eddie comes from a long line of Patches, and continuing that tradition, my son—our son, Owen—is a Patch, too.

Eddie and I were never married, and though he was once the love of my life who altered my trajectory forever, our relationship is still loving, in its way, but purely platonic.

A former field technician, Eddie is a high-level supervisor

and Professor of Interstellar and Cosmologic Infrastructure at the Patch Institute, where we are now.

Given my lifestyle and the cases I work—my job isn't exactly 9-to-5 and puts me in close contact with all sorts of unsavory figures on-realm and off—I finally accepted it was best for Owen that he also live at the Institute. Where he can get the training and guidance he needs to help him become the best version of himself he can be. Another Patch.

I still get Owen on weekends, and we VidChat almost every day. But as he gets older, and his mind and skills continue to grow, I feel like I know him less and less, even as I want to know him more and more.

"Whoa." Olin stares through the wall-length reinforced viewing window on our left and into the reaches of the Cosmos. Three gas planets of varying densities and hues are so close to our field of view it feels as if we could reach out and whoosh our hands right through them. "This is the Patch Institute."

"It is," Eddie says.

Olin is still struggling to get her bearings. "I knew it existed... *somewhere* on-realm, but... I had no idea."

"Kinda the point," I say.

Dozens of mechanics, engineers, and astrophysicists are wearing jumpsuits and noise-filtering headphones. They mill around lifts, platforms, supply pallets, ten-foot rolls of industrial wire, hydraulic lifts, staging equipment, and cosmic construction equipment.

The one before us now is new to me, at least twenty feet high and half as wide, perched on giant arms. Thick tubes and cables feed into its belly. A hiss of steam releases. Shrouded in orange and gold sparks, a handful of helper drones hover at the top, welding plates to the equipment.

"Your visit is... unexpected," Eddie says. "Another case?"

"Kinda." I move closer to him so that only he can hear me above the thrum of activity. "I gotta talk to you." I shoot him one of my this-is-serious-shit-I-need-you-now looks. "Alone."

Eddie eyes Olin, nods. He talks into a handheld device. "Amon. It's Eddie. Can you come to Hangar Five? I need you to give a tour." Eddie listens, nods again. "Yeah, I know we're backed up. But do me a solid?" Eddie's gaze never leaves Olin. "Thanks. I owe you."

"What"—Olin is mesmerized by the equipment—"is that?"

"Retraction Mole."

Olin looks perplexed. "A what?"

Like most specialists accustomed to communicating with other specialists in shorthand, Eddie needs a moment to recalibrate his mind so that he can better articulate complex terminology to a layperson. The classic dumbing-down.

"There are weak spots in the fabric of spacetime. Sometimes an asteroid, comet, or other debris gets... wedged into the weak spots. See the long, mechanical arms with the big grippers on the end? We use those to pull out the debris."

"Like removing a splinter," Olin says.

Eddie smiles. "Exactly like that. And the machine looks like a mole, so..."

"Retraction mole." Olin seems more settled, the overwhelm having washed past her. "But how did we get here so fast? I've never seen any—?"

"Amon," Eddie says. "Detective Olin is just visiting. Can you take her to the observation deck? I think she'd like to see the Wurlac System. The work's almost done."

"Sure thing, boss."

"Hang on," Olin says. "What about the—?"

"I apologize," Eddie says. "It's nothing personal. But this is a restricted area, and you don't have clearance. Amon will show you around."

"Hardwicke!" Olin shouts as Eddie leads me out of the hangar, in the opposite direction of where Amon is leading her. "Where are you going? What are you doing? We..."

A metal security door closes behind us. Her voice disappears.

Eddie stops us in the hallway, sighs. He knows me too well.

"Angela," he says worriedly. "You know you can't do this. What's wrong?"

I'm not sure what my expression conveys, but I'm filled with dread. "It's Whistler. He's in real trouble. He told me to find you."

"Eddie hive?" Eddie's face contorts into a pucker of confusion. "What does that mean?"

"Don't know. That's why I'm here."

"You certain that's what he said? *Eddie hive?*"

"No, not certain. But Bernice ran the filtering program. It's the best we could get."

The mention of Bernice gives Eddie pause.

A former Patch herself—before Eddie's time—Bernice was injured on a jobsite, resulting in her amputations. Regardless of the NDAs she signed after leaving the Institute, she's never told me what happened. And I've never asked.

"If Bernice says it's the best she can get, she's probably right," Eddie says finally. "But we can rerun the data if you want. We're always upgrading our tech, so you never know."

Reaching for my phone, I hesitate. "I don't know what this means or what it's tied to. This has to stay..."

"It's in the vault," he says with a nod. "I'll use an encrypted server to analyze the code. My access only."

"The way he phased? He was almost entirely out of focus, and his voice sounded like he was talking through wax paper." I shrug.

Eddie leads me into a secure room, barely larger than a closet. We're surrounded by server racks embedded in the walls, lights blinking in a blitzkrieg of alternating sequences. Above and below us are clear panes of custom-designed reinforced plexiglass offering a view of distant constellations, as if we're standing in the heart of the Cosmos. Maybe we are.

"Tell me more," Eddie demands. "The phasing. What else?"

This isn't like Eddie, his hands balled into fists. He's making me nervous. As a Patch, he's always been physically strong and fit. But after a jobsite accident of his own that destroyed nearly half his body, he's now as much a network of artificial limbs, joints, and synthetic organs as he is organic. He still walks with a slight limp, although he's ditched the cane.

"Eddie, is this a Patch thing? You guys are connected to spacetime in ways we're not. Can you... feel it? Can you sense it? Can you—?"

"Angela." Eddie isn't aggressive by nature. But he can be

intractable when it comes to his job. He has considerable knowledge about the nature of the Cosmos he'll never share with me.
Assuming I could even understand. Maybe I can't. "The phasing. It's important. Tell me *everything*."

I try to explain what I saw. "It was like... he was caught in
a flume of water, fighting to stay in place. He kept... phasing.
There, not there. Barely there. And then he was gone."

"Like a signal caught in a distortion field."

"Kinda," I say with a nod. "Why? What does it mean?"

"It means..." With a nasal inhalation and exhalation, he
offers a closed-mouthed smile and rubs his hands on my fore-
arms, as if he's trying to pacify me. Though I suspect he's trying
to pacify himself. "I need to check something."

Annoyed, I pull my arms away. "So you *do* know."

"I don't. But what you're describing sounds like... and this
is pure speculation... like he's caught in an artificial orbit, moving through time or dimension. He can't break free."

"What do you mean *artificial*? As in... tech-based?"

"Possibly."

If Whistler's caught in the folds of spacetime, which does
not happen easily or often, he either fell into it by accident during an investigation, or he was targeted.

"Who has that kinda tech?" I ask.

Eddie stares at me wordlessly. From his expression, it's clear
he's holding back. I don't know if it's a security issue, fear, or
something else altogether, but I can't remember him ever being
so intensely torn over how to handle himself. He takes a series
of short breaths when I feel his entire body shudder. His chest
rises with a large inhalation, and then deflates with an exhale.

"*We* do."

Without further explanation, Eddie shuffles me out of the server
closet. He leads us down a series of tight hallways, then through
a guarded security checkpoint requiring his retinal scan and ID
badge confirmation. The armed security guard lets us through
the barrier, leaving the Institute's hangars and entering the edu-
cational wing.

"In here." We cross an expansive foyer outside a series of

large classrooms, workshops, and anti-gravity training pods, toward another door, when I hear my favorite word of all.

"Mommy!"

Owen jumps into my arms. He's almost at the point where I won't be able to hold him any longer. Unless his arms are wrapped around my neck and his legs around my waist, he's just too heavy for me now. I've already damaged ligaments in both wrists from when I used to pick him up and hold him at the armpits, the front of his sockets pulling down on my thumbs. I could've gotten nanobot physical therapy, but I don't do nanobots. Never again.

With hordes of other students hustling to their various destinations, I feel the strain in my shoulders, back, and knees. Yet caught between two baffling cases—my missing partner, and a cop who hijacked her way to this facility, camouflaged deep within the snow-capped Baldamere Mountains—the angst of it all immediately evaporates.

Call me a sap, a sucker, a cliché. I don't care. Feeling my son in my arms, the warmth and weight of his body against mine, his arms wrapped tight around my neck, is worth all the sharp pains radiating down my vertebrae. There is no pill that can replicate the feelings we share for each other. The love. The bond.

He's my boy. And I'm his mother.

But seriously, he's getting heavy. And I still can't let go. I run my fingers through the back of his hair, feeling him squeeze me even tighter.

"Okay, buddy. I'm gonna put you down." I do. Standing on his own, he's now up to my shoulders. It seems like just yesterday he was barely up to my hips.

"Mommy! It's not your day to visit. Come see what I did!"

"Love to, pal, but I need to talk to your dad for a—" Owen's already off, running toward one of the workshops. I let out a half-chuckle, half-sigh. I shrug. "Two minutes."

Eddie nods begrudgingly. Not that he doesn't care what Owen wants to show me. It's that Eddie's probably seen it, and there's something urgent he needs to tell me. Something I need to hear. But Patch, private eye... whatever. When your kid's excited, you get excited, too. And more often than is convenient, what *they* want supersedes what *you* need.

Inside the workshop several other children are tinkering with one project or another, with more helper drones buzzing over various contraptions. On the walls in bright painted colors are aspirational phrases like *Dream Today, Build Today* and *Experiments Are Great Ideas Just Waiting to Happen.*

"Whadaya got, bud?"

Owen hands me what looks and feels like a damp washcloth.

"Uh...," I start. "It's...?"

Standing behind a series of consoles positioned for his height, Owen presses a button. In front of us, a section of wall slides back, revealing, behind a blast-shield window, a portion of the Cosmos. He takes hold of two handgrips, like video game joysticks, and uses them to maneuver two mechanical arms. Snared between the grips are opposite edges of the washcloth.

"What, uh... what are you doing here, pal?"

Owen's tongue juts out to the side. He concentrates intently, let's out a little smile. "You'll see." I look to Eddie, who raises his eyebrows at me, and shrugs knowingly, as if to say, *What are you gonna do? He's your kid.*

"Mommy," Owen says, "you see how that section of space-time is wounded?"

"Uh... not really." I watch as Owen magnifies the screen. "Oh, yeah. There it is."

Manipulating the arms, he layers the washcloth against the wounded area. Confident it's secure, Owen releases the cloth, which fuses against the damaged section of spacetime. The wound shimmers, then smooths out. No more irritation.

Owen looks up at me, beaming. "It's a wound patch! I made it myself!"

I look to Eddie, who nods agreeably. "He did. He created the formulation in the lab. Once we've done another round or two of fine-tuning, we'll test it against larger wounds. If it goes well, we might use it on live projects within a year or so."

The emotion overwhelms me, the amazement and pride. My chest swells. My eyes fill with water. "Amazing, buddy. Great stuff." I offer him a smile and a wink, then wipe my eyes with my sleeve.

"Thanks, Mom!" He looks at the clock. "Time for snack! Gotta go! Love ya!"

"Love you, too, buddy. How about a hug goodbye..." He's already off. I'm about to lament how little I'm in the know about his life when Eddie intervenes.

"Five minutes of your attention is like five weeks to him." Eddie takes my hand. "And whether you want to believe it or not, he's much more excited to show you than he is to show me."

Tears flow out of me so fast I can't stop them. "You're right. I don't believe it." I wipe my eyes again with one hand, squeeze his hand with the other. My way of saying I appreciate his kindness, and hopes he says things like that to me again. I need those words more than I used to.

With a deep breath I soak up this room and my memory of the experience. It'll have to tide me over for a while. I have no idea when I'll be back.

Eddie checks his phone, grimaces. "Your friend is getting antsy. You need to get her out of here."

"She's not my friend." Eddie gives me a look. "Okay. I hear you. But what about the tech you said you—"

A harsh buzzer goes off. Red security lights whir.

Eddie looks about, checks his phone. "Damn. Another dead system. I gotta go."

"Dead system? But what about—?"

"Get Olin outta here," he repeats, running for the door. "I'll talk to you later."

"But—"

Like father, like son. My two boys have left me here alone, in the middle of a crisis, because they have the audacity to have lives that don't entirely revolve around mine.

"*There* you are," Olin says as her Patch escort waits impatiently for me to take her off the premises. "What the fuck is going on?"

I take a quick breath to center myself. "I have no idea."

CHAPTER 5

I teleport Olin and me back to Kimmie-slash-Nóirín's apartment. Jarring if you're not accustomed to it, she's less rattled by the instantaneous mode of transportation this time, but she's a bit wobbly. It helps being in this small, confined space, a way to reacclimate, the scale and dimensions more tractable.

It's understood that what Olin saw at the Institute, and how we got to and from, isn't for public consumption. I remind her anyway. She's got more questions than answers—I know the feeling—but before we can get into it, she's pinged by Headquarters. Apparently, there's a break in her double homicide case. As lead detective, she has no choice but to follow up.

We agree to reconvene tomorrow, well, later—it's well past midnight—because despite myself, I need to sleep. And if not sleep, close my eyes, and let my mind swirl until the disparate fragments of my life can settle down.

On the walk back to my apartment I get two texts from Darren, my kinda/sorta boyfriend. I ignore them for now. A professional drummer, he's been doing local gigs for the last two years. But he's got a new band now, about to start a new tour, and he wants to see me before he goes on the road.

I'm tempted to have him come to my place, so I can fall deep into his embrace and maybe even sex the stress out of me, but I can't bring myself to get there. He stuck by me after my arrest. And he's been patient with me since, even though I've barely been present with him, even when we've been in the same room, which has been less frequent as the months have gone by.

It's not that I don't care about him, or us. And as healthy as it would probably be to let my PI life fall away for a few hours and scratch some other itches that have gone unsatisfied for far too long, I can't do that right now.

How can I, when I'm surrounded by a nasty pimp, my missing partner, a sketchy homicide detective, my son, my ex, sweat-inducing nightmares, an inner-sanctum friend who won't talk to me, and one of the highest-ranking law-enforcement officers on-realm?

Sorry, Darren. If my blowing you off right now means we're over... we're over. I'll cry about it later. And yes, the tears will be real. So will the self-loathing.

Named after her former owner's love of books, Page greets me at the door, wagging her tail. On the table is a note from Rosemary, my new dog walker, telling me Page did her business, eyeballed some squirrels, and had dinner. But Page is staring at me, her head tilted, eyes shifted, as if guiding me into the bedroom. Because there's work to be done. I need to sleep, and she needs to watch over me.

I take a quick shower to wash off the grime, letting the hot water beat down on my flesh. I towel off, slip into my sweats and t-shirt, shut off the lights. I check on Owen's room, purely out of instinct. And because I miss him. I crawl into bed.

I'm a side-sleeper, curled on my right shoulder, pillow bunched beneath my neck. Page is perched on the floor, watching me, but angled so that she can easily spy the door and the window, moonlight creeping through the blinds.

Page would be great with me on a stakeout. My mind goes there, envisioning my dog sitting in a parked car, in the next seat, waiting for the target to show, when there's a thick, gray fog all around me. I'm walking through a forest.

Someone's walking ahead of me, in the dense fog, just out of reach. But I can see the arch of his shoulders, the sway of his arms. I want to call out, to ask who he is, the thoughts lingering in the folds of my mind. But now isn't the time to talk. It's a feeling I have, knowing I need to pay attention to my surroundings, to figure out where we are. And where we're going.

Through the fog I see a man—I know through dream logic he's my guide. He reaches out his arm, tugs on a skinny tree branch covered with poisonous tendrils. He pulls it away, ducks under, and moves past it. As he does, he turns back to me, and though I can't quite make out his fog-shrouded face, there's something around his neck.

It's a collar. A dog's collar. I reach for it, to read the name tag. My guide brushes my hand away, even though we don't make physical contact, and shakes his finger at me.

Him in front, me still behind, we hike deeper into the forest. As the fog dissipates that low *whumming* returns. The headaches I've been having. I then notice that the leaves, fungi, and tree stumps are covered in bioluminescent moss. The glowing blues, greens, reds, and yellows glowing brighter even as the forest becomes denser, the trees so tall I can't see their tops.

Then I hear it again, a whisper so faint it tugs on my heart, sending shudders through me. It's Dolores. I can't see her. I don't know where she is. But in my dream mind's eye, she's there, again, somewhere, on the ground, leaning against an old, mossy tree, holding her gut, blood leaking out.

Don't leave me. I'm hurt.

I turn this way and that, through the thick, bioluminescent forest. But the more I look, the more the branches, twigs, and leaves hit me in face. As if trying to keep me away.

I'm bleeding. I'm in so much pain. I'm gonna die.

"She's out there," I say to my guide. "We have to find her. It's Dolores. She needs me."

He turns back to me, shakes his head *no*, then head gestures to follow.

"No," I demand, feeling my voice getting stronger. "Where are we going? Who *are* you?"

My guide stops. He remains perfectly still, then turns to face me. The fog completely gone now, he looks at me like he's been there all along. Because he has. With a film across his mouth.

"Whistler," I mumble. "Why are you so small?" I don't know why I ask that, but it makes sense to me somehow, even though he's a half-foot taller than me.

Beneath our feet, a groove appears in the moss-covered dirt. A jagged, bioluminescent line, slowly trickling through the forest, like an expanding crack along the ice of a frozen lake. He narrows his eyes, which glow red, as the forest descends on me. He gets up in my face. Covered with the film, his mouth opens in the shape of a yawn. Stretching wider, the film splits apart in elastic fronds until they tear away. Freed to speak, he exposes deadly fangs, a drip of blood leaking off the bicuspids. His mouth opens, slow at first, until his jaw expands wider than physiology permits. His chest and shoulders expand.

Whistler rises, two feet taller than me. Three feet. Four. For just a few seconds, ghosted atop him, is another man. Fiftyish, spiky, brown hair, hazel eyes. I don't know if that's another version of Whistler, someone else, or morphing dream logic.

This ghosted man seems important somehow, like I'm supposed to know him. Or fear him.

I do.

Sensing my terror, he offers me a crooked, demented smile. But I can't let him scare me off. I steel myself, straighten my back, and ask: "Why do you hate Whistler?"

I'm not sure how I know he hates Whistler. I just know that he does. And that whatever he's done to Whistler, he won't let go.

"I'm sorry I hurt you," I say, unsure why I've said that, too.

With that admission my heart races, beating so loudly it nearly deafens me. I cover my ears. But in doing so, I've raised my arms, elbows out and extending past my face, initiating a panic, because I've done what he wanted all along. For me to physically expose my heart. I've left it unprotected, that four-chambered muscle now on the outside of my chest, thumping away faster, faster, faster-faster-faster.

The ghosted man stares at his crimson target, takes a deep inhalation, displaying his canine teeth. He holds his pose, escalating my fear. As if thrusted by a disentangled spring, he lunges at me through the thicket of branches. With blood-curling force and intensity, he grabs for me, and barks so disturbingly loud, the glowing forest retracts in terror.

I jolt awake. I'm drenched in sweat. Page is on my bed. She barks at me, then again, the forest replaced with my bedroom walls. I breathe in short, awkward gasps. I rub my chest—my heart on the inside, not out—to soothe myself.

As my breathing slows, I wipe sweat from my forehead, reach forward, scratch Page under the chin. "Good puppy," I say. "You're a good dog."

She follows me as I go to the kitchen and pour myself a glass of water. I sit at the dining room table, letting the cold liquid slide down my throat. It cools my entire body. The headache, the *whumming*, is still there, but it's muted now. Not quite gone, but almost.

I'm no expert, but I get why Whistler might have been in my dream. But why *this* dream? He's missing, stuck in some kind of orbital loop, and I need to find him. He was also one of the last people to see Dolores before she died on the galaxy cruiser, Whistler wounded almost as badly as she was.

I hate feeling so out of control. And nothing good will come from me sitting here, tugging at my guilt and self-doubt, falling down the cavernous rabbit hole of nightmares and theories and *maybes* and *what ifs*. I need to take charge of myself. I need to suit up.

During my third year as an independent investigator, I was hired by a bank teller to find out if his wife was cheating on him. I don't take infidelity cases anymore. Back then it was the easiest way to get my business going. Turns out my client was both right and wrong. He was wrong, in that his wife wasn't cheating him, but his instincts were correct in that she was up to something.

Through an intermediary she'd hired a lowlife named Jackie Two-Turns to kill her husband so she could collect on a sizeable life insurance policy, which he'd taken out at her behest. I was able to connect the dots because I got a tip.

From Dante Maurice Browning.

Do I owe Dante for that? Yeah, he did me a solid, in that he helped me close the case before the wife was able to have my client killed. So, in his way, Dante saved his life. And got me paid in full.

But pimps, and certainly Dante, are not typically known for their acts of kindness. Pimps like him are monsters. Not because they work in the sex trade, but because of how they manipulate already broken women to line their pockets. Women who think they have options, or that they deserve better, do not work for a pimp like Dante.

And when a pimp like Dante calculates the investment in a particular prostitute no longer pencils out, they sell her to another pimp on the cheap or through barter, or cuts her loose—often destitute, demoralized, and drug addicted, and on a fast-track to an early grave. For some of these women, the damage can never be undone.

In the case of Jackie Two-Turns, he had roughed up one of Dante's girls to the point where her prostitution days were over. That violated Dante's pimping code of ethics—and hurt his bottom line. That's when Dante suggested I visit The Side Door, a dirty, underground watering hole in Sinner's Row. Jackie Two-Turns was a regular. It wasn't hard to piece it together.

Which makes me wonder if Kimmie-slash-Nóirín had picked up either vague or specific intel about another crime, and that's what got her killed. Sex workers are a fountain of information, their johns revealing all manner of secrets. Some want to impress the girl as an act of puffery, bragging about their clever little schemes. Others are sad and lonely, and once they start talking, all sorts of dirty deeds spill out. And sometimes, they're just that stupid.

Thinking they can talk shit without it coming back on them. Or they not-so-secretly want to be caught, dropping breadcrumbs that lead to their demise.

Entering a scuzz hole like The Side Door during the day is like bathing in rancid dumpster water. Leaving the harsh glint of sunlight for a dark cave below street level, everything about it makes me want to vomit. The stink and seediness find their way into my pores, soaking into my nasal cavity, even pasting on my taste buds and down my throat.

Aiko Yoshida, one of Dante's girls, is sitting at the bar, looking every bit the sex worker coming off a long shift.

"I'll get this one." I nod to the gaunt, tattooed bartender. His scrawny left arm from elbow to fingertips is cheap chrome. Based on the track marks on his right arm, he's likely a heavy heroine user, his cybernetic limb the result of medical amputation and replacement from an infected needle. Although it could've been elective surgery.

I toss a few credits on the bar. He scowls at me, then with long chrome fingers, claws them into his palm.

"I don't do girls," Aiko says, her black eyeliner smudged. Spaghetti straps dangle off her tiny shoulders. She's sporting bruise marks on her wrists, and a black left eye that's almost healed, but not quite. There's a drop of dried blood on her left earlobe. My guess, an earring was torn away. "And I'm done for the night."

I stare at the bartender, telling him wordlessly to fuck off. He eyes me, Aiko, then me again, demonstrating it's his bar and he makes the rules. Satisfied he's made his point, he lazily goes to the other end near a scruffy old man hunched over a shot glass of well-grade bourbon.

"I'm here about Kimmie."

Aiko stiffens but keeps herself together. "Got nothin to say."

"I'm Hardwicke. Dante sent me."

Aiko rolls her tongue, sips her cocktail. I hand her a business card. She studies it, looks me up and down, then slips it into her tiny black purse.

"Booth," I say. "We can talk over there."

A few other customers are drinking quietly, sadly, up toward the front of the bar. The most intact booth of the four back here, this one is littered with scratches and puncture marks in the old brown leather, with patches of exposed foam.

"Bad night?" I gesture at her bruises.

She pulls her shoulders in close, hides her wrists beneath the table. Squirming, she's acting like someone's who been punished, fearful of being punished again.

"Got jumped," she mumbles.

"By who?"

"Couple'a junkies. They took my purse, my ID. My night's roll."

"Dante pissed?" Aiko drops her eyes, avoiding me. "What can you tell me about Kimmie?"

Fidgety, Aiko pulls her hands up from underneath the table, toying with knock-off spiral bracelets hanging loosely on each wrist. "Top Slot."

"I know. Any idea who killed her?"

"I don't know shit about shit." Aiko keeps eying the bartender, as if he's keeping tabs on her. Maybe he is.

"Kimmie worked the high-end hotels. Dante said that's the model for all you girls. No street walkers. Hotels only. Which are yours?"

Her head is tipped down, eyes furrowed, protecting herself by humoring me without giving me anything that can come back on her. With her right hand, she rubs her left wrist. Nervous habit. The bracelets jangle. "The Wander Inn. The Hint. A few others."

Those are seedy motels. Nothing good ever happens there.

"You get along with Kimmie?"

Only nineteen, Aiko looks twice her age, used up, with gloomy bags under her eyes. She's underweight to the point her skin might slip off her bones. She doesn't answer, so I shift tactics.

"What happened to your eye?"

She pulls back, instinctively reaching up to the bruise, to hide it. "It's nothing."

I'm not sure what she's processing, but like the first crack in a dam, her eyes soften in the corners. She sits upright and reaches across the table, grabbing my hands. The dam breaking open wide now, she's nearly in tears. She keeps her voice low but speaks with clarity. And desperation.

"You gotta get me out." Her hands exposed, there's a red irritation mark on her left wrist where she was rubbing it.

"Out of what?" I ask but can take a good guess.

"The life. Kimmie looked after me, was teaching me how to play it right. But now…"

Aiko tells me her story. She ran away from home when she was sixteen because her uncle, a dentist with a thriving family practice, had repeatedly molested her since she was eight years old. When she finally marshaled the bravery to confess what he'd been doing, the family blamed her for making up lies. For trying to ruin a good man's life and bringing disgrace to them all.

Tormented by their rejection, she contemplated suicide, going so far as to procure razor blades to slit her wrist in the bathtub. She ran away instead, hustling to get by. Dante pulled her into his stable a few months ago.

In addition to her bruised eye, there's a spot of dried blood under her left nostril. Probably from doing too much blow. Or meth. The corner-girl sex workers I know tell me they lose a month off their lives for every week on the street. Some sex workers ply their trade in safe environments. Others do not.

Aiko's shaking. "I can't do it without Kimmie. I'll never make it."

"When's the last time you saw her?"

She wipes her messy eyes. "Monday, I think. At the crib."

"What crib?"

"On Winchester. Me and the girls. We all live together in an apartment. Dante's rules."

"But Kimmie has her own place. Had her own place."

"She's Top Slot. She's got privileges. She stays with us once, maybe twice a week, to make sure we're okay, the counts are right, and we ain't getting hooked on no shit. Dante says we can use to get in the groove and turn those tricks. But if the shit starts to own us, he's keepin our cut and tossin us out. Says you can't trust a junkie whore. But it's so hard, you know. You get a taste, get all dreamy. Makes it easier to forget what you're doin. And who you're doin it with."

It's a rough life when you feel trapped by a pimp like Dante, with very few happily-ever-afters.

"Anyone want to hurt Kimmie? Enemies? Possessive johns? A stalker?"

"Nobody I seen. She was..." More tears. "Kimmie was good people. I just couldn't figure out the deal with her and Dante. It's like... she decided to take care of us girls. Not because she was Top Slot. More like... she made her job that way. Kimmie said just because we sold our bodies didn't mean we had to sell our souls. I didn't believe that. Not sure she did either, or if she was just giving us hope in a hopeless life. Either way, she cared about us. That's how it seemed to me. But now she's gone... I don't know how Dante's gonna keep us together. He needed Kimmie more than she needed him."

"Dante," I say, nodding at her wrist. I'm not sure she even realizes she's rubbing it again. "He get rough with you?"

Aiko can't look at me. She shakes her head *no*. She's not convincing.

"How about the other girls?" I leave the question intentionally vague, to see if she interprets me to be asking if Dante ever gets rough with the other girls or if they ever get rough with her.

A stable of sex workers like this one isn't a slumber party. It's a harem of desperate women who, all day, every day, submit to the sexual gratification of strangers, surviving the persistent onslaught of depravity, kinks, and perversities however they can, for as long as they can.

Sex workers tend to look out for each other, bonded by the life. But when they feel hopeless, it's no surprise when they turn on each other. They can only take so much working for a pimp like Dante. And when they do lash out, it's often at the person standing right beside them, earned or not.

"What about a john?" I ask. "You get slapped around?" She'd hardly be the first sex worker to get more than she asked for.

Aiko tenses up. Her body language tells me I'm onto something. Or it could be her reaction to the opened door, a streak of hazy light let into this dank cavern. The bartender looks our way, then to the man who sits down at the bar. Aiko curls the loose spaghetti straps back on her bare shoulders. They fall right off again. With jangling bracelets, she clutches her purse and gets up from the booth.

"Talk to Kayla," Aiko says. "She's next in line for Top Slot."

Possible suspect. "You think she had beef with Kimmie? Enough to knock her off?"

"I'm terrified twenty-four seven. Dante's always in our shit, playin mind games, makin sure we don't lose focus, or get lazy. We gotta hit our numbers every week. We do, we get to stay. We don't…" She side-eyes the bartender. "I don't wanna be in the middle of anyone's shit. I got enough of my own."

CHAPTER 6

I call Dante. Tell him I want to stop by his apartment. Talk to the other girls and catch him up on what I've learned so far. Ever the charmer, he's in a good mood.

"What the fuck you waitin for? Move yer ass." He hangs up.

Times like this, my attentions split between cases, were so much easier when Whistler and I worked them together. Something I never thought I'd admit.

After nearly fifteen years on my own I resented his presence when he crowbarred his way into my life, doing everything I could to push him away. But he stuck with it, taking his lumps until he became a heck of an investigator, a partner, and, as much as I did not want to accept it, a friend. And now that I'm on my own again, a lone wolf, all I want is to reunite my pack.

Not to mention that my other case... is Whistler.

Which makes me realize I need to get back to the office, see what he may have left behind. And what did Eddie mean when he said the kind of tech that might've swept Whistler up in an artificial orbit was from the Institute?

Was Whistler investigating them?

Did the Guild we've been trying to infiltrate actually infiltrate the Institute? If so, does that mean that Eddie has been compromised? And if so, has it reached our son?

My heart is back in my throat. Blood rushes to my ears, drowning out the mid-day roar of an active construction site erecting a new residential tower in the shadow of the nearby monorail station.

Just another element of how quickly the realm is changing before our eyes.

As the story goes, Eternity went through an industrial phase eons ago. The Minders of the Universe—three existential beings who created and now oversee Existence and everything in it— figured automation would speed things up throughout the realm, allowing for greater efficiency in our ability to design, build, and maintain the Cosmos at their behest.

But the environment in Eternity became so toxic as a result, the illness rates so high, the Minders scrapped it completely.

With a blink of their unfathomable eyes, the Minders supposedly replaced that model with a wintry habitat, positing that constant frigid conditions would keep everyone moving, just to stay warm. Can you imagine? Freezing my tits off year-round? No thanks.

Not sure how long that tundra lasted, but as the Minders do, they changed their minds once again, going in the opposite extreme. They completely reinvented Eternity as a tropical paradise, figuring that happy, relaxed, and well-rested workers would consistently give their all. Another misfire. Eternitarians spent too much time windsurfing, fornicating, and getting drunk on the beach.

So the Minders gave Eternity yet another new look and feel, the one I've known.

Yet the realm as a whole and E-Town in particular are being increasingly devoured by a new wave of technology. AI, androids, cybernets, synthetic organs, and increasingly complex computer algorithms, holograms, virtual reality, augmented reality, hover and driverless vehicles, and intergalactic travel are ubiquitous. Changes are being implemented so rapidly we can barely keep up.

It's only when I get back to my office do I notice the burn in my legs and the grip in my thighs. I'd been walking so fast and in short, controlled bursts I nearly pulled every muscle from Achille's heel to ass.

Up on the second floor landing I reach for my keys, and stare at the frosted glass, with the wording in black stenciled ink: *ANGELA HARDWICKE: PRIVATE INVESTIGATIONS*

I'd meant to add Whistler's name to the door, but I got arrested for murder before I could. And since I've been out, my future—our future—has felt uncertain, if not bleak. I've been repositioned against my will to feel like an unwanted guest, an intruder, in my own office. My name's still on the lease, so technically... it's still mine.

Kinda. Sorta.

But Tarrish put my business into a quasi-receivership, such that Whistler is, for now, the legal administrator, paying the bills from revenue he's been bringing in from cases he works, while Tarrish pays me less than minimum wage to serve as a non-agent agent, indefinitely out on loan.

Another reason I haven't stopped by the office much since I got out of prison.

My key still works, so that's something. The space is just how it used to be, only Whistler seems to have moved out of the back room he'd been using as his private area, and over to my desk. It's littered with files, papers, 3-D holocubes, maps, and tablets, likely loaded with all sorts of intel and research for cases I know nothing about. I wonder if Whistler thinks of it as his desk now, or if it's just a matter of convenience.

It's *my* desk. I bought it, stressed over cases from there, met with more clients than I'll ever remember. Yet I feel like I'm violating *his* space just by touching the surface, rummaging through the piles, letting my fingertips run along the back of the leather chair I spent more than a decade breaking in.

The circular table is still here, opposite my desk, loaded with more piles, books, and, underneath a recent newspaper winged open... a laptop. His laptop. Whistler's. I can't help but smile. My heart flutters. Because if his laptop is here, it means he's likely using the table as his desk. Leaving my desk alone. Preserving the sanctity of my space.

I know it seems petty, to be so concerned over which slab of wood is more mine and which is more his, but it's symbolic. Whistler's way of communicating to me that he still sees this box and four walls as *my* office, and he's just holding down the fort until I resume my place at the head of the physical and metaphorical table. That he still respects me. That he values what I've built. And has no interest in trying to take it away from me when I'm down and not quite out.

I'm not typically a day drinker, but I take off my jacket, drape it on the hook on the wall. I pull a rocks glass and my bottle of Scotch from the bottom drawer and pour myself a snort. I take the drink and sit in my chair, reclaiming what's mine.

My chair feels like it always did, the years and the cases I've worked soaked into the fabric. The leather is contorted to the shape of my body, including my butt print, and the arch in the small of my back. And yet, it doesn't feel quite right. Like a college student who comes home from their first semester away, the space is the same. And yet utterly different, a shrunken, distorted version of what you'd remembered.

That's the funny thing about growing up. It means you can never go back to the way things were, even if you'd spent most of that time wishing things could be different.

"Enough," I say as much to myself as to Whistler's ghost, then toss back the liquor. "Let's get to work."

Dante texts me twice, demanding I get over to the apartment. I tell him I'm on my way. I'll see how long that holds him off. I instead rummage through Whistler's table, sifting through the files of cases he's worked on—a kidnapping, an inside job at a warehouse theft, insurance fraud—and an electronic file of receipts he hasn't submitted yet and billed back to the clients.

But nothing about the Guild, the Institute, or Eddie. And yet sifting through the last year of Whistler's life makes me feel more connected to him, more grounded, the muscle memory from our years together kicking back in.

Unsure where to look next, I switch on my contact lens, and try to sync with Whistler's. I'm not even sure if he's got it in his eye, or if he's working only with ICD tech. Tarrish made him sever the link with my lens after he put Whistler in charge, putting a wall between us, a way of keeping ICD intel from getting to me. Even Bernice couldn't re-establish the link.

But Whistler's always had a little Angela Hardwicke in him, a rogue spirit, willing to skirt the rules when the rules didn't hold up to scrutiny. Or got in the way.

"Come on. There's gotta be a workaround—ow! Fuck!"

Dropping me to one knee, I squint, lean forward. I wedge the pad of my hand against my right eye to smother the blistering pain. My lens is shooting signals, like grains of broken glass, through my optic nerve, into my brain, and piercing what feels like a puss-filled blister.

"Damn it!"

But squeezing my eyes shut doesn't prevent images from ripping across the frontal-parietal control regions of my brain.

"*Mayzhhhh!*" It's Whistler again, his voice distorted with the buzzing wax paper effect. Only he's coming into focus. "*Mayzhhhh! Mache!*"

To establish boundaries, I made Whistler call me Ms. Hardwicke the first few months he was under my charge. But eventually he started calling me Ms. H, which devolved to Mizzache and finally, Mache. As far as nicknames go, I've had better. I've definitely had worse.

"*Mache,*" he says again, clearly. "*Can you hear me?*"

I fight through the assault in my mind.

"Er... Eric. Is that you?"

Six feet tall with light brown skin, Whistler's about ten years younger than me. Yet right now, he looks so much older.

"*I'm boosting the signal the best I can. I gotta talk fast.*"

"What happened to you? Where are you? What's—?"

I reach out to grab him. But as my hand makes contact with the orbital field he's encased in, I get an intense shock. It knocks me back on my ass, spraining my wrist. Stunned from the recoil, I pick myself up, favoring my injured hand.

"Whistler, what's happening?"

"*I'm caught in some kind of temporal loop. I was able to re-route the coordinates to get me here, but it won't hold, and I can't get loose. You need to go to the...*"

He's starting to phase, his image, clear just seconds ago, buzzy and distorted again.

"*Mayzhhhh! Go tzzooo the.... Eddie... the Eddie... the Eddie... the Eddie... hiiiive.*"

"What's the Eddie Hive? Whistler? Whistler! Do you mean my Eddie? At the Institute?"

"*N...nzz... no. Not... Ed...eee.*" He's becoming increasingly distorted. "*EDSNDIE... IIIIIIIIVE. I foundzzzz... him. Tu-tu... tel-lzzz Tu... Taar... Tarr... Tarrish. I found him. And get in the queue.*"

Fffzzz...or ... the a...a...a... apzz."

"Tarrish? I don't understand. Tell him you found *who*? Found Eddie? What's Eddie Hive? What queue?"

"Nnnn... no. Not... Eh.. eh... IVE. Get in the que—"

He's gone.

The shock of the moment distracted me, but now I can feel my hand throbbing. I rush into the bathroom, see my hand is red and swollen. I let the cold water from the faucet cool me down. It's not enough. Out in the main space I dig through the mini fridge for an ice pack, steam nearly hissing off my hand.

"Whistler," I say with a sigh. "What the...?"

Stop, Angela. Think.

Whistler phased here. When *I* was here. But how did he *know* I'd be here? Which means he suspected, or knew for certain, that I *was* here. Can he... see me, from wherever he is? Can he... sense me? Is he tracking me? And what does that mean?

Eddie but not Eddie. Eddie Hive.

I have no idea. But he said to tell Tarrish that he found him. That he found Eddie not Eddie Hive. Eddie not Eddie.

Does that mean I need to find *an* Eddie, but not *my* Eddie? And if not my Eddie, then who? There are countless Eddies out there. But if Whistler's caught in a temporal loop of some kind, an artificial orbit, who would know more about that than my Eddie?

And why isn't Tarrish getting back to me? If he's got Whistler working on a case that's caught him up in... whatever the hell this is, wouldn't he want every piece of intel he could get? One way to find out. I make a call. Tarrish actually picks up.

"T," I say hurriedly. "It's Whistler. He phased in again. I just saw him."

"I know."

"What do you mean *you know*?"

Tarrish mutes me to take another call. Or is that his way of buying time to think without me knowing he's not sure what to do either?

He's back. "Hardwicke. If Whistler shows up again, you ping me immediately. Not after. Not later. During. Immediately. That very second."

"Why? What are you trying to—?"

"Just do it."

I hate this fucking arrangement. But Tarrish holds the keys to my freedom, and until I can learn more about what he's up to, what's happening with Whistler, I have no choice but to play along.

"Okay. If it happens again, I'll ping you during. I'm going to talk to some of the contacts I made in the Guild. Maybe they have a lead on Whistler."

"No," he retorts forcefully. "Stand down."

"What do you mean *stand down*? Fuck that. I'm not standing down."

"Yes, you will. *Don't* investigate, *don't* follow. Don't do anything. Just work your one-for-you until I tell you different."

"You gotta be kidding me. We're past that, T."

"We're not."

"It's Whistler!" I hear him sigh with restrained frustration. "T. You know who I am. You know what I do." I let my fear and anger subside enough to let myself be vulnerable with him. Not something I'm prone to do. "And who Eric is to me."

His tone is gentler. "I know. And I know it's hard for you. But I need you to sit tight."

"But—"

"Angela. Telling me to sit tight would make me do the opposite. I get it. But as always, things are more complicated than you think. Give me a day. I'm working on it. I promise. But for now…"

"Stand down?"

He pauses before answering. "I'm sorry, but… yes."

He never apologizes. Ever.

I press the ice pack deeper into my burned hand and bite my bottom lip, fierce enough to draw blood. I sigh through gritted teeth. "Fine. I'll stand down."

"Thank you."

There's silence between us, until I break it. "But, T?"

He hesitates before responding. "Yes?"

"Not for long."

He sighs again. "I know that, too." He hangs up.

Like a wild animal in captivity, I'm pacing my office as if it's my cage, counting off in my head as I stare through iron bars.

One... two... three...

Fuck it.

That's long enough.

I don't know what Tarrish and Whistler have been up to or why he doesn't want me near the investigation. I also don't know what Whistler meant by *Eddie not my Eddie, Eddie Hive,* or what Eddie meant about the Institute's tech being the possible link to Whistler's phasing. But I intend to find out. And I don't I care if Eddie's ready to see me. I'm ready to see him.

I remove my sidearm from my shoulder holster and confirm that it's loaded, graze the grip on my boot knife snug against my ankle, and pat the retractable taser secured in an updated sheath strapped to my jeans along the hip.

From the wall I snag my jacket and slip it back on.

"Okay, Eddie not Eddie Hive." I produce the device Eddie gave me to transport from wherever I am. "I'm getting in the queue. Knock-knock."

I press the button, ready to reappear in the Patch Institute.

Except I'm still here. I look at the device oddly, try again. Same deal. Nothing.

"What the...?" I lean forward, examining the device, as if I know what to look for. I shake it, then tap the button repeatedly to get this teleportation under way. "Why aren't you...?"

Then it hits me. I raise my head, staring at the frosted glass on the door, my name, in black ink, appearing backwards. Out of sequence. Misplaced.

"Eddie. Damn it."

He deactivated my device.

CHAPTER 7

Looks like I'm going to have to get back to the Institute the old-fashioned way. I call Esteban to pick me up. He's working the end of the afternoon shift, so it takes him nearly an hour to get here in rush hour.

Night descending on the city, his cab pulls up outside my office, flashers blinking. I hop into the backseat. The motor hums. A nearby streetlamp reflects off my side window.

"Sorry, I'm late." Banny's wearing a midnight blue infantryman's military uniform with a double-bar insignia on the sleeve. On his time off he works as an extra on movie, TV, and commercial sets. The gigs don't pay much, but it feeds that part of his soul he can't satisfy in any other way. He likes to be seen, even if he's not heard. "My last fare was a casting director I've worked with a couple of times. She commented on my uniform. I had to go for it."

"And?"

He gazes at me through the rearview. "You know..."

"Well," I say, "at least—"

"I got a part!" He turns around to face me. "She knows the director of the TV movie I'm auditioning for! I'm getting"—he exhales slowly—"I... am getting... a scene with... check it... Gloria Mandalapali!" He punches the air in victory. "Yeah, baby!"

"Wow! Really?"

"Well," he says through the bulletproof partition, "I still need to audition, but this part... it's bigger, it's got lines, and it's with..."

"Gloria Mandalapali?"

"I can't believe it! After all these years. This is it!"

I lean back against the backrest. "I hope so, Ban. I really do."

He starts the fare—he doesn't drive me for free—shifts into gear, then waits at the red light at the corner. Traffic blares around us.

"Anj," he says. "Lay it on me." Banny has always been great this way, helping me out on cases when I'm in a jam. I haven't called on him lately. Not after the galaxy cruiser. "You don't have to worry. I'm not mad at you."

Which is good. Because he's still close with Nini. And no matter what I told Olin, I can't risk losing any more friends. I really need him.

Banny rips through the intersection, barely avoiding a black and chrome hover car and a dinged up rental truck. "Don't do that. Dolores was her own woman who made her own choices. You didn't cause that clusterfuck up there. And you didn't force them to be involved. The way it played out... it's not your fault."

He's twisting himself into knots to help relieve my guilt, and I love him for it. But when it comes to the life I lead, the cases I take, there always seems to be collateral damage.

"Some of it was."

"Without you, it would've been a whole lot worse."

"Maybe," I say. "But Dolores is still dead. And Nini... she won't talk to me."

Nini's a nurse at E-Town General. Even after a decade in the ER, she'd never seen anything like what went down on the cruiser. A freak accident unleashed a murderous frenzy with humans and androids alike tearing each other apart. Me, Whistler, Tarrish, Dolores, and Nini got caught in the crossfire. Dolores never made it out. The rest of us survived, barely, but we haven't been the same. We never will be.

"Give her time." A fleet of security drones cut us off. Lights blaring, they whisk in front, down the avenue, perpendicular to us.

"It's been a year, Ban. How much time does she need?"

He eyes me through the rearview. "You deal with it your way," he says, "she'll deal with it hers."

We sit in silence, navigating traffic until finally we make our way to the West Side, around the monorail's line of elevated track and onto the Rubiyat Highway, curving around the Chabaqua River. Across from those choppy and dangerous waters are the Manuela Projects. Another case that still haunts me.

We're flanked by a delivery truck, its sides a digital billboard. The ads scroll from a cheery blonde in *Donna B's Fun Panties & Bras*, to a starburst that blooms into a patch of bright red strawberries—*Order fresh fruit today from Meadow Lane!* The screen blinks into white bulbs and then over to a cylindrical bed floating amongst a background of stars to *Visit Lucid's Dream Pods*, and finally to a sexy babe with flowing red hair, crystal blue eyes, a cranial implant, and cybernetic limbs. She pops her hip, and winks. *Why be organic when you can be Organic Plus?*

An aggressive driver, Banny finds an opening in the logjam. He shoots ahead, speeding along the busy highway. "Why are we driving? What happened to your device?"

I'm reluctant to bring him in too deep, so I give him the short version. Instead of giving me shit about risking Whistler's life again—Nini would have been right to do so—Esteban picks up like old times, focusing on the task at hand. The driver next to us notices Banny's uniform and salutes him. Banny nods in appreciation.

"Whadaya think Whistler meant?"

"I don't know." The tension in my chest loosens now that I'm talking about it. "But Eddie's never locked me out before. The Institute's into all sorts of shit we don't know about. The research, the tech. The access to... everywhere. No matter how many times I've been out there, Eddie's only shown me a fraction of what they've got. Now that I think about it—"

My phone buzzes. Dante.

I hesitate before answering. "I know," I say to him, "I'm running a little late."

"You gotta help me." A desperate whisper. Panicked female voice. "Hurry!"

"Aiko?"

"He's gone crazy. He's so *angry*. He's..." She hangs up.

"Aiko!" I shout into a line that's gone dead. "Aiko!"

Banny eyes me through the rearview. "Problem?"

I clench my fists, accept my fate. "Change of plans. We gotta turn around."

It takes us another hour to get off the highway and track back through the urban streetscape. Given traffic flows we have no choice but to cut through Upper Midtown West, a canyon of skyscrapers, blaring lights, and more holographic billboards competing for digital space throughout the frenetic skyline.

I try not to focus on them, but it's hard not to notice the galaxy cruisers far overhead. Their transmitter lights blinking, the luxury ships transport thousands of people throughout the Cosmos.

But are those blinking lights standard operating procedure? Or coded distress calls?

I want to think they're all safe, with enhanced protocols in place. And they probably are. But if another psychotic rampage has been unleashed among any or all the cruisers, I wonder if I'll hear the screams.

"Hey." Banny seems to have noticed I drifted back into my PTSD. "We're almost there."

We're back in Sinner's Row. The ETPD has an unofficial look-the-other-way policy about the neighborhood. It's mostly populated by old tenement buildings, seedy bars, drug corners, strip clubs, pawn shops, liquor stores, cheap diners, and underground mod shops where, for a fee, unlicensed ModDocs perform cybernetic surgeries.

Members of the Vice Squad are permanently embedded in Sinner's Row. The unwritten policy is that, as long as you keep the sin within this underworld enclave, they won't kick in too many doors. But if bodies drop, or you drag minors into your kink, they're coming for you. Murder and minors. It's good to know they have standards.

We drive past the Side Door, where I met Aiko. I didn't realize Dante's crib was so close. Two blocks away, Esteban finds a spot on an unlit side street. Overflowing garbage cans line the curb.

"I'm coming up," Banny says, locking up his cab.

"No!" I command aggressively, an unchecked anxiety reflex. "Too dangerous."

A gunshot rings out in the distance, followed by shouting, a car alarm, and the quick patter of footsteps. "You think it's safer out here?"

Esteban is tough and wiry, ready to brawl. His fists are small but hit like jackhammers—quick, repetitive, destructive. His uncle, an old flyweight boxer who fell into a bottle, used to beat the crap out of him. Esteban learned to hit back.

I pat the butt of my gun to reassure me. "Fine. But stay close. And take off that uniform. You'll get shot crossing the street."

We turn the corner and look up. Black metal numbers nailed into the brick face above the apartment building's entrance mark the address. At the top of the stoop, Banny one step below me, I press the buzzer for 5B. Top floor. Above the door frame, a small black globe, a security camera, shifts in my direction.

An aggressive buzz unlocks the black metal security gate. I pull it open on its squeaky hinge. The front door, made from heavy wood with reinforced metal edges, also unlocks. It opens in.

Inside the foyer the stench hits me in the face like a cinderblock. A combination of trash, spicy food, cheap sex, and even cheaper perfumes. I go to the elevator.

A gaunt teenager in a sleeveless tank top and track marks up and down his emaciated arms leans against the dirty wall. He bounces a pink rubber ball against the side of the stairwell, perfectly timing it so the ball lands in his open palm without having to move. "It's broke. Dante upstairs."

Banny and I trudge cautiously up the dimly lit stairwell, the stench lessening the higher we go. There are five apartments on each floor, the landings guarded by rickety wooden bannisters. The stairs creak with each step we take, no way to sneak up.

A large, burly girl with an afro and a thatch of freckles on her brown cheeks is waiting for us on the fifth-floor landing. In gray parachute pants, black t-shirt, and a red, white, and yellow bandana around her neck, she's wielding a metal baseball bat. Dried blood is soaked into the stained white tape wrapped around the grip.

"Whatchu want?"

"Dante," I say.

"Fuh what?"

"Spiritual advisor. I'm here to save his soul."

Burly Girl grips the bat. "You funny. But ain't no souls left to save in there." With the weapon's thick end, she taps the door three times. "Comin in. That skinny white bitch is here. She gotta friend."

We hear some rustling on the other side of the door, then a series of chains and bolts being undone. The door opens. It's Dante. Bright red shirt tail yanked from black trousers, he's sweaty and agitated. Blood marks his knuckles.

"Getcher ass in here."

He grabs me by the arm, pulls me inside. Banny follows. Dante slams the door. Railroad apartment, bigger than I thought. One of his girls is on a couch, her eye swollen shut. Dante eyes Banny. "Whooda fuck is this?"

"My driver."

Dante scrapes his big pink tongue beneath the edge of his top teeth. "Whatchu got for me? What happened to Kimmie?"

"What happened *here?*"

"Mindja fuckin business, Hardwicke. It ain't work that way. *I* ask, *you* tell. You feel me?"

"Daddy," demurs the beaten girl, her bare legs curled beneath her on the couch. Pretty other than the battered face, she's medium height with ebony skin and wild black hair pinned messily in a bun. Her swollen left eye is purple, with a small square gash over it. She appears to be naked beneath a black satin robe with a roaring red dragon embroidered into the fabric. "You don't gotta be like this."

Cold like a serpent, Dante's eyes nearly glow red. He scowls and leans in her direction. He pulls his shoulder back like he's about to smack her again.

"What I tell you, Simone? I'm gonna fuck yer face into next week you don't shut the fuck up."

Simone squirms into the corner of the couch, a shaded window behind her head. But I've been around enough beaten women to see she's looking to strike back. You beat a dog long and hard enough, it'll bite its master. You beat a woman long enough, she'll stab you in the heart.

From what I can tell it's a three-bedroom apartment, two on one end, one on the other, the kitchen and bathroom side by side. The space is surprisingly uncluttered, with a few couches and chairs, quilts, and end tables. Bizarre, erotic art dangles on the walls. Used paper plates, grungy napkins, and a greasy bag on the coffee table.

A bedroom door on the opposite side of the living room opens enough that I can see a sliver of Aiko's face, the rest of her hiding behind the door. Dante sees me see her. She's wearing a white teddy, covered by a jade green satin robe, sash tied at the waist.

"It's okay, baby girl." He coos at Aiko as if he's an entirely different monster than the one who just beat his employee to a pulp, for reasons I've yet to determine. "Daddy ain't mad. You know you my girl. Daddy's loves you."

"I don't like this," Banny whispers to me.

"There's nothing to like." I'm not sure what's happening, but Aiko's distress call was real. "So... Dante." I glide into the center of the apartment, keeping him equidistant from each girl, me closer to Simone, Esteban closer to Aiko. "You're riled up. What's the problem?"

"The problem," Dante says, glaring at me, then roars, "the PROBLEM?" He huffs curtly through wide nostrils. "Fuck." He clenches both fists, one set of clock rings sparkling beneath the muted lighting, the other smeared in blood. "It's Kayla. Bitch is gone."

I know who she is, but I ask anyway. "She one of your girls?"

"Kayla was next up for Top Slot. And now I got *these* two bitches and Jasmine. She the only one..." He lunges toward Simone, but I pull him back. He eyes me, yanks his arm free. "She the only one out there makin my *muthafuckin money!*"

I gotta chill him out. We're getting nowhere fast. "How about a drink? It's been a long few days."

"I ain't want no drink." Typical pimp. He needs to feel like he's in control. I let him come to it on his own.

"I'll get it," Simone says.

Dante's temper erupts. "Shut your hole and know your role!"

He turns to Aiko who, from still inside her bedroom, is clutching the barely ajar door. He's all sweetness again. "Aiko, baby. S'okay. Get Daddy a drink, will ya? The way I like it."

With renewed vigor, Simone gets up from the couch. "I got it."

"I *said*," Dante repeats, yet another reminder of who's boss, "Aiko."

Simone ignores him, goes into sex kitten mode, running her fingers down the inside of her smooth black thigh. "She ain't know how to satisfy you," she purrs. "Not like I do. Sit in yer chair, Daddy." Simone goes to the open bar, pours two fingers of amber liquor into a rocks glass. "I'll"—with metal tongs, she rubs the ice cubes between her legs, then, with a clink, suggestively drops one cube into the glass, then another—"do it right."

Seemingly pacified, Dante permits her to approach. Simone saunters toward him like the trained prisoner she is. Shorter than Dante, she offers him the glass with one hand, rubs her other along his crotch. "Drink it slow and smooth, Daddy. It'll go down *real* nice." She twirls her tongue around a maraschino cherry. "Just like me."

As if it's his throne, Dante sits in a high-backed chair opposite the windows overlooking the street. The blinds are three-quarters closed. He can watch the action out on the streetscape as needed, while also being shielded from prying eyes. I sit on the couch kitty corner to his chair. Esteban remains by the door, ready to bolt or fight.

"Love on one," I say to Dante, "hate on the other. What gives?"

"It's the Pimp's Credo. Kick ass or kiss ass but leave no ass unattended. If not, you get a coup up in this bitch."

The streets may be dirty, but they teach you the dirty truth. "You should train CEOs."

He rolls his eyes. "Don't I know it."

Simone and Aiko take their places on either side of his throne. Aiko is petrified, rubbing her sore wrist, the same one from the other day. Simone is all business, collected after the beating she took. My guess, she'll need a week or more to recover physically. Psychologically? No telling.

When ruled by a pimp like Dante, sex workers only have so many moves. And if you can't run, even fewer.

"You said Kayla's gone," I say. "Gone, as in, she took off, gone? Or...?"

Dante takes a chug of liquor. The amber liquid smears his lips. "She dead."

CHAPTER 8

"**D**ead? How?"

"Whatchu mean... how? Like... she ain't breathin no more. That's how."

"No shit," Banny says. "Who killed her?"

Dante's eyes shift to him like the security camera's black soulless globe. "You ain't on my payroll. Which means I don't wanna hear shit come outcha mouth unless it's got my hairy asshole on it." Dante's upping his inner pimp poison. Trying to make everything and everyone around him dead, vulgar, and foul so we're easier to dominate.

Banny should know better, but he punches back. "You kiss your mother with that mouth?"

"Momma dead," Dante says, rising from this throne. His two girls pull his arms, trying to hold him back from inciting more violence. Once punches get thrown, anyone can end up with broken bones. Or worse. Including them. "You ain't shut the fuck up... you next."

"Where is she?" I interject, getting us back into the details. This is why I didn't want Banny up here. "Where's Kayla? Where's her body?"

Dante shifts his gaze from the hand on one shoulder, then to the other, giving Simone and Aiko the death stare. They both let go.

"Chabaqua River. Olin on the dial."

This is getting more complicated. That Olin's been first on the scene, twice, is more than a bit suspicious. "How'd she die?"

"Shot in the head. Stabbed in the gut. Then dumped. It ain't no coincidence."

"And with Aiko getting jumped the other night..." I let that statement linger. I'm not sold she was attacked by two junkies. Either she got into some other kind of mess, and Dante gave her some homeschooling, or she was the first on the list, but managed to get away. Though the way she's shaken up, it seems unlikely. Regardless, Dante says aloud what's becoming clear.

"Someone's gunnin for my girls."

With frantic, shifty eyes, Simone surveils the apartment, as if looking for an escape route. Aiko shrinks into the corner, nervously rubbing her wrist.

"Or someone's gunning for *you*," I say. "And using them to do it."

Dante's not ready to relocate, feeling safer holed up in the apartment where he knows the streets and the local players. He says Olin's got people in Vice who can watch his back. But he also knows that if he's relying on the police to keep him alive, he won't be sucking air much longer.

I ask about enemies, but when it comes to the pimp life, it's more efficient to make a list of anyone who doesn't hate you. Targeting sex workers is rarely the work of a rival pimp. It's bad for business. But if Dante borrowed money from the wrong people or is mixed up in the drug game, all bets are off.

And if his girls are being hunted, right now Jasmine is the most vulnerable, out on the street. Dante called, told her to come back to the crib. She's too scared to come back alone. Which means I'm going to her.

Amy's is another dive bar in Sinner's Row. It's also a cybernets hangout. I worked a case here awhile back involving Nini's cousin. His implant malfunctioned. Didn't end well.

Punk metal thrashes inside as the bouncer pats me down. We've done this dance before. Six-foot-two with three nose rings, a pink mohawk, and a cybernetic implant next to her left eye, Siobhán reminds me of the tavern's policy, mounted on the wall behind her: *Check all Weapons… or Get the Fuck Out.*

She makes me check my gun, retractable taser, and switchblade, but lets me hang onto my silver scout orb. It's no clear threat.

Wearing spiked, fingerless gloves, Siobhán hands me a ticket for my gear. "Who's your friend?" She gestures at Esteban. "He's cute."

"Not for you. He only dates men."

"Who said anything about *dating*? Whadaya say, sunshine? Meet me after my shift?" She cranes her neck from side to side. It cracks loudly. "Have a little fun?"

Banny follows me into the bar. "Rain check. But I know where to find you."

Modest crowd, the ratio about three-to-one cybernets to not. The regular bartender isn't working. I don't know this guy. "Whatever you've got on tap," I say. He pours me a pint, hands it to me. "Charlie working?"

The bartender stares at me as if he's about to slit my throat. The lights on his cranial implant scroll in a red-red-black pattern. *Suspicion.* "You a cop?"

"I look like one?"

"I've seen you here before, asking questions."

"That a crime?"

"Should be."

"Fair enough. But no. I'm not a cop. Looking for some company. I'm lonely."

He nods, but mostly to himself. "Charlie doesn't do that anymore."

I take a large swallow from the pint, wipe foam from my lip. "I know. They're a friend."

Friend might be overstating it.

The bartender pulls empties off the bar. "In back. By the dart board."

Banny and I serpentine through the crowd, drawing all manner of stares, unsurprising given that we have no cranial implants. We stick out. The dart board is on the other side of three laser pool tables, all occupied, with credit-loaded star drives on the railings to secure whatever wagers are on the line.

I spot a server with a snake tattoo on the back of their neck. They turn with an empty beer bottle in each hand. Upon seeing me, their cranial implant activates in a frantic pattern.

Charlie used to trick out by the Rubiyat Highway. Got beaten within an inch of their life by some trans-hating fuckweasels who did unspeakable things to them with a baton—before and after they were unconscious. Cybernetic implant repaired most of the damage. Charlie quit the streets after that. Been working here ever since.

"Charlie," I say. "Life treating you okay?"

A hundred pounds soaking wet, they shake their head. "Let me guess. You're looking for someone."

"Guilty as charged."

"I haven't seen them."

"Seen who?"

"Whoever. Can't help."

"I got two dead sex workers in the last week. Another's in trouble. I'm supposed to meet her here. I'm trying to keep her safe."

Charlie tenses up, then expels a sigh of aggravation. Their implant blinks several times. "Order a drink from me."

I know the code. "Beer. And a club soda for him."

"With two orange wedges." Esteban looks at me. "What? I like it that way."

In short order Charlie comes back with our drinks. I raise my phone to pay for them. A photo of Jasmine I got from Dante is up on the screen. Twenty-five or so, Jasmine is a stunning brunette with an hour-glass figure. But she has an old scar on her left temple, likely from a burn mark. Don't know how she got it.

"How old's the photo?" Charlie asks.

I look at them curiously. "Why?"

"Near the restrooms. By the back exit."

Banny and I make our way through the increasingly crowded bar. A double-bass drum rock song pounds through the speaker. The lead singer barks out a long, throaty scream.

"Hey," Banny says. "Over there. I think that's her."

I follow his gaze. "Could be, but she's got a..." I make my approach.

"Not tonight," she says, pawing nervously at her drink.

"I'm Hardwicke. This is Esteban. Dante sent us. To take you home."

The cranial implant flashes where her burn scar used to

be. That's why Charlie asked about the photo. Implant must be new. Jasmine is a classic beauty, but the look behind her eyes tells me she's caught between the life she had and the life she has. Sex workers don't typically have long careers. The half-life wears you down.

She slides her hand into her purse. I see a cannister of pepper spray. "He with you?"

"Who? Dante? No. He's at his crib."

"Not him." Her eyes dart back and forth, scanning every inch of the bar. Her implant flashes red-red-red. Red-red-red. *Panic.* "The other guy."

"What guy?"

Jasmine stares at me dead in the eyes. "The one who's trying to kill me."

This case is escalating quickly. I hate that my gear's been checked. But I still have my scout orb. The size of a large marble, the silver orb has a 360-degree camera system that's synced to my lens. I surreptitiously drop it from my pocket. The orb hovers just above the floor, circulating throughout the bar, sending images back to me, and storing them on file.

"I was with a client," she says nervously. "Dante wants me to call them *clients* now. Not *johns.* It's classier that way. His words."

"The client tried to kill you?"

"No. I was at the Strident Hotel, on the North Side of Sinner's Row."

"I don't know it."

"It's a half-decent hotel. Better than the shitholes around here. The client's got a mod kink. Been a regular since I got my implant."

"If it wasn't him, what happened?"

"Shelly... the client... he's got a foot fetish, too. He was... playing with my foot when I flinched. It'd been bothering me all day. I thought I needed new shoes. But there was something on the arch of my foot. I must've stepped on something. Thin as an eyelash and sharp as a kitten's claw. No idea where it came from. The cut is tiny. Just a smear. But Shelly's super squeamish about blood. So he left."

"If it wasn't Shelly, then who?"

"I don't know. I never saw him before."

"How'd you actually see him? And how'd you get away?"

She says she has a deal with the night girl at the concierge desk.

"Laura said some guy slipped her credits on a star drive, saying he was supposed to meet me, but forgot the room number. Wanted to know where to find me."

"No offense," I say as the scout orb sends images through my lens. No vital intel, other than all the eyes on us. "But you *are* a sex worker."

"That's not our system. They're supposed to meet me in the bar. Laura got suspicious and gave me a heads up. I took the freight elevator down so I could slip out behind him. And after I heard about Kayla... I had to get outta there."

"But not to Dante's?"

"He's on a rampage. He acts all cool and in control, like he's king of all pimps. Trust me. He's not. He's paranoid. And not half as smart as he thinks he is. This is the only place I could think of."

Because she feels safer here. With her people.

Charlie swings by, presumably to check on Jasmine. Before she reaches the table, Jasmine subtly raises her hand, as if to give her the all-clear. They communicate via implant. Charlie's flashes yellow, red-red-yellow. *Trouble? Need help?*

Jasmine's responds blue, yellow-yellow-red. *Safe for now, but stay close.*

"Banny," I say. "Go out the back. Get the cab running. We may need to bolt." Without saying a word, he slips away. "What's he look like? The guy?"

"Black. Sorta tall, middle-aged. Real fit. Muscular, but not bulky. Like he works out. A lot. And knows what he's doing."

"Does he have a mod?"

"No. He's a reg." A regular. No implant. "Spiky brown hair. And hazel eyes."

My heartrate kicks into overdrive. My internal systems scream out to me like a creepy breath on the back of my neck. I dive into the recess of my mind. Black, with spiky brown hair, hazel eyes... spiky brown hair, hazel eyes...

"His hair. Was it brown and spiky? Not a mohawk, but with short, tight spikes?"

"Yeah, actually. I think it was." Her implant is flashing. "You know who it is?"

I'm struggling to conceal just how intensely I'm shaking. "No. But I've seen him before."

She tenses up. "Where?"

I do a visual scan of the bar and check the images from my scout orb. No reg males in here. Which means I know him from the most dangerous place of all.

"My nightmares."

I have Jasmine head out back and into Banny's cab while I collect my gear.

"Don't be a stranger," Siobhán says, seeing Banny pull up. "And bring your friend."

I can't bring Jasmine back to Dante's place, and I'm not bringing her back to mine. I need to know more. I call Olin. Straight to voicemail.

My mind is flooded with horrifying images of the ghosted man with the canine teeth in the bioluminescent forest. Staring at me. Ready to rip out my throat. I'm starting to panic. Gotta get outta my head.

"Jasmine," I ask. "When did you get the mod?"

"Does it matter?"

"Maybe."

"About a year ago."

"You had a scar there, on your temple. Was that...?" Then I realize. "You tried once before, didn't you? It didn't take."

She nods faintly. "It was my fault. Dante said it would be good for business, to have a mod in his stable. I didn't want to do it, but... he has this way, you know?" Her shoulders slump. She's relinquished her guarded streetwise persona. As if she's drifted off to some dark and distant region where the boundary between her will and Dante's has eroded into wet sand. "He knows just the right way to mess with my head. And he never lets up."

That's how pimps like Dante operate. Dominate. Always. The more successful pimps break in new sex workers who don't know any better. They prey on vulnerable girls who were already lost or on the run from lives they wanted to escape yet were unprepared for the evil they would soon endure. Others are sold in sex trafficking rings.

But pimps like Dante physically, emotionally, psychologically, sexually, and financially grind the girls down until their resolves are broken. And then remind their girls day and night that the only way to feel safe is to keep Daddy happy. No matter what it takes.

Jasmine shakes it off, comes back to me. "I tried being a dominatrix for a while, but it's more physically demanding than I anticipated. And you have to be in tight control all the time. That wore me down. So I went for the implant. I got in the chair, then the doctor... this scrawny pervert type... leaned over and got close, you know? Close like a dentist. He's leaning over me, almost on top. And even though he was wearing a surgical mask, his breath reeked of cheap cigarettes. I could feel the heat on my face. He was lining up the implant to mark where it would fuse to my head. Then I saw the metal tray of drills, hooks, and tools next to me and..." Jasmine's nearly shaking. "I yanked my head away. It dragged against the bottom of the implant. It's how I got the scar."

"I'm not judging," I say. "Everyone's got their kinks, and the need to have them satisfied. We could all use a little more understanding. But you're a beautiful woman, and you've got brains. I get how Dante can mess with your head. But why this life at all? You don't seem to like it."

"Long story."

"No doubt." I immediately feel horrible I brought it up. But it's my job. "We've all got a story." Including me. "None of them good."

Jasmine shakes her head *no*, agreeing with me.

"Anj," Banny says. "Where am I going?"

I look out the window. Sinner's Row is kicking into full gear beneath a dark and bleak sky. Three moons tonight, all draped behind dense clouds. Police drones fly overhead. I get the very real suspicion they're only there for show.

"Get back on the Highway. We'll figure it out from there."

I text Olin this time. *Need you. Call me. Now.*

We stop at a red light. On one side of the street is a tattoo parlor with three hoverbikes parked out front. Through the front window we see patrons getting inked up. On the other side of the street, sinners and more duck in and out of a hardcore sex shop called Gnarly's. Two doors down is CyberNaughty, a night club with flashing bulb lights: *LIVE GIRLS. REGS. MODS.*

"Let me see your foot," I say.

Jasmine clutches her purse, rolls her shoulder away from me as if into a protective cocoon. Her implant flashes frenetically.

"Sorry. That was..." I was way too aggressive. She's already terrified. I soften my gaze. "If you don't mind. I'd like to see the cut on your foot. It's probably nothing." I open both hands, palms out, to show I'm not a threat. "But..."

Always looking for an escape route, she views the streetscape, then looks back at me.

"Okay. Just... be gentle. It's sore."

I slip on surgical gloves I retrieve from an inside jacket pocket as she curls into the corner of the backseat. Pressing down on the front of her dress to conceal her groin, she shifts her body, one leg tucked beneath her. She slips off her other shoe, and extends her left leg, placing her bare foot in my gloved hands. From her heel, I raise her leg high enough to get a clear look at the arch of her foot.

"I don't see the cut." I activate my lens, zoom in two hundred percent. "Wait. There it is. It's razor thin." Gently, I graze my thumbs against her skin on either side of the incision.

She recoils slightly, though I keep a grip on her heel.

With my lens, I take multiple photos, zoom in another two hundred percent. Blown up, I can see the wound more clearly. No jagged edges. I take more images, then send the entire batch to Bernice. Maybe she's got an idea.

A tap at the window. It startles me. A couple of lowlifes, one on each side of the cab.

"Well-hell-hell," says the skank on my side. Lots of tats, lots of piercings. "Whuduhwe got here?"

"That's a sweet leg," the other says, nearly drooling. Two huge hoop rings in his lower lip. He tries to peek up Jasmine's dress. "I bet she's sweet between the legs, too. And nasty. *Just the way I like it.*"

I drop Jasmine's leg. She shifts into the center of the cab, pressed up against me.

They have no obvious weapons, but you never know. "Listen, boys," I say. "You're looking for love in all the wrong places."

They both pull on door handles. Locked.

Tats and Piercings smirks fiendishly. "Looks right to me."

Banny pulls a shotgun from beneath his seat. "Me, too." He pumps the stock. "Wanna find out?"

"No pussy's worth this," Lip Ring says, and the two scumbags back away until they're on the curb, shouting obscenities at us.

I eye the shotgun. "You know it's not loaded."

"I know. It was that or run them over. But my girl here"— Banny pats the dashboard—"doesn't like blood on her fenders. I just had her washed."

He slips the shotgun back beneath the seat and peels out when the light turns green.

My phone buzzes. Olin. Finally.

"Jasmine's on the hitlist," I say. "I've got her with me now. She won't go back to Dante's. I need you to stash her. Someplace safe."

There's a delay before she responds. "I can't."

"Whadaya mean *can't*? I can't keep her with *me*."

There's a long and deafening hush, its meaning ambiguous. It's impossible to accurately interpret silence. "Because," Olin says finally. "We have a big fucking problem."

CHAPTER 9

When you're a private investigator, the range and intensity of those very problems are staggering. "You'll need to be more specific."

"The OD I cleaned up at the Love Star motel. We stepped in the shit."

My faces scrunches. "What OD? What are you talking about?"

Silence from Olin. And then, "Shit."

She explains that Aiko wasn't jumped by a couple of junkies. No surprise there. I figured the bruises came from Dante. Kicking her ass, not kissing it. But that's not what happened. Aiko was with a john on a meth bender. He got a little rough. The john OD'd in the room. Aiko freaked, took off. The Love Star is such a scuzz hole even Vice doesn't get worked up when a john goes down. But dead bodies tend to smell. It wasn't the first OD there, won't be the last.

Dante called Olin to make sure there were no loose ends that could link back to Aiko or, more importantly, to him. And that it was ruled an accidental overdose. Which it was. The coroner signed off on it. Unclear if Olin paid off or pressured the coroner on Dante's behalf.

"So what's the problem?"

Olin clears her throat. "Ever hear the name Gabriel Graniel Zavala? GGZ?"

I search my memory banks. GGZ? "Yeah, actually. It sounds familiar. Why do I know that name?"

"Because he's—"

Then I remember. "Part of the Guild."

"Scumbag for hire. Muscle work. Murder. Arson. Whatever pays."

"Which means…," I start.

"The ICD just got flagged. He's under their jurisdiction."

Just what I need. But still. "So why's that our problem?"

"GGZ was linked to something. Something big."

"Big?" I stare at Jasmine, who seems clueless about the part of the phone conversation she's picking up. Lights from the overhead monorail trestle shine through the front windshield as we motor towards the onramp to the Rubiyat Highway. "Big how?"

Olin hesitates. "Not over the phone. I need you to meet me." She texts me the address. "I'll be waiting." She hangs up.

I'm now caught between Tarrish, Olin, Dante, and Whistler, and what to do with Jasmine. Part of me wants to drown myself in Scotch. The other wants to punch someone in the face. Instead, I grip and regrip my hands, digging my fingernails into my palms. But I don't like to live in fear.

So I do what I need to, in the way I need to do it. I check my gear, a way to feel in control, then lean forward and talk through the partition. I tell Banny where to go.

"Seriously? But it's dark out."

Seeing my affirmative nod through the rearview, he reaches back under the seat, pulls out the shotgun, places it next to him.

"Don't worry," he says to Jasmine as he switches the meter to double fare. "This time it'll be loaded."

I close my eyes for what only feels like a few seconds. Before I realize what's happening, I'm back in that bioluminescent forest. I don't know if I'm dreaming again or if it's a memory of that dream.

But what are dreams? Are they coded messages we can't access while we're awake, unable to break through the filter of our conscious minds? Are they unconscious wishes and desires? Are they stress relief? The mind's way of processing the unending bombardment of noise in all its forms?

And how do you discern between dreams and nightmares? The experts say that if you have the same dream, the same nightmare, over and over, it's your subconscious's way of telling you something important. But if so, why are the images so confusing and amorphous? Why do our minds play such laborious games?

Dolores suffered and died on that galaxy cruiser, on my watch. Nini was beaten within an inch of her life. Whistler almost died from a gunshot wound. And a lot of other people were literally ripped into bloody, mangled pieces, some of them by me, while we were all caught in a relentless, psychotic rage. And now my subconscious is telling me I feel guilty about it? That it shook me to my core?

No shit. I don't need a recurring nightmare to remind me. I already know.

Accessible by an unkept roadway and perched along the river on the Saiwyn Peninsula, the Hurling-Aberdeen Psychiatric Center was once considered the leading institution for the treatment of mental health. Until one of the patients, who'd been horribly abused as a child, found his way into the basement, and tampered with the fire suppression matrix.

Fusing it with an experimental formulation to help treat debilitating insomnia, he released toxic gas through the vents while the facility was fully staffed. Eighty-three people died from inhaling those poison fumes, their lungs peeled away on a cellular level. Another twenty-three suffered permanent brain damage.

A HAZMAT team cleared out the toxicity, but the facility's run as a functional psychiatric center died that same day. The City still hasn't figured out what to do with the site. The psych center now lying dormant on the river's edge. Abandoned.

Surrounded by the thrashing river on three sides, a cold wind blows in, teasing the distant winter. Out here in such a desolate, forgotten corner of E-Town, just miles away from the heartbeat of the urban circus, I wonder how many jumpers have gone in the drink tonight alone, how many murdered bodies were dumped.

The psych center's newest wing was modern, with a chrome-plated entrance and glassed-in foyer. Further expansion and upgrades had been planned before the mass murder did those plans in. Connected by a series of arched corridors, the rest of the nine-building campus was constructed with Xanthian brick and brown sandstone, with five pavilions.

Olin is waiting for me out by the dock, the old, deserted tower hovering over us. I'm not sure if I believe in ghosts, but if I did, they'd definitely live there. Banny is parked at the bottom of the short hill below us, the cab fueled up and ready to go. Jasmine isn't happy being down there with him. But given the circumstances, where else could she be?

"Psych center," I say to Olin. "You trying to tell me something?"

Sprayed with mist from the river's crashing waves, from here we see a haze of distant light hovering over the heart of the city. 3-D holograms, digital billboards, hovercrafts, interior lights from apartment buildings and office towers and the elevated tracks of the citywide monorail, all combined into an acrobatic kaleidoscope of relentless energy.

Olin takes a heavy drag off a vape pen, holds it, then exhales a loose cloud of what smells like a fruity sativa blend. Cops aren't supposed to smoke weed, much less on duty. Not sure what that says about Olin. Maybe it means she can be trusted after all. If she's willing to break one rule, who knows how many others she's willing to ignore. Then again, she's working for Dante. The lines of right and wrong blurred for her a long time ago. I know the feeling.

"My great aunt Sara spent time in there," she says. "She died"—Olin turns to find the right building—"in *that* wing. She had another in a long line of psychotic breaks. She slashed her wrist with a rusty screw she found underneath her bed, then jumped out that window right there. She threw a chair through the glass. Then she jumped. She landed on the asphalt. They replaced the window with stained glass. The called it *The Shadow of Life.*"

I don't know why she's telling me this. She continues.

"When I got my shield, I looked through her file, saw the crime scene photos. I shouldn't've done that. I still have nightmares." Olin takes another toke. "Story of my life. Too curious for my own good."

I scan the area. Down at Banny's cab, to make sure he's still there, up at the gothic tower hovering behind us, back to Olin, then out over the violent river. My head is throbbing again, that low persistent *whum*.

"GGZ? What do you have on him?"

Olin shows me a photo on her phone. I squint and shake my head, as if that will somehow open my memory banks. "Vaguely familiar. I'm not sure."

"You know much about astrophysics?"

I look at her curiously. "A little. Why?"

"From Eddie? Because he's a Patch?"

"That's some of it. But I get around."

"I bet." She takes another hit off the vape. "What's that like? Being with a Patch? Having a Patch for a son?"

That stops me short. My closest friends never ask me about it. Because they know I don't want to talk about it. I'm not sure *how* to talk about it. But she's a cop. No boundaries.

"Where do Patches even come from?" she asks. "They're Eternitarians. Human. And yet they're... I don't know what they are. Children of the Cosmos? Descendants of the Minders of the Universe? Everyone's afraid of them, Angela. Except maybe you. Makes you wonder."

"Makes you wonder *what?*"

"If they're glorified construction workers. Or our jailers."

I've had the very same thoughts. I still do. Not that I'm gonna confess that to her. "What about astrophysics?"

"I've got a buddy in the ICD. File clerk. Doesn't do field work, but..."

"He sees the intel."

She nods affirmatively. "He owes me a favor back from when I was working Vice. I helped his brother out of a jam. He couldn't give me much, but he says the ICD is all twisted up about a dead system in the ass-crack of whatever sector they were scanning. Every star, every planet, every particle... destroyed. Nothing left but dust and debris."

"Dead system? I... wait. Eddie said that. At the Institute."

"Yeah," Olin says as if she's now just remembering that, too. But I still can't trust her. Like any good detective, she knows when to play dumb. She held out on me all this time about Aiko's attack, so who knows how much she's still keeping from me. "He said it was a dead system."

"No," I correct, realizing it myself. "He said *another* dead system."

"Shit. You're right. He did say *another*."

And one more link to Whistler. Does this dead system have anything to do with the *Eddie Hive*, whatever that is? And why he's gone missing? Which gets me thinking about how Olin acted when we were inside Kimmie-slash-Nóirín's apartment.

"Why did you ask about astrophysics? What's GGZ into? What's he doing for the Guild?"

Olin fidgets with the vape pen, down by her side, rolling it between her fingers down by her side. She squints in my direction, then looks out over the river.

"I come out here a lot. It's the only place I know where even the security drones don't go. It's why I took my motorcycle. I disabled the GPS. Station can't track me. Funny, right? A cop trying to avoid the law?" She tugs on the vape. "Maybe it's not funny. Tragic is more like it. I never wanted to be this kind of cop. Dante got his hooks in me early. I'm not a piece'a shit, Hardwicke. I'm not." I stand next to her, take the vape pen. I take a quick draw, then give it back to her. "Maybe I am. I don't even know anymore."

A light buzz kicks in. Cops always have the best shit. "There's no *easy* in this life. Not that I've seen."

She nods. "Yeah."

Either she's dropped her guard, or she's playing a long con. I don't think she's that good. If she was, she wouldn't be trapped like this. Then again, neither would I.

"What's the link?" I ask. "To GGZ?"

"Another scumbag named Adrian Odirozzi was listed in his file under *known associates*."

Odirozzi. Nasty piece of work. "Contract killer," I say. "Who knows what else."

"I can't get access to the files. They're classified. I'm pretty sure the ICD has been trying to flip Odirozzi. I don't see that happening. But GGZ had a bag with him loaded with star drives."

That's new. "I thought the Love Star was clean?"

"Yeah," she says. "About that…"

My adrenaline spikes. Whatever she's about to tell me, I'm pretty sure I'm not gonna like it.

"Aiko's just a kid, scared shitless. Only been with Dante a few months. You know these girls. Most of 'em don't last more than a few weeks. It's a brutal life. When she took GGZ to the Love Star, she had no idea who he was. He had a black duffel bag full of gear, including a change of clothes, some tech, and a roll of credits-loaded star drives. And a shit-ton of meth."

I look at her suspiciously. "How do you know all this?"

Olin wipes mist off her face. "Aiko told me."

Yeah. I knew I was gonna hate this. But I control my outrage. Not gonna do me any good right now. I exhale a restrained, frustrated sigh. "What else?"

"GGZ was tweaked. Rambling about a huge score he was about to close. Aiko said he kept going in his bag for more meth. He'd crush it on the nightstand, snort it off his knife, then look in the mirror and ask, 'Can you see me? Can you see me now?'"

"What does that mean?"

"No idea. He could've been hallucinating. Aiko wanted to bolt, but she was terrified of him. Said he was losing his grip, getting more paranoid. He dropped some kind of bracelet. When she went to pick it up, he backhanded her across the face, then grabbed her by the wrists."

"The bruises," I say.

"GGZ took another hit of meth, then grabbed his chest. Massive coronary. Aiko panicked. She called Kimmie-slash-Nóirín."

"Top Slot. And the mamma bear. Figured it was better than calling Dante."

Olin pockets the vape pen. "Much. Except…"

"Kimmie-slash-Nóirín ended up dead."

"Yep."

Fuck me. It's coming together. "You think her death is linked to GGZ."

"I've got no proof. But yeah, it's what I think."

"And you knew all this when we got started? About the attack?"

"Sorry. Dante wanted the star drives for himself. Thought he'd get rich."

"Hold on," I say. "Where's the bag?"

"That's the other problem. It's gone."

Of course it is. "You think Dante's got it?"

Olin says Aiko left the bag at the Love Star. She tried to take the star drives, but they were secured in a slotted pouch. They wouldn't release.

"So that means..." Damn. "You think Kimmie-slash-Nóirín went back for the bag."

"Again, I got no proof, but yeah. That's what I think."

"Then Dante went to her place, looking for the bag. But instead he found her dead, and the bag was gone."

"Looks that way."

"Any chance he killed her? Fought over the bag?"

Olin raises an eyebrow. "It crossed my mind. But the way he's losing his shit, I don't think so. I think he was shocked to find her like that. He's really shaken up."

"So you're thinking... what? That someone linked to GGZ, and maybe even to Odirozzi, killed her for it? That it's..." I turn to face the cab. I see two silhouettes, when an image shoots before my eyes. "The guy Jasmine saw. The guy with the spiky brown hair."

From my nightmare.

"I'd need to know more," Olin says, "but best I can put together, Aiko was in the wrong place at the wrong time with the wrong guy. And it all links back to Dante."

"Which," I say, connecting this unfortunate line of dots, "links back to us. If we assume that whoever killed Kimmie-slash-Nóirín has the bag, and he still came after Jasmine, it means he wants something else. Maybe she thinks Aiko killed GGZ, and this is all payback. Or maybe he's part of the Guild, too, and he's covering his tracks. Tying up loose ends. Whatever it is, there's a killer on the loose. And we're caught in the crosshairs."

"That's why I'm standing in the shadow of the psych center smoking weed. I can't go to my Unit about this. And I can't go to the ICD."

"So you came to me."

"No one's more surprised than I am," she says. "But after the Institute, where else could I go?"

It's late. I'm tired, I'm cold. There's a burn in my back and both legs, too many hours on my feet. I want this night to be over. Unfortunately, it's just getting started.

"All right," I say to Olin. "See what else you can find out about GGZ. But don't raise any flags. We don't want more eyes on us."

"And what are you gonna do?"

I reach into my pocket. "I gotta call in a favor."

CHAPTER 10

ACCESS DENIED.

Bernice has never rejected me three times in a row. I pound on the outer door, but I doubt the sound gets through Diradium this thick. The dim hallway lights flicker on and off, like from a temporary power drain. It's an old building. I know she's installed her own power grid and replaced all the systems and mechanicals, but I have no clue what kind of advanced tech she's got stashed back there or how much juice they require.

"Bernice." I know she's watching me through her security feed. "Come on. It's Angela. Open up."

Banny and Jasmine stand behind me as I stare at the camera. Her voice comes through the intercom. *"No strangers, no visitors. Go away."*

"Don't be like that." I zip open my jacket enough to reveal my neck. "I've got another scarf for you," I sing-song, threading my fingers down the fabric. I have no idea where her scarf fetish comes from, but it's real. She's already got one of mine in her collection.

I can almost hear her aching for it. And then: *"No sale."*

Bernice came out of her bunker a few years back to help me on another case. I thought that night would've kickstarted her return to circulation. It didn't. If she's left her bunker since then, I don't know about it.

Unsure what to do next, I turn to Banny. He side-eyes Jasmine. I hate to go there, to do this to either of them, but I'm desperate. "Bernice. I brought a friend."

"She's not my friend."

"She could be." I pull Jasmine into the camera's sightline.

Jasmine is a voluptuous woman, a temptation for anyone,

regardless of gender. Bernice has a type. Jasmine is that type. I'm hoping her cybernetic implant will seal the deal. The security globe's blue orb rotates a few degrees so that it can zoom in on her.

"I'm sorry," I whisper to Jasmine. "I didn't want to go there."

She shrugs. "I'm used to it."

"I know." I'm disgusted with myself for using her like this. But when you're in the field, you use what's available. "That's why I'm sorry."

The security globe shifts back to me. *"I don't do favors,"* Bernice finally says. *"Not for her. Not even for you."*

"I know, but it's not a favor." I steel myself. I never thought I'd do this, but I'm stuck. Everyone I'd go to first is either missing, dead, won't talk to me, can't help me, or is potentially compromised. Even considering this ask makes me sick in the deepest recess of what is clearly my murky, twisted soul. "It's *the* favor."

I first met Bernice working a case. A former Patch herself, she was still shell-shocked from the amputations. I never got the full story about what happened, but it was Patch-related. Before the accident, apparently she'd been a superior athlete and dancer.

The cybernetic implants, synthetic organs, chrome limbs, and hoverchair saved her life, even gave her a new one. But the invasive surgeries and the knowledge she was no longer a fully organic being, with a computer interface wired directly into her brain, destroyed the image she had of her former self—a traumatizing psycho/spiritual death.

After her transformation, Bernice being Bernice, no one was going to tell her who she could and couldn't be or what she could and couldn't do. But the harsh realities of the physical limitations and augmentations she endured forced her to face the necessity of having to reinvent herself… or complete her suicide.

She'd had it all planned out. Shotgun in her mouth, trigger-pull by way of a guttural voice command. When I found her, the gun was already loaded. It's a blur to me now, but I talked her down. Good thing, too. Because the gun went off seconds after it left her lips.

When she was most vulnerable, and at a time of her most genuine connection, she couldn't bring herself to speak the words *thank you*. I never needed nor expected those words. In the years since, we found ourselves drawn to each other, two wounded warriors who have faced the bleakest of moments.

Our connection grew over time, to the point where she often gave me preferential treatment over her other clients—and revealed a part of herself I'd secretly suspected was lingering deep beneath the surface. Including one rainy night in her bunker when, after many cocktails, she acknowledged that she owed me a debt.

If I was ever backed into a corner, she said, one I couldn't escape in any other way, I could activate the *in case of emergency, break glass* rider of our friendship.

Once.

I was hoping to never need it, much less use it. I didn't help her that night so she'd owe me one. I just didn't want her to hurt herself. Yet here I am.

I take a deep breath, let out a sigh. This isn't something I do lightly. "Bernice," I say. "This is me, breaking the glass."

There's a long silence in the brick-faced hallway. After a time, the scanner lights up again: *ANGELA HARDWICKE—AUTHENTICATED*

Inside the bunker, Bernice faces us in her hoverchair. Her long gray hair is woven into a tight braid running down her back.

"Greetings. You must be Esteban."

Banny nods. "And you must be Bernice."

She lets a smirk slip out. "How deductive we are."

"And you, dear," Bernice says, her gaze on Jasmine—Bernice's hoverchair eases closer to us—"you are a welcomed guest."

Jasmine keeps her cool under pressure. Maybe even flirting a little. "I thought you didn't have guests."

"When they're as magnificent as you, I make an exception."

If I didn't know any better, I'd say Jasmine is blushing. You don't see that often from sex workers. They've heard every come-on there is. You can't fake a blush response.

"Thanks for doing this, Bernie, but we're kind of in a—"

Bernice extends her chrome arm, opens her chrome palm. She wiggles her chrome fingers. "You know what to do."

"But I," I start, quickly realizing it's a lost cause. I thread the scarf off my neck, place it in her hand.

"Esteban," she says. "Be a doll and hang it with the others."

Banny approaches slowly, eases the scarf from her hand as if it were a rattlesnake. Satisfied he's safe, he drapes the scarf over a latticework bar between three server racks loaded with tech. My scarf takes its place with more than a dozen others of various colors, patterns, and textures. Three have frills.

Other than Whistler, I've never brought anyone into her bunker. I've never even considered it. Because Bernice has made it clear just how much she despises her inner sanctum being violated. I don't want to waste her time or outstay her patience. I get to it.

"I should tell you about—"

Bernice raises a hand. "Angela. Don't be rude to my guest. Esteban. Do us a good turn. There's a tea kettle in the kitchen. Get a boil going, will you? I'm sure Jasmine would appreciate a hot beverage."

"Oh," Jasmine says awkwardly, as if surprised to be the center of attention. "I'm okay."

Bernice offers a sultry gaze. "Don't be silly, dear. We're all far from okay. It'll just take a tick. Assuming Esteban follows directions better than he drives his cab." She eye-gestures to the small kitchen area. "Selection of teas are on the counter in the wood box."

Banny eyes me. I give him a half-shrug.

"Santsi Black tea for me, with just a touch of honey," she instructs Banny. "Jasmine, I have a robust collection. What can I get for you?"

"I'll have the same, thank you."

"I'll have—"

"Catch me up," Bernice says, cutting me off. Her way of tossing me attitude about calling in a chit we both thought would never be raised.

As Banny boils the water, I tell Bernice about GGZ, my

investigation, my bizarre trip to the Institute, and what Eddie said about the dead systems.

She leads us around her multi-tabled workstations and to a section of brick wall. With her left chrome forefinger, she presses a button on the armrest. It activates a projection onto the wall.

"The Invidi system. What's left of it anyhow."

Projected on the wall are the remnants of what once was, chunks and dust particles drifting in a debris field to nowhere. Bernice slowly zooms out so that the Invidi system is smaller while that quadrant of the Cosmos now appears larger.

She zooms out by several magnifications until the Invidi system is now just a tiny black dot within a spiral galaxy. She reverses the sequence process for contrast, zooming back in, such that all we see again is the Invidi system—a dead system of debris.

Satisfied we're starting to understand, she zooms out much farther than before. Now on the wall are dozens of galaxies—spiral, elliptical, and irregular—innumerable stars, planets, nebulas, and other celestial phenomena glowing and twinkling in a haze of brilliant colors.

She then zooms backs in so that we're focused again on the dead system. The debris field. Zooms out, giving us the wider perspective, back in. Out, then back into the Invidi system.

"As you'll plainly see," Bernice says. "There's very little left."

"Like you said." Banny hands steaming cups of tea, one each, to Jasmine and Bernice. "It's dead."

"Not dead. Annihilated. That region of the Cosmos has been pulverized at a subatomic level. That pocket of spacetime cracked open. And what seeped out... is toxic."

I've spent my share of time in the Cosmos. I've never heard of anything like this. Except when the Big Bang erased all of Existence and replaced it with a new one.

"As a singular phenomenon," Bernice says, "one could chalk this event up to the mysteries of Existence."

"What do you mean *singular?*" My chest tightens. The *whum* in my head is getting worse, more intense. The pressure is building. "It's happened before?"

"I apologize for being unclear," Bernice says as the lights flicker again. "I assumed, which is certainly my mistake, that the inference was obvious. You are an investigator, are you not?"

Yeah. She's pissed. More than that. She's embarrassed—and giving me payback for it. And showing off for Jasmine.

I open my mouth, inhale air. I'm about to respond. Bernice doesn't give me the chance.

"Among my *many* and varied interests that occur on-realm and off," she says and winks at Jasmine—her cranial interface flashes blue-magenta-blue, magenta-magenta, *flirting*—"I study odd cosmic phenomena." Bernice zooms back out, then whirs the controls. Untold galaxies spin by faster than we can focus on them. On the wall now are dozens of galaxies. She holds that vantage point, then zooms back in, taking us from nine galaxies, to four, down to one. "This is the Fua'yar Galaxy." Zooms in closer. "This is the Phynn System." Zooms in again.

I step forward so that my silhouette appears on the wall on top of the projected image. I put my finger against the wall. I feel the brick against my skin. "Nothing but debris. Dead systems." I turn to face them. "This has happened twice. Eddie said as much. But here's what I don't get. Outside the Institute, nobody noticed? No one, anywhere?"

Bernice eyes me, exasperated. "Look at the coordinates. Check again."

I'd been so focused on space itself I didn't read the data at the bottom of the projection screen. She scrolls back to the Invidi system. I take note of the interstellar coordinates. She quickly scrolls all the way back to the second system, the Quinquela System. I note the coordinates.

"Not the same," I say.

Bernice chuckles with bemused arrogance. "You have the gift of understatement, Angela. These coordinates are five point two one seven three four trillion light years apart. Remarkable distances by nearly any metric, and with vastly different cosmologic characteristics. The Invidi system supported only microscopic life forms. The Quinquela system consisted of gaseous planets and dead moons. There is no unifying quality among them I can determine other than that they have suffered the same fate. Unless they were under direct observation, there is no plausible reason anyone would have noticed their destruction, much less established a causal link."

"But Eddie seemed worried, which means…" The picture in my mind starts to crystalize. "It's happened in other systems, too."

"Three others that I've detected. In each case, no less than two point seven six trillion light years apart."

"That's pretty damn far," Banny says.

"And still too close for comfort," I say. "And with five systems we know of now, there's a pattern."

I stand in the center of the image, my back to the wall. Blinded by the projection source, I see a bright halo around Bernice, Banny, and Jasmine.

"*That's* why Eddie kicked me out. They think it's gonna happen again and don't know how to stop it." I step out of the projection cone, take my place by Bernice's side. I stare at the dead systems. The annihilation. And why Eddie cut off my access. "Bernie, do you still have contacts at the Institute?"

"Of course."

"Have you heard about this? What are they saying?"

That she doesn't launch into a soliloquy tells me something important. "My contacts are being unusually non-responsive, even through encrypted channels."

I rub my eyes. "What could cause this kind of damage? A black hole? Radiation? An intruding alternate reality? Sabotage?"

Bernice sips her tea. "The fabric of spacetime is highly imperfect, suffering all manner of rips, tears, burns, and bruises, in need of repair. Patches wouldn't exist otherwise."

As a former Patch, she explains there were old rumors of fault lines scattered throughout the Cosmos. The earliest Patches feared if one fault line were to implode, the resulting shock waves would ripple throughout Eternity in a cascading event, one imploding fault line setting off another.

Each subsequent implosion would ripple across the various quadrants, further weakening the structural integrity of spacetime itself. Like a fist-sized rock dropped onto a frozen lake, the microfractures would expand the radius, until they were beyond repair.

"It could crash the whole system," I say. "The Cosmos would collapse."

"Yes," Bernice says. "That was the theory."

Even if the odds were one in several billion that those fault lines even existed, the fear was impactful enough that the Institute created a special division to research the potential phenomena, allocating time, personnel, and resources to scour the Cosmos.

"Did they find them?" Jasmine asks, appearing more curious than terrified. "The fault lines?"

"No, dear. Never. Eventually—millennia later, as I understand it, after exhaustive search and analysis—there was no evidence to support them. The Institute wound down the search, then finally closed the investigation. The theory about fault lines ultimately became more legend than reality, until the rumors were all but forgotten."

"Until now," I say.

Bernice concurs. "Based on the information you're sharing, and on my own analysis, the Institute fears those theoretical fault lines have finally been confirmed."

"And now that they have, we'll get more dead systems. Until there's nothing left."

Bernice shuts down the projection, exposing the brick wall. It's a lot to take in. My eyes readjust to the dim lighting, the humming computer racks, and cooling systems, even the scarves hanging from the beam. Then it hits me. In my mind I get a single face against utter blackness. The man with the spiky brown hair.

"If you're telling me that rumors of cosmic-level fault lines across spacetime are real, and systems are imploding..."

"A map," Jasmine surmises. "Maybe that's what he had on the star drives."

We all look to her.

"Good," Bernice says, impressed, her cranial implant lighting up. Jasmine blushes, tilts her head in an aw-shucks kinda way. Her implant also lights up. "Very good."

Banny cuts through their flirting. "Also... not so good."

"Not good at all. Which is why"—Bernice checks the controls on her armrest, gazes at them intently, adjusts two dials, then propels her chair to the nearest console, and activates other switches—"I need to show you this."

She opens the right-side arm rest on her hoverchair, flips one switch, then turns a dial. I paw at my temples to deaden the pain. A thin beam of light seeps through the center of the brick wall that had just served as a projection screen. From the midpoint, the wall retracts in two halves, in opposite directions. Sliding along grooves in the floor and ceiling, it exposes a hidden room.

From within we see various computers, advanced tech, and machinery, including a circular platform in the center. The platform is surrounded by black boxes with inverted cones, like giant subwoofers. A brimming blue-white light, much like from shuttlecraft plumes, shines down on the platform.

In her hoverchair, Bernice leads us into this hidden room. She goes to one of the consoles, activates various switches, dials, and levers. The mechanism draws immense power, such that the interior bunker lights flicker off and on until there's barely any illumination.

She seems to increase the power, until something appears within the cone of the blue-white light. Or more to the point... someone.

"Whistler!" I call out. He hovers above the platform, my headache so intense now I can barely see straight. "Are you okay?" I turn to Bernice. "Is he okay?"

"Unclear. The quantum field generator is pulling him away from the orbit. It's holding him in place. But not for much longer."

No wonder she didn't want to let me in. It wasn't out of guilt, embarrassment, or jealousy. She was hiding a secret. But still.

"He's been here the whole time? What the hell?"

"I had him earlier, then lost him. The signal goes in and out. It didn't want to say until I knew what I was dealing with. It just came in again."

"Can we get him out?" I reach toward him and into the cone of light. "Can we pull him down—?"

"Angela!" Bernice warns. "Don't!"

Like sticking a fork into a nuclear accelerator, the reaction tosses me back a dozen feet. I crash to the floor, hitting my head, kidney, and shoulder. I ache all over.

"*Maydgzz,*" Whistler's still a bit fuzzy, his voice like speaking through wax paper. Bernice adjusts the setting. His image and his voice are clearer. "*Mache. There's more. They're coming. The star systems. They're going to...*"

He fades again. Bernice frantically manipulates the console. Multiple light bulbs pop into glass confetti. One of the computer consoles crackles dangerously with electricity. Melted wires and fried circuits spew out trails of smoke.

"*Find,*" Whistler says, "*fffiindzz... the... edneee... ive.*" He fluctuates. There. Not there. Barely there. "*Check... ugzzz... duh... zzz... Dzzoug... Finer... Be...beforezzz... itzz too latezzzzzzzz.*"

"Doug Finer? Whistler! Who's Doug Finer?"

The consoles switch off. Dead. Whistler disappears.

Bernice drops her gaze, exhales a sad sigh. She looks to me as Banny helps me up. I'm in so much pain I can barely move.

"I'm sorry, Angela. I tried."

"I know you did," I say with an understanding grimace. Suddenly woozy, I start to black out. But I catch myself. "Banny. Juice up the cab."

"Okay. But where to? And to do what?"

My breaths clog my throat like quicksand. "What I need to do." I look to Banny, to Jasmine, to Bernice. "Get my partner back."

PART II:
ZENO'S PARADOX

CHAPTER 11

"**Y**ou'll never get in." Bernice is upgrading my contact lens and recalibrating my scout orb. "Even I don't have access. The Institute is a persistent frustration." The power drain from trying to pull Whistler in from the elliptical orbit overloaded her system. "Especially on lockdown."

The synthetic painkiller cocktail Bernice whipped up is doing the trick, but I'm still sore all over from being shock-blasted across the room. "I know. But I have another way."

Bernice raises an eyebrow. "Do tell." I do. Esteban looks away. Bernice chortles. It's only the third time I've ever seen her laugh. "You have my sympathies, Angela Hardwicke. I will use all of my skills and resources to get a better lock on young Mister Eric. I'm sorry I couldn't do more. I... enjoy his company."

She escorts Banny and me to the door.

"Jasmine," I say. "You coming?"

She hides behind her mug of reheated tea.

"Actually." Bernice smiles knowingly at Jasmine, then turns back to me. "She'll be staying here for a while. It's safer with me."

"Uh," I start. Jasmine is my only eyewitness who can identify Spiky Hair. Besides, she's my responsibility. "I'm not sure if—"

Bernice directs us into the hallway. "Be careful," she says, the vault door closing them in—and us out. "And give my regards to Betty."

E-Town emerges from the long dark night. The pinkish blue creamsicle of dusk washes over the sky. Banny's cab is parked in an alley behind a dumpster facing a brick-faced apartment building.

Banny starts the motor, turns on the meter. I get in back.

"I gotta go home and shower," he says. "My audition's in a

few hours. I want to look the part, not smell like it."

"There's a shower where we're going. And some not terrible food."

"Anj. It's been a long night."

"You're right. I know. It's just..." I exhale a deep, exhausted sigh, then slump into the seat. "It's Whistler, Banny. If it were anybody else, I wouldn't ask. But it's Whistler."

Banny loosely regrips the steering wheel. "I've been waiting for this break my whole life. I wanna help you. I want to help him, too. But I have to come first sometimes. Nini warned me about this. Being sucked into your..."

He's right. I do this, leaning on my friends as a support squad when I get in over my head. They've been there for me more times than I can count. More times than I've been there for them. They didn't sign up for the private eye life. I know it makes me a shitty, manipulative friend, but this is one of those times where my being right has to outweigh his being right.

"It's a great audition," I concede. "You'll bring it home."

Although I can only see him from the back, I get his eyes in the rearview mirror. He seems to relax at my response. But the truth is, I didn't need Banny to take me. I could get another ride. He's not my personal driver, even though I treat him like it. Maybe he knows me well enough to see through my facade, maybe not. But my friends center me, give me a sense of self I sometimes lose during an investigation, when I'm out there in the dark.

I've had Whistler with me the last few years. And even though I gave him all sorts of shit for cramping my style, my style doesn't work like it used to without him. Which is my lame-ass way of saying... I miss him.

I'm lonely. I'm scared. And this case might be too big for me.

Even during the times I've felt this way before, I would never validate those doubts by defining them. Angela Hardwicke, hardboiled private eye, doesn't back down from any case, any place, or anyone.

Sorry, Banny. I'm not about to start now.

I know. I really am a shitty, manipulative friend.

"Okay, Angela," I say aloud, laying out the variables. It's a performance—a bad one—for a singular audience. "Dolores is dead, Nini won't talk to me. I have no access to my son. I've got two dead sex workers with more in trouble. Whistler's caught in some kind of elliptical orbit, chunks of the Cosmos are imploding, and I've got no easy way to get where I need to be." I pop my lips with a hearty exhale. "Fuck it." Seeing Banny eyeing me through the rearview, I squint and nod, as if I'm coming to grips with my reality. "You can drop me at the office. I'll get there on my own."

A totally. Shit. Friend.

Banny cranes his neck, the skin bunching up between his shoulders and the back of his head. "Fine. But you'd better make this one up to me. And not with a round of drinks or an I.O.U. You need to make sure I'm in good with the casting director, with an audition that's mine to lose. And in a movie with Gloria Mandalapali! Or someone better. I'm not joking. It took my whole life to get this far. So you have to come through for me. You have to."

"I will," I say reflexively, although I have no idea how I'll honor that agreement. "You're the best."

"You're damn right I am." Banny shifts into gear, gets us back onto the streetscape. "Food better be hot. I'm fucking hungry."

Banny maneuvers us through the early morning traffic, the streets and sidewalks already bustling, security drones whisking overhead. E-Town feels like an entirely different city during the day. Morning sunshine gleaming off the glass skin of majestic skyscrapers. The suit-and-tie crowd trudging off to work. Kids hustling to school. Diners packed with breakfast crowds and sex workers out on their corners, either coming off the night shift, or starting a new one.

We motor past the El Walk, a public park above the streets on E-Town's old industrial zone, snaking between high-rise residential buildings and boutique hotels, with distant views of the Chabaqua River. Along the path are various plant and flower gardens, art installations, neon lights, and galactic viewing stations, as well as a teleportation hub that jumps you ten feet across the width of the path.

Finally making it through the gridlock, we drive though Cobblestone Alley, past Calico Terrace, and the newly built Downtown marina, then onto MaCaleesh Highway. Nothing but open fields on both sides of the road as we head toward the horizon. Toward the Infinity Cloud just outside E-Town's border.

The Infinity Cloud. An all-encompassing fog with no dimensions, no discernible top or bottom, no beginning or end. It's the fastest way to leave E-Town, an express route to anywhere. If you want to travel from one point on-realm to another, you enter the Infinity Cloud, envision in your mind's eye where you to want to go, and whoosh, there you are.

Unlike the dense urban street grid of E-Town, Elden Grove is a sphere consisting of mostly residential, single-family neighborhoods, parks, schools, libraries, and shopping centers. I rarely come out here.

Suburban sprawl might work for some people, but not me. Can't help it. I'm a city girl. I can't sleep unless police sirens, blustering traffic jams, and the streets are screeching with madness. Suburban life has too much stillness, too much quiet. And it's not that I don't appreciate tranquil moments. It's that, in my experience, the silence isn't an absence of chaos. It's a confection of untold truths and repressions to keep the neighbors at bay.

There's more than enough domestic trauma, drama, drug addiction, crime, prostitution, suicide, greed, and boredom-based bad decisions in the suburbs to keep any private investigator busy. But I know myself well enough that I would go insane in a place like this. How can you peel back the layers of time, space, and dimension when you spend half your time cleaning out the gutters?

"Hey," Banny says as we turn off the highway, onto Main Street, and along, yes, a strip mall. Lined side-by-side is a Dim-Sum restaurant, nail salon, hardware store, and memory vacation station. There's a steady flow of daytime traffic, cars in the jigsaw puzzle of parking lots, shoppers going in and out of the establishments. "We're getting close. Where to?"

We drive past Elden Grove Middle School and yet another strip mall. "Up there. Turn left. At the corner."

The houses here all have nice curb appeal, with a car or two in the driveways and on the tree-lined streets. Soft cloud cover dims the sunshine. "That's it. Fourth house on the right. Blue house with the white door."

Banny parks on the street. The motor rattles as it starts to cool down.

"You ready?" He unlocks his door.

I usually don't get nervous while working a case. But this one's got my heart pumping. I exhale three short breaths, inhale through my nose, feel my lungs expand. Let it all out. From the back seat I exit the cab. Banny follows me as I lead him up the walk, then the four steps up to the covered porch.

I knock on the door. We wait. We hear footsteps approaching from inside. The door opens in. My heart pounds. I'm greeted with a look of conflicted surprise. So I get right to it.

"Hi, Ma. Got a minute?"

CHAPTER 12

It's always weird being back here. I grew up in this house.

"Angela." My mom pulls me in for a hug. She squeezes tight, kisses me on the cheek. "I didn't know you were coming. Why didn't you tell me?"

"Sorry, Ma. It was kind of a last-minute thing."

"I'm Esteban," Banny says and extends his hand.

"Yes, sorry. Ma... this is Banny. That's his cab out front. He's a—"

"I'm an actor," he interjects. "I got a big audition."

"An actor! That's so exciting! Come in, come in."

My mom shuffles us into the house, the living room laid out just as I remembered. One couch, a sleeper, and three terribly uncomfortable swivel chairs my mother refuses to give up because they were a gift from my grandmother. Picture frames above the mantle, including two of Owen, one as a baby playing with a galactic pinwheel, one on a jungle gym from about three years ago.

And a large, framed photograph of Denise. My older sister. When I was just a teenager she died from metastatic cancer, the kind with a cellular anomaly resistant to even the most aggressive treatments. The oncologists were confident their next generation nanobot protocol, though still experimental, would permanently eradicate the cancer. It didn't.

"Where's Daddy?"

"You know him. Playing golf."

Banny offers a confused look. "He can play golf? I thought he had trouble walking."

My mom chuckles amiably. "Computer golf." My dad has an advanced spinal condition that's compromised his neck and lungs. He won't consider cybernetic augmentation. Comes too close to my world. A world he's not ready to accept. "He sits in his wheelchair all day, clicking the mouse until his fingers go numb. The doctors say it's not making the condition worse. And it keeps him busy."

"And out of your hair?" Banny winks. "Which looks lovely, by the way."

Blatant sucking up or not, my mom blushes at Banny's compliment. Curvier than me and with curly blond hair, she always looked more like Denise.

"Aren't you sweet?" She brushes her finger through my hair, curls it behind my ear, then drifts to a place I'm not sure she wants to go. "You could use a haircut yourself. Blow it out. Maybe some highlights."

Just that tiny maternal gesture, the edge of her fingers grazing my earlobe and the wisps of my side skull, send a jolt through my heart that nearly has me in convulsions. The subtle yet significant physical contact, and the proximity between us—mother and only surviving daughter—rips off the titanium lock of my emotional vault, where the totality of my confounding childhood gushes through my consciousness.

She holds her gaze, staring at me, but also past me, as if torn between her joy of seeing me, and her resentment of me, my presence too painful to face. I understand. I feel the same way.

"But yes, Esteban," she says, pulling herself back from the drift. "If Arthur's occupied, it frees up my day. Are you hungry? What am I saying? Of course, you're hungry. Let's see what I've got."

My mother trundles into the kitchen, poking around in the refrigerator and freezer. "I can make you a sandwich or... no. Forget that. Here we go. I've got a tray of home-made lasagna with sweet sausage, and some leftover roast chicken and red potatoes. Or if you wait, I can make my famous shrimp scampi in garlic butter sauce."

I quietly shake my head *no* about that one.

"I'd love some lasagna," Banny says, "if that's not too much trouble."

"Not all. Here. Sit at the kitchen table. It's cozier that way.

Angela, why don't you say hi to Daddy. He's in the den. He sleeps down here now."

With my mom busy with Banny, I head back through the living room. The furniture, the knick-knacks. It's all coming back to me, unlocking a tidal wave of memories and feelings from the years I spent here—and the ones I didn't. I turn down the hall toward the den, but something holds me back. I'd rather face the unknown horrors of the Cosmos than what I fear I'll see.

After Denise died, it was impossible not to feel my dad's disappointment in me. At the way I lived my life, the choices I made. I guess I can't blame him. For a long time, I didn't make things easier. On any of us. Then again, they didn't make it easier on me.

I push the door in. "Hi, Da..." He's sleeping in his chair, the golf simulator on his oversized monitor. Digital green space looking out over a sparking digital ocean. The blinds are half open. Green leaves from the cranberry tree outside the house have begun their seasonal change of color.

I always remembered my dad as being this giant man, tall and strong. But in his wheelchair, with his decompensating spine, he's 65 going on 90. He's thin. Pale. A shell of his former self. He's gotten much worse.

Which means my mom's been carrying this weight on her own. It also means I didn't know. And fuck me in the spleen for not knowing. If Denise were alive, she'd be here to help out, the dutiful daughter. But she's not. And it's not like I've picked up the slack. My dad's insurance covers most of his care, so financially at least, they've been okay. I offered to pay the balance, but my parents won't have it. Too much pride. Too much resentment.

My absence here is yet another reminder that I've failed the people closest to me, wrapped up in the variables of my own life while conveniently ignoring theirs.

I lean over, drape my hand on my dad's slumped shoulder, then kiss him on the forehead. He may be a weaker, older version of the man I grew up with, but he still has the same smell. From a single whiff I can tell he still uses the same soap, same shampoo, same deodorant. I find it oddly comforting, knowing some things never change. Yet it's unsettling, too. Because some things never change, even when they should.

In the distance I hear my mom chatting away, which gives me cover to sneak upstairs.

The bathroom is at the top of the landing, my parents' room on the left, my old room to the right. And Denise's old room next to it. For years they kept her room as it was, a shrine to her memory. But eventually they had to move on and converted it to my mom's sewing room. Another way for her to feel close to Denise.

My old room is now the guest room, with a desk and a computer my mom uses to pay bills and shop online. There are two beds, one each for me and Owen when we visit. Which isn't often. The closets are filled with my mom's seasonal clothes—blouses, slacks, dresses, and skirts hanging from hooks. Shoe racks on the floor, as well as boxes of toys for Owen, and assorted junk.

I look under the bed for something I need, then in all the cabinet draws. Nothing. "Where was it...?"

Owen's box of toys. I pull it out of the closet, sit on the bed. I rummage through the items. Various action figures, little trucks and cars, a model galaxy, and a tin box with a nebula emblem on the front. I open the tin. There's a half-pack of playing cards, some game dice, a rubber ball, a handheld video language game, two holocubes, and a levitating holographic spaceship.

And magnetized to the inside of the tin, a paper-thin chrome sheath, half the length of my index finger.

I dig my fingernail between the tin and sheath, prying it loose. I clutch the sheath in my palm, exhale, and nod to myself.

Bernice gave this to me a few years ago. I had it on me during my last visit here. I needed to reorganize the gear I keep in the pouch sewed into the back of my jacket. I was nearly done, the sheath and MedKit still on the nightstand, when my mother started in with me again about my job, and the way I live my life. I left in a huff.

I didn't have the heart—I was scared shitless—to tell Bernice I'd lost it. I figured I'd come get the sheath, eventually.

But then I got arrested for murder. Just one more heart-ache and embarrassment I put my parents through. I promised myself I wasn't going to come back here until I was free and clear of Tarrish, when I was back at the top of my game and could carry myself with a strut. Yet here I am, pretty far from the top.

Why is it that I can hunt dangerous criminals, or put myself at the mercy of the Cosmos, but can't face my mother?

I secure the sheath to a magnetic band inside my pocket, then head back downstairs.

"Okay, Ma. I hate to rush off, but there's a lot going on."

"Already? You haven't eaten."

"I'm not hungry."

"Angela—"

"Can't, Ma. Banny's got an audition. I promised to get him back."

"It's okay," he says. "I'm stuffed. Thank you so much. It was delicious. I need to run my lines anyway. Why don't you guys chat while I get into character."

I almost protest again, but it's clear I'm trying way too hard to avoid my mother. And we both know that can't go on forever. I almost feel Denise's eyes staring at me from the photograph, telling me from beyond the grave that being uncomfortable around my mother is a whole lot better than being dead.

"I guess I could eat," I say finally. "Ma? Grated cheese?"

She takes a beat before answering, probably surprised I agreed to stay, even if a part of her wished I would go. "I've got some in the fridge. But let me say goodbye to Esteban." She hugs and kisses him like he's the son she never had. "You're always welcome. Any time."

"Thank you, Betty. I'd like that."

I sit at the table and pull off my jacket. My mother heats up a plate in the microwave. After the timer bings she puts the plate in front of me. I take a bite, then grimace.

"That good?" my mother says, annoyed.

"It's fine, Ma. I've got a headache. Allergies, I think. Been having them a lot."

"It's what I've been telling you. With that job you have, the hours you keep. And the arrest..." She retracts, as if she wished she hadn't gone there. Or at least, not so soon.

"I know, Ma. I know. I got a lot on my plate right now. But my parole's almost over."

My mother goes to the cabinet, produces a bottle of red wine. She pours a glass.

"A little early, no?"

She looks at me like a boxer who's gone one round too many but knows the bout's not over. And when the bell rings, she'll have no choice but to answer.

"With you, Angela, it's never too early."

That one stings. But I had it coming. For almost twenty years we've been avoiding each other in the ways that matter most. Maybe it's my fault, maybe it's hers. Not sure it's important. Because we're here now. And like I tell my clients, the longer you hide from the truth, the deeper it burrows into your soul. In our case, if we don't excise the wound there won't be any healthy tissue left to save.

If we're doing this, let's do it. I push the plate aside. I come out swinging.

"I know you're mad at me, Ma. I'm sorry. But I can't take her place."

"Oh, for fuck's sake, Angela." She takes a drink. "It's not about Denise."

"Yes, it is! You just won't admit it. I know I'm not perfect. Far from it. But Denise wasn't either. Comparing me to a ghost is bullshit, Ma. It's fucking bullshit."

She takes another drink. "Seriously. Angela. How can anyone so smart be so dumb?"

Ouch. That one lands, too. Not because she's wrong. I'm just not ready to hear it.

I'm sweating everywhere, riddled with nervous, humiliated energy, on the verge of explosive tears.

"Ma... come on."

"Don't *Ma* me," she scolds. "Don't *Ma* me. Why are you so mean?"

"*Me?* I'm the one who's mean?"

She finishes off her glass of wine, pours another. "You

really think it's about Denise?" Still standing, she takes another drink. "You think *that's* why I'm upset?"

"Well... yeah. Kinda." Although I'm starting to doubt myself about that.

She sits across from me. "No, Angela. I'm upset because it's always something with you. Denise died, which was hard enough. But then you got pregnant... at sixteen. Then the baby died. Then all your drugs and drinking and slutting around. Then it was your private eye life, doing who knows what with who knows who. Do you have *any* idea what it's like to be your mother? Never knowing where you are, or when I'm gonna get the call? That you're dead. Or in prison? Or worse? If there is a worse. And then you sent my only grandson to live at that... place... that no one can find, with his father, who I hardly know. I never see Owen. Or you. And I worry. Unless I drink it all away. But then it comes right back. Because there's nothing I can do to change it."

Damn. It's difficult to be upset with her when she makes a compelling argument, focused mostly on my legitimately bad and insensitive behavior. "I know, Ma. But Owen's in a safe place. Probably safer than you are here."

My mother shakes her head, exasperated. "Why are you so difficult, Angela? Why can't you be...?"

I don't know what my face looks like to her, but I can feel it contorted into a scowl. There's a judgmental edge to my tone. "More like you?"

That missive lands with the precision of a poisoned dart. I can almost see the wave of pain ripple through my mother's entire body. Her shoulders slump. Her eyes sag. Her upper lip quivers. That's all on me. I hurt her more than if I'd kicked her in the teeth.

"Ma," I say, softer, gentler. But I hold my ground. "I get that my life's not for everyone. Maybe it makes no sense at all. But it's the life I choose for the reasons I choose it... even if it's not the life you choose for yourself. I don't need you to get it, Ma. But I need you to get that *I* get it."

She exhales gently through her nose. "I know. I already lost a daughter, your father's gonna die, and you put yourself at risk just to prove that you can." Her eyes are getting red and moist, the years of pain mapped out on her face. "Why do you do this, Angela? What have I ever done to you? I love you the best I know how. I always have. I always will."

"I know that you love me, Ma. But you don't accept me."

"How *can* I? You freeze me out then blame me for it. How can I understand you if I don't even know you?"

That one stops me cold. Whistler accuses me of the same thing.

"Yeah," I admit. "Maybe. But I keep you at a distance because sometimes... not all the time... but sometimes, I deal with dangerous people. And I don't want them to hurt *you* as a means to hurt *me*."

"And you hurt me anyway. That's what I mean, Angela. You're a grown woman. You're a mother. Yet you act like you're neither. Why do *I* have to pay for *your* choices?"

"Why do I have to pay for yours?"

Her chin tilts down. Her voice quivers. "What do you mean?"

"When Denise got sick, then died... you *disappeared* from me, Ma. You and Dad both. I get that you were scared about her. That you were in pain. But you know what, Ma? *I* was in pain! I mattered, too! But it was all Denise, all the time. I hated her for it. And I hated you, too. So I found attention...comfort... anywhere I could."

My chest is tight. My eyes fill with water.

"I didn't *mean* to get pregnant. And how could I know the baby would die? It shattered me, Ma! It absolutely destroyed me. But all you did was let me know how much I let you down. How much I failed you."

My mother slumps back in the chair, wipes her eyes. She then leans forward. She takes my hand. I let her.

"Is *that* how you remember it? Oh. Angela. Baby. I tried day and night to connect with you. But you pushed me away."

I retract my hand. "No. You came back to me *after* Denise died. Suddenly there was time for me. And even then, all you tried to do was control me. Every second. Where I went, what I did, who I was with. I couldn't breathe!"

Her eyes go messy with tears. "I'm sorry, baby. I didn't know what to do."

My tears follow. "I didn't either."

My mother paws at her face, her voice gone quiet. There's a heavy stillness now. Back in my childhood kitchen, I'm seeing this space in a whole new light. I never realized how much truth had been soaked into the walls. She extends her hand again. This time, I take it.

She smiles sadly, hopefully. "Why is it so hard to love someone?"

Half-squinting, half-crying, I squeeze her fingers. "Because it's so hard to love ourselves."

We sit for a while, wordlessly, until finally my mother gets up from the table, her eyes red and rheumy. She clears my plate, goes to the sink. With her back to me, she scrapes leftovers into the garbage disposal, runs the motor, then rinses my plate. She faces me again.

"You look so tired. Do you sleep?"

I sigh. "Not really. A little. You know. Good nights and bad."

"You still having the dreams?"

Something stirs in me. "What dreams?"

"You don't remember?" She chuckles awkwardly. "You used to dream. About a forest."

Adrenaline spikes. With my eyes flared open, I push away from the table. "What forest?"

"I have no idea. I could never make sense of it. You used to tell me about a glowing forest." She looks down the hallway, as if remembering something. "Hang on."

I'm almost shaking in anticipation as she digs through a closet. She moves some things around, until she produces a large bin. It's labeled *Angela*. She opens the lid, rifles through the bin. Finds some old drawings. Done by me.

"Here it is." She shows it to me.

In my hand I'm holding a piece of construction paper. On it is a crayon forest, lots of green trees... and blue, glowing streaks. Lightning bolts. I study the paper. Closer.

The dreams pop back into my head. Flashes of the encroaching forest. The cries for help. I wince, the *whumming* pain behind my temple getting worse. I know this pain. But it couldn't be what I think it is, could it? But that was...

"There's me," I say, pointing to a crayon girl with brown crayon pigtails. "But what's this?" I point to a brown smear. And what looks like two eyes.

"Him?" My mother shakes her head. "That's the man with the brown hair."

My hands vibrate so hard I nearly rip the drawing in half. There's a question I need to ask, but the words catch in my throat. "*Spiky* brown hair?"

She thinks on it. "That's it. *The man with spiky brown hair.* You said he was coming to get you in the glowing blue forest. It was very important to you for a while. But then you stopped talking about it. I figured it was just a bad dream. And that it finally went away."

CHAPTER 13

"**W**hat does it mean?" I ask Banny as we speed our way back through the suburban sphere of my childhood. I'm clutching this old drawing at the edges, my fingertips chafing on the construction paper. "I saw this in a dream? Thirty years ago? I don't remember."

"I don't know, Anj. Dreams are fucked up."

"I know. But I drew this when I was *five*." It's little kid artwork, no definition, scratchy coloring. But there's me, the blue forest. Some birds. And the man with spiky brown hair. "How could I have known about him back then?"

When I was pregnant the first time, with my baby girl, I had recurring nightmares about us burning up in a fire. In my dreams, I'd be sitting in a rocking chair, baby at my breast, engulfed in a raging sea of flames. I could feel the rising heat, as if I was physically in that room. My baby would erupt into smoldering orange and black liquid, hotter than lava, her flesh melting off her as I cradled her in my arms.

Dream logic told me I'd done this to her. As if the very milk she was suckling from my nipple was the source of her incineration. As if I'd been feeding her the very accelerant that melted her flesh and bones and destroyed her soul. As if my own body had poisoned her. That I'd intentionally sabotaged her—murdered her—because I resented how she was going to irrevocably change, and even consume, the totality of my life when I was still just a child myself. And that I'd rather see her burn alive, in my arms, than deal with the anxiety and torment that go hand-in-hand with motherhood.

The doctors told me that the nightmares were normal. My subconscious processing the stress and fears about the physical and hormonal changes my body was going through, and the enormous responsibility I'd incurred, and would continue to incur, for the rest of my life. But also that I shouldn't worry. Every expectant mother had the same fears.

After the baby died from a rare genetic complication, I looked back on those dreams as an early warning system, my subconscious's way of preparing me for the inevitable tragedy I'd have to endure. And my scorched realm approach I would embrace in the years that followed, as a means of punishing myself for failing to protect my baby. For destroying her.

A mother's worst nightmare.

Or was it a self-fulfilling prophecy? Did I somehow permit those apocalyptic pregnancy dreams to dictate my path of self-destruction? Did I set fire to my life because my dreams told me to? Was I just following the blueprint my subconscious had mapped out for me? Or did I tap into the ether of all Existence?

Coming up on the Infinity Cloud again, I tell Banny where we need to go next.

"You sure?" he asks through the partition. "It messed you up last time."

I stare again at the old drawing I made as a child. Younger me talking to the older me. This me, the now me. "I know," I say, and with that admission, finally release my grip. I'd somehow tapped into the timestream, leaving myself a message that took thirty years to unfold. "I don't have a choice."

Back in the chaotic churn of the city, we dodge the midday bustle of the Harper and Cobblestone Districts, with the relentless assault of noise, lights, vehicles, people, tech, billboards, drones, commerce, crime, and chrome, and head into Praker Town.

We got caught in some traffic near Biotech Circle, the city's newest medical research and development corridor, bustling with new restaurants, retail, and the PaPei Forest and Observatory. PaPei Forest is a synthetic mountain encased in a glowing glass dome and populated with diverse vegetation, exotic plants, and waterfalls.

Banny does his usual magic and finds a prime parking

spot on a tight-angled side street. Heading around the corner on foot, I refocus with uncertain determination. I finally step into DreamHopper, an immersion center set between a juice smoothie shop and an augmentation polisher.

Soft blue light illuminates the small, carpeted intake room. I approach the counter. Behind bulletproof glass, the clerk is scrolling on her phone.

"Hey, Jody."

Jody looks up at me. She's sporting a nose ring, lip ring, one diamond stud each in her left eyebrow and right cheek, and a cluster of ear piercings. "Angela? Didn't think you'd come back."

I did some dream-hopping a while ago. Wanted to see what all the fuss was about. It kicked up some repressed memories I wish had stayed buried.

"You know how it goes."

Jody's natural jet-black hair is dyed purple, buzzed down to the scalp along the sides. Last we spoke, she was training to become a licensed physical therapist.

"One more year and I graduate." She flexes her fingers. "Time to put these babies to good use." She gives a head-nod to Banny. "So what'll it be. Tandem? Solo? I got three pods open."

"Just me," I say. "He's gonna wait."

Banny eyes me. "I am?" I eye him back. He nods as if my response was inevitable, which it was. "I'll be in the waiting room. Running my lines. Again."

Jody leads me to the intake center. She gives me a key on a lanyard, which I wear around my neck. I store my jacket and gear, including my weapons, in a locker. Jody hands me a mug of Dream Tea. It relaxes the mind, making it easier to enter the Dreamscape.

Mug in hand I sit on one of the couches opposite an elderly woman in a brown pantsuit, a younger woman with a cranial interface, and two teen boys holding hands. They're all in various stages of drift from the Dream Tea. Soon enough, they'll be ready to enter a Dream Room, then lay inside individual Dream Pods.

Tandem Dream Pods sit side-by-side, connected above by a series of tubes, cathodes, and wires. Once the session is initiated, Dreamers enter each other's subconscious, and 'hop' between their respective dreams. I'm flying solo. Last thing I need is yet another dream invader.

The tea slides down my throat and into my belly. Almost immediately I feel a warm glow inside me. I've done more than my share of drugs, but to escape. I don't like to let the walls down. Especially not the amorphous boundaries of the Dreamscape.

But my face unclenches, taking the pressure off the jawbone joint, releasing the stress I'd been carrying up to my eye sockets. My back and legs loosen. My hands, which had been balled into tight fists, open up and vibrate so that my fingers seem to float like jellyfish tendrils.

"You're there," Jody says, supervising. "Ready?"

It takes a few seconds to find my way through the Dream Fog. "Let's do it."

Eight feet long and three feet wide, Dream Pods are white chrome tubes, like tanning beds, with long, thick cables attached on both ends and mounted with reinforced plating.

Jody opens the pod like a clamshell. Or a coffin.

Both the interior bed and underside of the lid are padded for comfort. Also for protection, in case you thrash around while in the Dreamscape. I lie down in the pod. Jody attaches diodes to my temple, the other ends leading directly into the pod's interior access panel. There are cameras and microphones inside the pod, in case I call for help, or if it looks like I might hurt myself.

In cases of extreme exertion, the pod automatically initiates a safety shut-off, and releases a gentle anesthetic to calm the Dreamer down. Let's hope we don't need this.

"Once I close the lid, give it about thirty seconds," Jody explains. "After that, you'll hear three hums, which lets you know you're entering the Dreamscape. Got it?"

"Three hums," I say, feeling gigglier than I'd remembered from the last time I tried this. "Hum-hum-hum."

"You have any trouble, get claustrophobic, hit the panic button." She hands it to me. "I'll get you out."

"That's reassuring."

Jody smiles. "Have a good trip." She closes me in. Mounted on the pod's interior pads, wire-thin string-bulbs give off enough subtle violet illumination that I can see down the length of my body.

Falling deeper into myself, I think of an Earth philosopher I once read about, Carl Jung. He said dreams were the emissary of the unconscious, whose tasks were to reveal secrets hidden from the conscious mind, and that dreams do so with astounding completeness, whether we realize it or not.

The unconscious, Jung said, is the dark being within us all that hears what our conscious ears do not hear and sees what our conscious eyes do not perceive. We only become aware of this unheard hearing, this unseen seeing, when the unconscious sends us these forgotten images in dreams.

Here's hoping it does the trick for me.

I don't hear the three hums, but I'm in the Dreamscape. I'm in my office, shrouded in fog. All the elements—desk, table, bookshelf, window, door to Whistler's space—they're all half-in, half-out of the fog, as if they're on the border of reality and dissolving into the ether.

Page is by my side. She barks once and points her snout, directing me ahead. Toward my office door.

"What's that, girl? You hungry?" I know she's not, but my mind is having trouble locking onto solid thoughts. "Go for a walk?"

She barks again. Once. But sharper. That's not her hungry bark or her I-need-to-pee bark. She wants me to look. To move forward. To advance.

I'm wearing my jacket but realize I'm barefoot. And I can't tell if I'm wearing jeans. I think I'm naked from the waist down. Feeling exposed, unprotected. I search for my retractable taser, then for the gun in my shoulder holster. My pockets are empty.

I'm overcome with fear. Panic. Embarrassment. Humiliation. *I'm a disappointment. I'm a failure. I can't do this!*

I look under my desk and scour my bookshelves, searching for my gun, my gear. But then the room starts to spin. It swirls, like I'm a toddler lost in the mall, confused by all the giant people and cavernous storefronts, all of them getting bigger and more menacing until they swallow me up and I'm falling into a hole so black and deep I can't see the bottom and don't know where the top is anymore and...

I'm unprepared. I'm not ready. I can't...

Stop, Angela. Think. Breathe.

I'm unprepared. I'm unprepared. I'm unprepared.

I'm unprepared because...

I'm dreaming. And if I'm dreaming, and I know I'm dreaming, that means the dream can't take me over. I can control myself in my dreams. Lucid dreaming. Don't let the dream control me. Control the dream.

If only it were that easy.

Page is gone. It's just me. The elements of my office are nearly consumed by the fog, such that through a small funnel, through the thickening white-gray, I see my office door, and my name in black letters on the frosted glass. I know it says *Angela Hardwicke: Private Investigations*

Because it always has. But when I run my finger along the letters, it says something else:

Angela Hardwicke doesn't work here anymore.

"No. I'm still here." I reach out my hand. The door doesn't so much open as disappear.

"Because it's MINE!" a voice snarls at me.

The size of a rhino, Whistler leaps on me.

No. Not leaps. He whooshes on top of me. Consumes me, swirling around and through me like an apparition. Whistler's face is enormous, distorted. With sharp fangs, saliva dripping off them, he's staring at me, so close I can't see anything except him. His skin is ashen. Eyes red. His soul feels like a cold, lifeless vapor, a hiss of unforgiving brutality across the Cosmos' vast and incalculable expanse.

His mouth isn't moving, and yet I hear him. "You lost it all," he says. "You lost *me*! How could you *lose* me? You know how much I love you and you *hate* me for it. I gave you the right hand. Grab my wrist."

I don't know what he means, and though it feels like I'm desecrating sacred ground, I reach out for him. Through the fog Whistler *becomes* the fog. He *is* the fog. A fog with a face so large it could swallow the forest.

There's an evil glint in his eye, a signal of what's to come. The Whistler fog clamps down, severing me in half.

I shut my eyes and prepare for the moment. For my death.

Now I'm in the forest. It glimmers with bioluminescent trails, as if an animal had been gutted, its blue, glowing life force leaking from its innards, leaving a bloody trail for me to follow.

Oh shit.

Animal. Is that Page? Is she hurt? Is she dead? Is she...?

Beneath a tight canopy of growth, the crickets, cicadas, and frogs chirp and croak like an amphibious orchestra:

Wur-wur-wur

Weh-weh-weh

Wur-wur-wur

Weh-weh-weh

Wur-wur-wur

Weh-weh-weh

Wur-wur-wur

Weh-weh-weh

Yet beneath the chirping and croaking I hear another sound. I instinctively hunch, as if that will help me listen more acutely.

Wur-wur-wur

Weh-weh-weh

Wur-wur-wur

Weh-weh-weh

That *whum* in my head is back. Instinctively I clench my jaw again. I need to concentrate, to focus. I need to know if this pain is what I think it is, or if it's just my mind's way of getting my attention. Of all the things to tell me... why this? I shush the forest.

It doesn't comply. But I bear down. I hear it. It's a... pinch? A click. A... ticking?

You left me, the voice calls out again. *Why did you leave me?*

Dolores. I still can't find her. But I know she's close.

The bioluminescent blue radiates with greater intensity, the glowing life blood penetrating the soil and woody substrates. My headache worsens. Drops me to my knees. I brace my hands in the moss, damp and squishy like cold chunky vomit.

I hear Dolores calling to me again.

I'm bleeding. I'm in so much pain. I'm going to die. I've been calling you. Please. You have to find me. Before it's too late.

I feel the panic slowly swirling in my gut, bouncing off the bottom of my ribs. Every ounce of me wants to flop face-first onto the ground with the smelly moss smushed into my mouth, if for no other reason than to drown out the horrible, childish wails I want unleash.

To let out a sloppy, drooling, messy cry, a good, old-fashioned, pathetic, and whiny tantrum so I can feel important while ineffectually trying to smoother my reality. My shame. That after all the cases I've worked and the son I'm trying to raise, I am, in the final analysis, nothing but a helpless, impotent loser. Unable to pull myself out of my depression. Knowing I'll have to face the dishonor I've brought upon myself, and possibly lose everything I've tried to build.

I thought prison was my bottom. I was wrong.

I'm not back to square one. I'm back to zero. Less than zero.

Or I can slap the stupid off my face and look at my journey through the Dreamscape as an opportunity—and a warning. Whimpering doesn't solve cases or fix my life. Investigating, and taking action, does.

There's rustling in the bushes. Is it her? Is it Dolores? Is it...?

A cinnamon-colored rabbit hops out. It rumples its nose, sits on its haunches, and with little pink eyes, looks up at me. There's bruising on its face. Already kneeling, I reach out for it, slowly. The rabbit seems to want me to, so I pick it up, and cradle it my arms. It's trembling.

"I got you." I stroke its forehead. "I got you."

The rabbit nestles itself against me. For security. Safety. Protection.

Rabbit in my arms, I stand up and study the foggy forest, examining the trees, the leaves, the mossy stumps, the exposed roots and... something sparkles ahead.

It's small, so small I can barely see it. Seeing what I see, the rabbit hops down, looks back and up at me, then scurries ahead along the bioluminescent trail. I follow until we come upon a patch of leaves. The rabbit stops there. With its little paws, it digs, uncovering what's underneath.

I kneel, brush my hand through the damp leaves.

There it is. It's a watch. The band is damaged. The face is cracked.

But it's ticking. I hold it up to my ear. Yes. It's ticking. It's still working.

Tick-tick-tick-tick-tick-tick-tick.

I get a jolt of energy. Of optimism. If the watch is working, that means it's still alive. *She's* still alive.

"You shouldn't be here. It's not safe."

I know that voice. I smell his natural musk. It's Tarrish.

Tall, Black, and lithe with a full salt-and-pepper beard, he's wearing his raincoat.

"Here," he says, looking like him, but not exactly like him. "Take this."

He hands me a jar of moisturizer. Intuitively, I unscrew the cap, then knead the oily cream between my fingers. My hands are soft and smooth.

I sniff at it. "What flavor? Is this...?" My hands get sticky. The moisturizer turns to glue. My fingers fuse together. "I don't know my schedule. Where am I supposed to *be?*"

Tarrish is floating somehow, yet it makes sense to me that he is. He's wearing the watch now. "You've already been there. You left it behind."

"Left *what* behind?"

"Not what," Tarrish says. "When."

I'm so upset now I'm swirling again, the forest whooshing around me in a brown, green, and blue whir.

"When *what?*"

The fog creeps back in. "No!" Whistler yells. Strands of bioluminescent vines are wrapped around him. He's a prisoner. The vines squeezing this limbs and throat. The other ends of the vines are spiraled around an enormous oak tree. Tarrish coils the other end of the vines around his arms, using the tree for leverage, struggling to keep Whistler in place. "Not *when!*" Whistler shouts. "*Wednesday!*"

"Hurry," Tarrish says, his hands and face trembling at the strain of pulling on the vines. He's now wearing two watches. One on each wrist. Then two on each wrist. Then three. Then four. "I can't hold it."

Knots in the surrounding trees morph into watches. All of them ticking louder, louder, louder until their faces distort and melt, surrounding me.

Wur-wur-wur

Weh-weh-weh

Wur-wur-wur

Weh-weh-weh

I don't know what he means. "Wednesday? But it's *Monday!*"

Tick-tick-tick-tick-tick-tick-tick.

The ticking is so loud it's driving me insane.

"Mache," Whistler whispers. "He's coming."

"*Who's* coming?"

Stuck to my hands is the drawing I'd made. Me. The forest. And him.

It's the man with spiky brown hair.

He's coming.

And I'm almost out of time.

CHAPTER 14

I hit the panic button. Jody opens the lid. I pop up.

"I gotta go."

Jody gently presses her hand against my shoulder. "You need to let the tea wear off. You should hydrate. And take it easy."

I pull the diodes off my face. "If I had time for easy, I'd be somewhere else."

I grab my gear from the locker, but I'm a little wobbly from the tea. Banny helps me to his cab. I tell him where we're going—and why.

"You're gonna need backup."

"I know." I check that my gun is loaded, my taser fully charged. It crackles at the end. I send a quick text. "Doing it now."

It takes Banny a half-hour to get there. Anyone else driving, it would've taken twice as long.

A motorcycle screams among the chaotic streetscape, then shuts off, parks. The rider removes a black helmet. It's Olin.

"I don't like this." She's got her gun out, down by her side. "He can't be here."

Banny pumps the stock on his shotgun. "You gonna arrest me?"

Olin grits her teeth. "This is why everyone hates you, Hardwicke. You push past the edge when you know we're out of options."

I regrip my gun. "Cops hate me because I get to the scene before they do. Dante keeps one guard on the first floor, another up top. Let me do the talking."

Olin tries to get up the stoop ahead of me. "Doesn't work that way."

From my pocket I produce the chrome sheath I got from

my mom's house. "Today it does." The sheath, which I place on my forefinger, is a multi-surface skeleton key. It can open any lock, of any construction. Above the doorframe, the security globe shifts in our direction. I ignore it, employ a swift, two-phase approach. Brushing my sheathed finger on the mechanism, I unlock the black metal security gate. Banny pulls it open. I immediately unlock then push the heavy wood door with metal edges.

The gaunt teenager with track marks and the rubber ball jumps back. He's got a gun.

"What the fuck, yo? You can't be—"

"Dante's in the shit," I say, as Olin shows her badge and points her weapon, then takes the kid's gun. "You don't want to be here for this."

I send my scout orb up the stairwell. It sends back a video feed to my lens. Nobody hanging about except who I figured.

Me, Olin, and Banny side-step up the stairs until we get to the fifth-floor landing.

Burly Girl is pointing a shotgun at us. I stare down the barrel. It's definitely loaded.

"Dante ain't seein *nobody*. Get the fuck out."

"He said to get my ass here like it's on fire," I say. "This is my ass. It's on fire."

Burly Girl stares at us, her eyes scanning for lies and deceptions. She inches forward, raises the shotgun. "I don't *think* so."

"Police business," Olin says. "I *very* much think so."

"*Psh.* Whatchu gonna do? Jail ain't shit to me. I got people all over that bitch. You ain't give me orders. And you *definitely* ain't give Dante orders. He gives 'em to you. And his orders are to fuck yer momma, fuck yerselves, and get the fuck out. I don't trust nobody 'cept my boy right here." She nods at her weapon. "Unless you wanna suck on this bitch, take them stairs back where you came."

"All right then," I say. "If that's the way you wanna play it."

"Ain't no other way."

Synced to my lens, I direct the scout orb, which has been hovering down by her feet, to rise up near her face.

She flinches. "What the fuck?"

The orb sprays her with a mist. Burly Girl goes down with a thud. Newest upgrade from Bernice. Knock-out gas.

We step around Burly Girl, knock on the door.

"Dante," I say. "It's Hardwicke. Open up."

"Fuck off."

"Something's about to go down. Let me in."

I hear other voices. Muffled arguments. A screech.

"I *know* you dumb bitch. *Fuck. Off!*"

Me, Banny, and Olin quickly confer. We all have our weapons out. I kick the door in but hide behind the wall in case Dante does anything stupid.

On brand, he fires off two shots. Both hit the walls inside his apartment.

"Dante! Put that away!"

From a ducked position, I see Dante in his chair, gun out, hand shaking. Simone is hiding behind the couch. I zoom in with my lens. Dante's eyes are glossy and bloodshot.

"You ain't gettin me," he rambles. "None'a you are gettin me. How I know you ain't with him? He's pickin us off!"

"We're definitely not with him," Olin says. "We're not here to get you. Dante. Please, just put the gun down."

His knuckles sparkle. The clock rings. "How I know you ain't playin me?"

Nothing like negotiating with a stoned, violent, paranoid pimp.

Olin knows him better than I do. She appeals to his vanity. "How could *I* be playing *you?* Come on. You're Dante Maurice Browning. You don't *get* played. You *play.*"

Dante considers her logic. It seems to pacify him. Until it doesn't. "Don't tongue my gaping asshole, muthafucka. You ain't sweet-talkin shit."

"No sweet talk," I say. "Just regular talk. I swear." I ease into the doorframe, hold my gun pointed down. "We're here to help. That's all." Olin and Banny come in behind me. That gets his fur back up. Palms open, I put my hands down. "Dante. No bullshit."

Panting like he just got chased by a pack of wolves, he's eyeing the apartment, as if waiting for someone, one of his girls, maybe the new Top Slot, to tell him what to do. But

Kimmie-slash-Nóirín is dead, and Jasmine's with Bernice. His harem is shrinking by the day. Which is a problem. Pimps always need to be in control, for someone *to* control, until they realize they have no control at all. That's when the panic sets in.

Olin eases toward Dante as I shut the door and lock it behind me. Banny stands guard.

"You ain't gonna get me," Dante says. "You can't let 'em get me." There's a baggie on the coffee table, white powder spilled out. Some of it peppers the outside of his inflamed nostrils.

Simone is hunched behind the couch, panting.

"Nobody's getting anyone," Olin says calmly. "What we're all gonna do now is put down our guns, okay?" Slowly she retracts the hammer on her weapon and switches on the safety. Then slowly secures the gun in her hip holster. "See."

With a forced smile, Olin raises her eyebrows, and looks to me, so I'll do the same. I do.

"Him, too," Dante says.

"Banny," I say. "We're all friends here. Put it down."

"Not until *he* does."

"Make 'im do it!" Dante's gun-hand shakes. "Or I'm gonna kill someone."

Banny points the shotgun at Dante. "Anyone's getting killed, asshole, it's gonna be you."

My heartbeat is going triple time. "Banny! No one's getting killed. Put. It. Away."

Banny flares his nostrils, his face contorted into a scowl. "Angela—"

A crash comes from within Aiko's bedroom.

Dante shoots wildly at the door. A scream comes from behind it. Simone whimpers. I raise my hand and push up Banny's arm so he can't get his own shot off. Olin pounces on Dante, pinning his shoulder back, and secures his gun.

"Quiet!" I command. "Seriously. Chill... out."

Dante's already coked-up and paranoid. Last thing I need is to tell him I saw something in a dream that had me rush over here. He tries to get up from the chair. Olin intercepts with one hand, has him sit back down. With the other, she gestures to Simone.

"It's okay," she says. "It's all right."

Like a terrified racoon hiding behind a dumpster, Simone still has her hands clutched to the back lip of the couch, her fingernails dug in. She's trembling. Olin lets Dante up. He checks the lock on the apartment door, then goes to the window, to see if the gunfire and screams drew any attention. In this neighborhood, it's background noise. The police tend to take their time responding to calls around here. If anyone even bothers.

Meanwhile, I check to see if Dante didn't just commit murder.

"Aiko. It's me. It's Hardwicke. You can come out. It's safe. I promise." I hear rustling from behind the door. "Are you hurt? Are you okay?" No answer. I really hope Dante didn't shoot her. "I'm gonna come in. Don't worry. It's just me."

I sheath the door, open it. It's a small room, with a window, bed, and dresser, and a few exotic tapestries on the wall. A silk bathrobe hangs on the back of the door. Aiko's on the floor, hunched between the foot of the bed and the dresser. On visual inspection, she seems unhurt.

"Come on," I whisper, and offer my hand. She's trembling, her hands compressed into tiny fists. "It's okay. Nobody's gonna hurt you. It's okay."

Eyes peeled back in horror, Aiko exhales through gritted teeth. It takes a moment, but with the chaos over, she releases her fists. Her breathing slows.

"Okay?" I say hopefully.

She nods and takes my hand. "Okay."

I notice the bruise on her wrist is worse than before. It's red, irritated. It should've gotten better by now. She might've hurt it worse than I thought.

I lead her out of the bedroom and into the living room. Olin wisely removed the drugs. Don't want Dante taking another bump.

"Dante," I say, trying to lower the temperature. "You seem a little tense."

"A little?"

"Talk to me. What's up?"

With what appears to be a look of genuine disbelief, he eyes
Aiko, Simone... and Olin.

"You ain't tell her?"

"I was gonna," Olin says.

I turn to her. "Tell me what?"

"I kept as much as I could from Vice, but the desk clerk at
the Love Star? He's dead. Shot between the eyes, stabbed in the
side."

"And you didn't tell me?"

"I was doing my *job*. And then you said to come here.
Emergency. So I came. And yes, it's an emergency."

Without having noticed she'd slipped away, Simone comes
from the mini bar and hands Aiko a shot of vodka.

There's a lot going on here. I need to think.

"I'm a little unclear," I say to Aiko. "At the Love Star, how
did you get out of there? The clerk must've seen you. Especially
if you were roughed up."

"He," Aiko says, her voice barely audible, "he wasn't there.
Maybe he was on a break."

Yeah. Not buying it. "Thing is... I checked the security camera. Nobody went by the desk at the time you said." I didn't
check. There were no logs. But she doesn't know that.

"Uh, I mean," she says, and slugs down the vodka. She
wipes her mouth. "I..."

Aiko's gaze shifts to Dante, then to Olin, as if asking per-
mission to speak freely. Or if she should speak at all.

"Well?" Dante says. "Tell it straight."

Simone hands her another shot. Aiko drinks it. "I called
Kimmie. She sent me to the roof. Buildings are close together.
I took the rooftops, maybe three or four. I don't know, it was
dark, and I was fucked up. I found a fire escape. I took it to the
street."

"Why ain't you *say* that?" Dante springs up again, like he
wants to swat her face. "You can't be hidin shit from me when
there's a fuckin psycho out—"

Olin stands between them. Dante balls his hands into fists,
tapping the clock ring faces against each other.

"Dante," I say. "Let her finish."

Olin hands him her vape. He considers his options, snags it from her. He takes two deep drags and coughs. That drops him back into his chair.

"Go on," I say to Aiko. "What happened?"

"I couldn't find a cab, so I ran. But I was alone, and it was late. So I stopped to check for the pepper spray in my purse. That's when I realized... I dropped my wallet in the room." Her eyes explode with tears. "If the cops found it, with a body there, they were gonna..." Sobbing, she covers her face.

"That's why you called Kimmie-slash-Nóirín. To collect your purse."

Aiko nods from behind her hands. Her voice is weepy like a child's. "Yes."

"Hold the muthafuckin fort," Dante says. "You tellin me my Top Slot, my Kimmie, went to clean up your muthauckin *mess*? And that's what got her *killed*?"

"She didn't have to take the bag," Simone says with a bit of an edge to it. "Could'a left it."

Dante raises his arm like he's about to backhand her across the face. "*Don't* be talkin shit about my Kimmie! Nobody..."

Simone hides behind me. Dante's coked-up and weeded down, feeling his life spin out of control. We need to make order out of all this disorder.

"If Kimmie-slash-Nóirín got killed over the stash," Olin says, talking it through out loud, "and now the desk clerk got killed..." She looks to me.

"Whoever took the bag from her apartment is cleaning up loose ends." I turn to Aiko. "Which means—"

A thump above us draws our looks. As if powered by a high-powered laser, a circular chunk of ceiling, twice the radius of a manhole cover, is carved out. Orange sparks crackle around the edges. The ceiling slab crashes to the floor. Gas grenade explodes. We choke on the gas, ripping at our lungs. Through my lens I see a nylon rope drop through the cloud.

A man in black combat gear slides down.

Wearing a gas-protective face shield. And has spiky brown hair.

The man from my dreams. My nightmares.

Kayger 9.5 pulse rifle with laser-guided scope in one hand and various pistols, knives, and grenades secured to his belt and vest. He elbows me in the head, knocking me down.

Aiko shrieks, her eyes red like a rabid animal. Dante grabs Simone, using her as a human shield. She screams and scratches at his arm, drawing blood. Dante howls and pushes Simone forward. Spiky Hair fires off a burst of shots through the smoke screen. The high caliber round rips holes through Simone, shredding her heart into pulpy chunks. Another round catches Dante in the thigh. He lets out a throaty scream, then drops with a thud next to Simone's mutilated body, her bone and blood smeared on the wall.

Banny raises the shotgun but can't get a clear shot through the smoke. Spiky Hair launches a round-house kick at him, knocking the shotgun across the room, toward the kitchen, then flips his rifle butt at Olin. She counter-moves, partially deflecting the gun butt, but it still makes hard contact, bashing the tip of her right shoulder. She howls in pain and drops her gun.

Spiky Hair grabs Aiko by the arm. Shot from a wrist guard on his other hand, an infrared beam scans her bad wrist. He studies it. "You. Come."

She squeals, scratching at him. But he's too big, too strong. And we can barely see.

My lens cuts through the smoke. Down on the ground I employ an Arberian martial arts leg kick, swirling on my pelvis. I strike him in the knee, which slightly buckles. I roll over and hop back up on my feet. I bash his gun hand with my fully extended taser. I hear the bone break. He winces, then front kicks me in the chest, knocking me back. I think he broke another rib.

Banny scrambles for the shotgun. Olin dives behind the lip of the couch.

Spiky Hair still has a hold on Aiko. A black, mechanical brace extends from his outer gear, supporting his broken hand. Still camouflaged by the smoke screen, he secures a hand-held grip to the taught nylon cord, about to activate a pneumatic hoist.

This isn't an assault. It's an extraction. Aiko is the target.

The hoist launches him up, Aiko with him. In a desperate

move I pull out my boot knife, slash at him. The sharpened blade pierces his fatigues, somewhere between the Achille's heel and calf. He grumbles. Blood gushes from the wound. He drops Aiko on top of me.

I crawl out from underneath her, then grab the rope, to climb up and follow him.

The cord drops, cut from above. Which is probably just as well. If he'd been waiting for me on the roof, I would have been an easy shot. Above are heavy, lumbering footsteps, a series of thuds. Spiky Hair making his escape.

With the threat seemingly ended, we're left in Dante's damaged crib. And all we can hear are our desperate pants and whimpers and the sound of our own hearts, which, for now, minus Simone, are still beating.

CHAPTER 15

We gag on the smoke as the cloud dissipates, Dante's crib more like a bloody playpen. Simone is ripped to pieces on the floor, with the chair, couch, and wall shot up, and the coffee table smashed.

From a side angle, Olin's looking out the window, her right arm hanging like a dead limb. Aiko's in the corner, trembling. Banny has the shotgun, his gaze following a trail of smeared blood leading messily to the apartment door, with a bloody handprint on the doorknob and faceplate. The door is ajar.

"Angela," he says. "Dante's hurt bad. I'm gonna find him."

"Don't. He couldn't've gone far. Wait for me."

He looks angrily at Simone's mutilated body, pumps the stock. "Not asking."

I claw my way to my feet, cough again. The tiny hammer thumps in my head, throbbing from the smoke, violence, and persistent *whum* I can't get rid of. I press the pad of my hand to my temple.

"Hardwicke." Olin staggers toward me, winces. "My arm's totally numb. My shoulder's on fire."

"You need an ambulance?"

"Probably. But we gotta... ah... we gotta call this in. Can't leave like it like this."

"A lot of questions we don't wanna answer."

"I know. And *gas leak* won't fly."

I reach for my phone. "I'll make a call."

"Who I think?"

"No choice." I dial. Picks up after three rings. An unhappy voice answers. Angry exchange. I hang up. "They're coming."

There's rustling in the hallway. The neighbors are freaked

out, even for this neighborhood. I shut the front door so we can think.

Once again I ease Aiko out of a corner. There are markings on her wrist. She pulls her hand away from me.

"Aiko. Let me see."

Shaky, she offers me her wrist. I take it in my hand, roll it side to side. There's some minor bruising. But starting near the forearm and scrolling around to the underside are red markings, a series of symbols I don't recognize.

"Jo. What do you make of this?"

She staggers over, squints, examines Aiko's wrist. "No idea." She turns to the door. "I have to control the scene."

I look at her oddly. "How?"

Olin holds her gun in her weak hand, badge fastened to her belt. "After this shit, they'll be happy to see a cop."

I raise my eyes. "Let's hope you're right."

"I'll secure the hallway," she says. "My old partner's on the way."

"You trust him?"

She takes a deep breath, winces, exhales. "He's solid."

Olin lumbers toward the door, slips into the hallway. Closes the door behind her.

Aiko stares at the cavernous hole in the ceiling, down to the fallen debris, and to Simone's body on the floor. "He'll come back. He's gonna come back."

"I know. Help's on the way. You'll be all right."

"N-n-no," she objects and pulls away from me. "They won't listen, they won't care. I have to go."

"Aiko. I know you're scared. But we need to move you." She stares at me, as if debating whether to believe me. I'm not the police, but to her, I might as well be. "We can't stay here, and you can't be on your own. You're a witness to a murder. And a target."

Aiko cries again. Tears cascade down her face. "I can't be in the system. No *cops*."

"Oh, Aiko." I gently rub her arm. "It's too late for that. He busted in for a reason. For you. Come on. Let's see your wrist again." I reach for it. She retracts. "Aiko…"

She can't stop staring at Simone, another dead sex worker cut down way too soon, thinking she'll be next. If we don't figure this out, she might be.

I take her wrist again as some of the neighbors argue with Olin in the hallway. "I'm just gonna look," I say. "That's all." I examine the markings through my lens. They're symbols, scrolling around her wrist like on a digital readout.

My lens says: *ENCRYPTED*

Whatever these markings are for, wherever they're from, or whatever they mean, this is what Spiky Hair was after. Is it a message from GGZ? Directions? Instructions? Confirmation? I record the markings as they scroll around her wrist, then send a voice command: *"Bernice. Can you crack this? It's urgent. Please."*

My head still sore from where Spiky Hair clocked me, I scroll through my mind, sifting through the debris of the last few days.

"Aiko. Gimme your wrist again." She eyes me with seething disdain, like a teenager whose been secretly cutting herself. I get that she's scared, but I don't have time for this. I snatch her wrist. She struggles, but I overpower her. "Stay still." Her hand in mine, I graze my fingertip along her flesh. "It's firm. Like there's a metal band beneath the skin or a..."

I stare into her eyes. My gaze meets hers. "Aiko. What did you do?"

"N-nothing." She tries to pull away from me. I don't let her. "I didn't..."

"You see your friend over there? Whatever this guy wants... *she* paid the price. Kimmie-slash-Nóirín, too. It'll only get worse. Now cut the shit, Aiko. What happened at the Love Star? Second by second. All of it."

We're locked in a tense stare, her face puckered and tight. Her adrenaline, fear, and shame have her contorted inside and out, as if she's in a furious fugue state. She knows where she is, and yet, she doesn't. In her mind, she's gone somewhere else. Anywhere but here.

Aiko seems to fall deeper into her fantasy world, her eyes focused on a scene only she can experience until, like a suicide jumper who finally steps back from the ledge, she expels a silent sigh of acceptance. Her shoulders slump. Her chest deflates. Her body eases just enough to let me know she's submitted to her fate. Time to come clean.

Feeling her arm relax and wrist loosen, I let go. As my fingers retract from hers, she lets hers linger. I'm not holding onto her now. She's holding onto me.

"His vibe was fucked up," she says about GGZ at the Love Star. "Amped, twitchy. He was pacing back and forth. He got a big score. That's what he said. Over and over. 'Big score, baby. *Big* fucking score.'"

"What kinda score?"

"He didn't say. But he had this look, you know? Like he couldn't believe his luck. All that *money*."

"You saw the credits?"

Aiko nods. "The bag he had. He kept goin in for meth. But he had all these credit-loaded star drives. They were in this... I don't know... a nylon strap, with pouches. Ten. Maybe more. It was hard to tell."

"He never said what it was for? The bag? The money?"

She shakes her head. "I asked, but..." Aiko turns away with a wince, as if she's back in the Love Star, him threatening to slap her face. She turns back to me. "He said when he was done, everyone would see... would really see... what a guy like him could do. And get rich as shit. Those were his words. 'Rich as shit.'"

I can't follow her logic. "He's going after a bank?"

"No. I don't know. I don't think so. He said no one would see, until it was too late."

"And you'd never seen him before? GGZ?"

"No."

"How'd he even find you? Plenty of sex workers to choose from."

That stops her cold. She stares at the floor, then back to me. "Kimmie."

It was there the whole time. "Was that normal? For Kimmie-slash-Nóirín to set up your clients?"

"No. Not usual. But he had a kink for girls who look like me. That's what she said."

That may have been what Kimmie-slash-Nóirín told her. But is it what she meant? Then it hits me.

"How did she even meet this guy? I thought she kept to the high-class hotels?"

"She was Top Slot. Part of her job was, you know... to look out for me. I don't know how she knew him. I didn't ask. I just did what I was told. Dante's rules. What Kimmie says, goes."

I believe her. And I don't.

"Did she know about the bag? About the credits? On the star drives?" Aiko doesn't answer. Which itself is an answer. "Aiko. Was this a setup? Was that the deal? Were you supposed to get him drunk and high? Then snatch his bag? You wouldn't be the first pro to roll a john."

Aiko's face explodes into a howl of tears. "It was her idea," she whimpers. "Dante... he takes all our money. Especially at first. Says he has to earn our trust. But it's not trust. He *owns* us. Owns me." She's sobbing now. "He's got me out there twelve hours a day. One after another. I can't take it anymore. But I can't get out."

I wish her story was unique. It's not. Sex workers trapped by a pimp like Dante rarely last for more than a few years. A lot them, a few months. A few weeks. The violence and disease. The desecration and depravity. For most girls who get broken like this, it's all about survival.

My mind flashes to Kimmie-slash-Nóirín's apartment. Her glider. The mothering. Then I realize...

"She was helping you get out. Kimmie-slash-Nóirín. *His* big score became *your* big score. Take the money and run."

Aiko nods furiously, her face puckered like a red lemon. "Y-yes. She was holding my money. So Dante couldn't find it. I needed more."

I'm starting to see how this played out. "At the Love Star. He didn't hit you first, did he? GGZ... did what? Went to the bathroom? And you took a chance. You're a pickpocket. You went for a star drive. And he caught you."

"There were a few loose ones in the bag. I thought it would be easy. I've done it before. I had them in my hand. But he made me so nervous. So I dropped them on the floor and..."

"He grabbed your wrist." She nods again. "Then what happened?"

"He got this wild look in his eyes. Like he'd wanted me to do it. And now he had an excuse to…" She pants heavily. "He was gonna *kill* me. I know it! So I kicked him in the shin. Maybe he didn't expect it, so he dropped me. He latched the door so it was locked from the inside. He said the rougher he got the wetter I'd be. Then he snorted more meth and…"

"He dropped dead." But there's more to the story. "What about the bracelet? I know you took it. Your wrist."

Aiko rubs at it again, then confesses that, in a panic, she grabbed two loose star drives—and the bracelet.

"It was chrome. And so smooth. I put in on my wrist and then it…sunk beneath my skin. I can't get it off."

"Does it hurt?"

"No. But it's sore. It itches. And these markings come up. I don't know what they are."

"Whatever it is, it's got you marked. Probably being tracked. And it's a lot more valuable than the credits you stole. Spiky Hair's coming back. And he's coming for you."

Aiko turns green. "I'm gonna be sick." She races to the bathroom, slams the door behind her. I hear the thud of the toilet bowl lid, and a series of heaves, retches, and splatter.

"Hardwicke," Olin says, coming back into Dante's crib. "It's getting crowded out there. We better go."

"I'm gonna check on Banny. See if he's found Dante. Keep an eye on her?"

"Why? What's she…?" More retching. "Yeah. Fine. But be quick."

I make my way down the stairs, engendering all sorts of nasty and quizzical looks. But the pure shock of the event seems to be keeping them pacified. For now. Plus the two Vice cops outside the building, who look like they're in no mood to fuck around.

Using Dante's sloppy blood as my guide I follow the trail outside. It leads me around the corner, then down a tight alley, backed by a chain link fence, and littered with broken bottles, drug paraphernalia, and discarded prophylactics. I see Banny's outline, shotgun by his side.

"How's he holding up?" I ask. "He gonna make it?"

No. He is definitely not. Dante's on the ground, legs out, back against the wall, sitting in a pool of his own blood. Behind him and above his head, on the concrete wall, are various graffiti tags, including *Jackie's got a smelly dong*, *Fuck the Light*, and *Wishes ain't shit – do it yourself.*

"Them... them bitches," Dante wheezes, his eyes sagging. "Them bitches are stealin from me. I"—he coughs weakly— "I know it. Can't trust nobody no more. The fuh... fuck am I sayin? Never could."

There's a wide, black-and-red splotch on his thigh from the bullet wound and blood soaking through his trousers. I hadn't realized he'd been hit twice. He took another bullet in the side. His hands are on his belly, the faces of his clock rings smeared with blood.

"Kimmie," he starts. "She was the only one who..." He coughs up saliva and blood.

"Dante. What *about* her? What about Kimmie?"

He's struggling to keep his eyes open. "She said... she said I could'a been a good boy, if only I had a chance. It ain't true. None of it. But she was the only one who ever said it." I don't feel the least bit sorry for him. But once upon a time he had a mother. And he was her son. "Even a piece'a shit like me needs to hear the words. Whether I believed them or not."

I kneel to be close to him. I produce a water packet from a pouch in the back of my utility jacket. "Here. Drink this." I put the spout to his lips. He sips some, coughs. He drools down on his chin. It skeeves me out to do it, but I wipe it off his face. "GGZ. The john from the Love Star. Kimmie-slash-Nóirín sent Aiko to him. Was that her idea... or yours?"

Dante coughs up more blood. "Fuck it matter now?"

"It matters. The guy who busted in... he's coming back. He's not done."

"How that... my problem? I'm fucked either way."

"Remember how we met? How you found me?" I didn't want to go there with him, ever. Then again, I've done a lotta things I never wanted to do.

His eyes are barely open now, but he smiles as I hear a crowd forming around the corner. Cars burn down the avenue. "You were always a fuh... fine piece'a ass. Could'a put you to work. Made a fortune. Nice legs, wet tang. And a mouth that wouldn't quit." He coughs up a blood clot. "That's what I figured. Never did get me a taste."

It started when I was barely older than Aiko is now. Got lost in a drug haze that lasted five years. One bad turn led to another, when I ended up in an abandoned building, far worse than this one. I was laid out on a mattress, covered in my own filth. Dante showed up.

"Why'd you let me go? You could've turned me out easy. I was so far gone."

Dante's head drops to his chest, bouncing meekly. "Happened today, I would'a. I was too young then. Too green. Didn't know what the fuck. Didn't get my... pimpin credo down yet. Guess I felt suh... sorry for you. Cuz I was dumb as a wet shit. And fuh... figured... do somepin right... maybe even decent... someday it would'a come back on me." He coughs up another clot. "Looks like I was right. Just not how I thought."

He's running out of time. We both are.

"How'd you get onto him? GGZ. How'd you know about the score?"

He chuckles feebly. "Kuh... coffee."

"Coffee? What do you mean *coffee?*"

There's an unmistakable shift in Dante's face. A change.

"That's the thing about Death," he says. "He ain't show up when it's convenient"—with what little strength he has left, Dante wriggles his fingers, the clock rings covered in his blood—"but that muthafucka's always right on time."

Dante's head falls to his chest.

"Anj," Banny says. "He's dead. We need to go."

"I know. Get in the cab. I'll be there in a minute."

I take the stairs in Dante's building two at a time when my phone buzzes. Text from Tarrish: *10 min out. Don't make it worse.*

The kid with the rubber ball approaches from a side apartment. He's squeezing the ball as hard as he can.

"Dante," he says. "He dead?"

"I'd look for a new job."

"Shit. Muthafucka ain't paid me. Three weeks."

"Sorry. There's a lot of that going around."

At the top landing, Burly Girl is coming around, looking groggy, and holding her head.

Inside Dante's destroyed crib, Olin puts her phone away.

"Took you long enough. What's up?"

I tell her.

"No loss there."

"I guess you're free."

Olin grimaces from the pain in her shoulder. "This look free to you?"

I turn to the bathroom. "How's Aiko?"

"Don't know. Been dealing with the tenants. Not easy with a dead arm. And in this tiny slice of hell."

I stare at the bathroom door. "She's been in there a long time." We look at each other. I jiggle the doorknob. Locked. I knock. "Aiko." I knock three more times. "Aiko, you okay in there? Aiko? Aiko!"

Don't be dead don't be dead don't be dead.

I kick the door in. The good news? She's not dead. The bad news...

"She went out the window," Olin says. "How the hell'd she do that?"

I climb into the shower stall, then hoist myself up on the wet windowsill. My head outside the building, I crane my neck, and look up. Fire escape is just within reach.

"She took the roof."

"In this neighborhood?"

I climb back down into the shower stall, wet mark on my stomach. "She's done this before."

CHAPTER 16

"I just got an alert," Tarrish says through the phone as I survey Dante's crib for any other clues the girls might've left behind. Olin's on the phone with her ex-partner. "Tell me that wasn't you."

From outside I hear the wails of distant police sirens. "It wasn't me."

He curses under his breath. "How many dead?"

"Two."

"Yours?"

I get why he'd assume that, but it rankles my nerves, nonetheless. "No. This was a tactical assault and extraction. Whoever it was had the tools, weapons, and training. He knew what he was doing."

"You get a look? An ID?"

"Sort of."

"What's *sort of*? You saw him or you didn't."

"He had a plexi-shield face mask. But he's Black, about six foot one, maybe two hundred pounds. And spiky brown hair."

"You saw his hair? Beneath a mask?"

"Well... no. But he matches the description of another witness. Plus..."

He sighs aggressively. "Plus what?"

Ugh. He's gonna love this. "I saw him in my dreams."

I can almost hear the gears in his mind clank, rattle, and snap. "You know, Hardwicke. For someone looking to recapture their freedom, you got a funny way of showing it."

"I know. It's the joy that is me. Look. I'd love to keep chatting about the nuances of my investigative style, but I gotta find that kid. Whoever our shooter is, she's the target. And she's on the run."

"Give me a name and description. I'll put out a BOLO. And I have to clean up your mess. Again."

"That's what makes us such a good team. I knock 'em down and you do... well, I don't know what you do. What about Whistler? Any update?"

No answer.

"T. You there? Whistler? Anything?"

"Working on it," he says finally.

"Work faster. I'll hit you up later."

"No. Wait for me. I'm almost there."

"Gotta go."

"No, damnit! Don't—"

I hang up.

"Who was that?" Olin asks as we make our way down the stairs. "ICD?"

"They're en route. They're taking over."

Outside the building, four plain clothes officers and Olin's ex-partner are doing crowd control. Street walkers, drug pushers, addicts, johns, tenants, and passersby of all ages are all out here, in the middle of the night, talking all sorts of shit about what might've gone down.

"Yo!" a spectator shouts. "That's Dante's crib. Shit is *fucked* up."

"Yeah, bitch," someone else says. "Shit is *supercharged* fucked up. Where's Dante? Where he at?"

"Jo," I say. "I need you to run point. I'm going after Aiko."

Her ex-partner approaches. Black hair, goatee, black leather jacket. Badge dangles around his neck. "Jo. This is some party."

"No shit. Dex... Hardwicke. Hardwicke... Dex."

Dex chin-nods to me. "Heard you were on parole. What's all this?"

"My redemption tour."

He chuckles. "If this is how you make good, I'd hate to see you break bad."

"Yeah, well, I'm a little fuzzy on the whole good/bad thing. Jo, you got this?"

"Dex," she says. "Help me run the scene?"

"It's your show. I'm just here to look pretty. But yeah." He calls to his new partner. "Rusty. Come on. Let's do it up."

"Dante's in the alley," I say. "He's done. You'll need to block that off."

Dex throws up his hands. "What the fuck? You're gonna do me like that?"

"You guys have the badges." Banny honks, his cab fired up and waiting for me across the street. "Just hold down the fort. ICD's on the way. Actually... there they are."

I see Tarrish pull up just as I hit the backseat of the cab. And like the good girl she is, my scout orb zips low along the street then up and into my palm.

Dex shouts at me. "This is why everybody hates you!"

"I know! But you'll learn to love me anyway."

Banny drops me at the Love Star. "I'm done," he says. "You owe me a lotta money."

I transfer whatever credits I have. "I'm a little short. I'll get the rest."

In fairness to me, I always pay. In full. And usually right away. But I can barely afford to eat right now.

"Fine." He shakes his head. Angry. Frustrated. Annoyed. As much with himself as he is with me. "But until you make good—on *all* your promises—I'm off duty."

He peels off before I can apologize to him. He's heard them all before.

The small lobby smells like the edge of a sewer. The old overhead lighting casts a cirrhotic yellow haze on the dingy orange carpet and once-white walls. The droopy-eyed desk clerk has his nose down in a tablet.

"You the new guy?"

"Nah. Day shift. Now I'm night shift. It's just a different slice of the same hell."

"Cops didn't shut you down? After your buddy got shot?"

"In this neighborhood? A dead body's about as shocking as the rain. And he's not my buddy."

"Why's that?"

"Finn did his thing, I do mine."

"Finn? That was night-shift guy?"

He winks, points his finger, and clicks his finger gun.

"Brave man," I say. "He was killed in the chair you're sitting in."

"Bullet to the brain would be sweet relief."

An older sex worker with dyed red hair and smeared mascara exists the elevator. She eyes me like I'm out to get her, then heads out into the night. A sloppy guy with white and brown stubble fastens his belt, stumbles along about ten feet behind her. Without making eye contact, he tosses the key fob on the counter. "Later, Kurt," he says, and exits in the opposite direction of his date.

"Kurt, huh? A friend of mine dropped her wallet the other night. Nobody's turned it in. Mind if I check?"

Kurt sluggishly reaches for the key fob. As if it requires every ounce of dwindling energy, he slides it to the lip of the counter on his side, lets it fall into a drawer he opens beneath it. "Gotta pay for the room."

"It'll take five minutes."

"Then pay for five minutes."

I don't have time to argue. I kick him a few credits I have stashed for emergencies.

He eyes the total on his tablet. "You're a little light."

"You said five minutes."

"We charge by the hour. Full price. And let's not forget the dude who OD'd the other night. That warrants a premium. Don't like it, look somewhere else."

"Does that also buy me a look at your security cameras?"

"Nope."

"Why not?"

"They don't work. But mostly because they're none a'yer business. You have your hour. I'm gonna finish my book. I know who the killer is. I wanna see if they fuck it up."

I take the elevator up, put the key fob to the lock. I can't say the room has been cleaned so much as the cockroaches have been reorganized. Dresser drawers are empty. Nothing under it or the bed, or between the mattress and box spring. Shower stall is empty. Complimentary bar of re-wrapped soap on the sink. The mirror is rusted and cracked around the edges. Other than the general scumminess, there's no evidence someone just died here, and nothing I can trace back to Aiko.

From the muffled squeals and moans I hear, two of the six rooms on this floor are occupied. I pass the ice machine and go to the stairwell door. I push it open. Three flights down, two flights up. I take the barely lit stairwell up to the top. Adjacent to the fifth-floor access door is another marked KEEP OUT. ROOF ACCESS. MANAGEMENT ONLY.

I give myself a field promotion to management, push the door open, walk onto the roof. I'm met with a wet mist that's rolled in, damp on my face.

Nearby billboards, marquee lights, streetlamps, and wet droplets refracting tonight's twin moons illuminate the black-top landscape up here. The squat buildings are close enough together I could take rooftops halfway across Sinner's Row. But where did Aiko go? What path did she...?

My lens picks up a twinkle on the blacktop. My sneakers crunch on the pebbles. Near the edge, I find a cherry blossom earring. Dried blood on the clasp. My guess, it's Aiko's. In the far distance I see the blue-white plume of cargo ships rocketing into the expanse.

A waist-high concrete barrier is all that separates the edge of this rooftop from the next. I climb over, serenaded by the late-night concerto of shouts, cries, honks, and wailing sirens.

To avoid a steam pipe jutting out I shift to the side, but I stumble, my foot hitting a rooftop divot hidden in darkness. I reach out to brace myself. The pad of my right palm goes down on the blacktop. In a half-squat, I land on something hard and sharp, right on that sensitive bump between the bottom of my kneecap and top of my shinbone.

I grimace, grab my knee. I brush my hand for whatever I landed on.

Credit-loaded star drive. Which means... I look around for... what did Olin say? Aiko hit the street near a chicken and rib joint. The one Dante liked to order from. The greasy bag was on the table in his crib. Andy's. Anthony's. Andre's. "Archie's!"

I rush to the north ledge, palms against the brick face. I scan the streetscape. Nothing here. All apartment buildings. I hustle to the other side of the roof. Tattoo parlor, pub, cranial implant adjuster, laundromat, hardware store, laser pool hall. I check the east side streetscape. Free clinic, moon rock mining company, grocer, apartments, and pawn shop. Frustrated, I scan the adjacent corner, when I get a whiff of tangy barbeque.

"Gotcha!" Set against a bright yellow background, red globe lights blink, advertising the establishment's name: ARCHIE'S CHICKEN & RIBS

I hop down to a lower, connected rooftop, find the fire escape. I take the metal stairs down to the street. There's a crowd outside the rib joint, hungry patrons tearing at food wrapped in wax paper, others carrying takeout bags. I'm in the right place, but where did Aiko go immediately after this? Dante's crib is a dozen blocks away. There are gaps in her timeline.

If I was a young sex worker, who ran from a crime scene, what would be my next move? Can't go home. Don't wanna go home. So where do I go?

Stevie's Pawn Shop. Light is on. I zoom in with my lens. There it is. Security camera above. Metal bars line the storefront window and door. Inside, I enter a chain-link security cage with laser shielding, then wait to be buzzed in.

I'm buzzed in.

A brown-skinned clerk in a white t-shirt and black and silver vest is sitting on a stool behind the counter. Secondhand clothes and various trinkets on racks and in bins, though the more valuable merchandise is secured behind bullet-proof glass counters and lockers.

"You Stevie?"

"Yup."

"You're open late."

Wire-thin, Stevie has a chrome right arm from shoulder to fingers. "Two to two." Looking through a dentist's loupe, she fiddles with an antique music box, manipulating a metal pick into the lock port. "About to close up."

"Lotta loot in this place. Afraid you'll get robbed?"

Stevie chuckles. "Many have tried. Many have failed." With her foot, she bonks the lower end of her side of the cabinet. "Between the security gate, suppression gas I can activate

through the vents, and a few surprises I keep in arm's reach...
I think I'm okay."

I like this chick. Stevie's my kind of people. And foxy, too.

"Wondering if you can do me a solid."

"Don't be shy." She looks down her nose through the enhanced
lenses, two inverted cones strapped to her eyes. "That's why I'm
here. To make deals."

No point bullshitting her. "I'm a PI. Looking for a girl. A pro.
She was last seen a few nights ago. Out on the street. Hoping to
check your security camera."

Stevie continues to fiddle with the music box. "Well..." She
side-eyes me, then shifts her gaze back to the music box. "That
depends."

"On what?"

"You're a PI?"

"What it says on my business card."

"Can you open this?"

I smile, offer my hand. She gives me the music box and pick.
Normally I'd use my skeleton key, but I don't want her to know I
have it. Instead, I produce a black leather pouch from inside my
jacket. I unzip it, remove my own pick.

"It's got a serrated tip. Works better." In short order I pick
the lock. The top of the music box pops open. Displayed in 3-D
hologram is a young boy on a mountain top. A meteor shower
soars overhead. Dainty classical music accompanies the scene. I
hand it back to Stevie.

"Sonuvabitch. Been at this all night." She smiles, impressed.
"You got yourself a deal."

From behind the counter, she lets me scroll through the
video feed for the last several days. I find the right time stamp,
various customers coming in and out, street and foot traffic
going by.

"There she is." I freeze the screen and zoom in. Not a great
shot of her from this angle, but good enough. She's agitated,
frantic, looking this way and that. Until a cab pulls up. Two men
exit. Aiko jumps in the back.

Aiko said she couldn't find a cab. What else did she lie about?

The cab pulls away. And there's the license plate. From this angle I can't tell which cab company it's registered with.

I make an awkward call to Banny, but I wear him down. Again. I give him the license plate number, which he passes to his pal at dispatch. Medallion isn't registered with them, but his pal has connections at the other cab companies. It takes some doing, but they finally ID the driver I'm looking for and get access to his log. Another debt I owe.

"Thanks for the help," I say to Stevie. "You ever need a favor… or wanna grab a drink"—I hand her my card—"hit me up."

Stevie is all smiles, admiring the lovely tune jangling from the music box. "I just might. You be careful. Some shady characters out there."

I give her a side-smile. "Shady characters in here."

Running on fumes, I grab a coffee at the all-night bodega. Two extra shots of caffeine. The black crack races through my veins and up into my brain. I focus on the driver's log.

I know this address. I think on it, realize where it is. I do a web search to confirm. I'd blame it on the coffee, but my blood is boiling for an entirely other reason.

"I fucking knew it."

CHAPTER 17

Back at Kimmie-slash-Nóirín's apartment.

Why would Aiko lie about coming here after the Love Star? What could it matter? What's she hiding? Unless she was trying to sever a direct link that night between her and Kimmie-slash...

Fuckety fuck fuck fuck.

Did *Aiko* kill her? Have I been looking for the wrong person all along? Kimmie-slash-Nóirín was likely pushed, but she was much taller than Aiko. Not sure the physicality works unless she was already off-balance. Still, on average, one woman is killed in E-Town every ten minutes, with more than half of those homicides committed by an intimate partner or family member, with about eighty percent of all violent crimes committed by men.

But the ratio of female-on-female homicide is only about two percent. Aiko is desperate to get away from Dante and out of the sex-worker life. Aiko said Kimmie-slash-Nóirín was helping her escape. Was that true? Did something go wrong? Did she threaten to rat Aiko out to Dante?

No. I don't think so. From what I know about Kimmie-slash-Nóirín, as Top Slot, she was dedicated to those girls, while keeping Dante pacified. Dante said the girls were stealing from him. Did he know that for sure? And if he did, did he know it was Aiko? Or Kimmie-slash-Nóirín? Or both? Or maybe Aiko and Spiky Hair are in this together somehow, and she's in over her head.

I need a fresh perspective. I re-examine Kimmie-slash-Nóirín's apartment as if I've never been here before. There's a compact kitchen area. On one side, the marble counter-top extends from the support beam across where it meets a stainless-steel refrigerator in the corner. Within arm's reach on the opposite side is another counter with more cabinets above, a stainless-steel sink in the middle, and a compact dishwasher. Wine rack on the wall. Seven bottles, three re-corked, four unopened. Track lighting is mounted into the ceiling.

Wearing surgical gloves, I run my fingers over the surfaces, feeling for imperfections. I don't find anything of value in the kitchen, then inspect the hallway closets. One is filled with Kimmie-slash-Nóirín's casual wear—sweaters, jeans, blouses, t-shirts, sneakers, sandals.

The other contains her work clothes—slinky dresses, high-heel shoes, two ball gowns, overnight bag, and red leather pouch with condoms, anti-inflammatories, prescription antibiotics, morning-after pills, taser, and rape whistle.

Around the apartment I find a few holocubes with rotating digital photographs of Kimmie-slash-Nóirín and some video tablets saved for binge-watching.

I climb the wood staircase up to the loft bed, go through the nightstand. Usual assortment, nothing useful.

Beneath the loft is the desk with a tablet on top, a framed picture of Kimmie-slash-Nóirín with two other women I don't recognize. I run my fingers along the wall and behind a mounted print of a tropical beach, then over to the drapes framing the steel-barre windows. I open the lock to the glass door and head out to the balcony, breathe in the air. It's cleaner here than in Sinnner's Row, filtered by the greenery lining the streets, and the nearby park lush with plants and trees.

Pedestrians stroll along the sidewalks, cars parked on both sides of the street. A hover car and a cab drive by. They stop at the corner, wait for the light.

I head back inside, do a web search on her. Graduated Lakebridge High School with a mid-high GPA. Braces, some minor chin acne. Long brown hair with awkward bangs. Graduated Ellsworth K'bein College, degree in business administration. She worked for a few different investment banks over ten years and then no formal work history I can find other than the ambiguous designation of *consultant*.

There's a decade-long gap in-between. For some women,

trading in a soulless corporate career to become a sex worker holds a lot of appeal. They're drawn to it. They get to be their own boss, set their own hours, and feel in control of their body. And their destiny.

They also help others explore sexual desires that otherwise go unfilled, while satisfying some of their own. And if they manage their business well, they can make good money, able to pay off debts, and support themselves, their children, and extended families.

Plus, it can be fun. More power to them.

But not when it's for a pimp like Dante. You don't end up in his stable unless you took a few bad turns.

She may have worked high-end hotels, but that didn't make the job any more glamorous, or any less violent. Hotel sex workers can find themselves in more danger than working the streets. Private rooms with locked doors and a window of time can give johns a sense of invulnerability and entitlement they don't feel on the streets, where prying eyes are everywhere.

Sex workers like Kimmie-slash-Nóirín are called *high-class call girls*. But there's nothing classy about the exchange of sex for money when it's as an indentured servant.

One of my sources, Latisha, is a thirty-six-year-old, self-employed prostitute who services mostly older clientele. She enjoys safe, consensual experiences with various partners and is well-compensated for her time.

Her husband is on board with her career, in a don't-ask-don't-tell kind of situation. It works for them. The life works for a lot of sex workers. Call it what you want, but the truth is, we're all on the hustle in one way or another. Theirs is more honest than most.

Yet many women enter the sex trade—whether as a stripper, porn star, or prostitute—as teens who come from a physically, sexually, or emotionally abusive home life, suffer from mental illness or drug addiction, or combinations of all of these.

Come on, Kimmie-slash-Nóirín. Talk to me. What happened here?

Back inside I take in the mounted television, with tablets

open to various novels, mostly political thrillers set in exotic locales.

And the couch, chair, coffee table, and the glider. Maybe it's the mother in me, clamoring for the baby days again, or maybe it's just comfortable, but I love this chair.

Sitting here, staring out the window, I still need to dig deeper, find someone who knew her back when. But I'm getting a better sense of who she was. There's a convergence, the home of someone who knew how to construct layers.

Kimmie was her work persona, a character she played, a way to protect Nóirín. But as Top Slot, she wasn't just a sex worker. She was a pseudo-pimp herself, a madam. Upper management. And you don't become Top Slot by keeping to yourself.

I'm a woman of two worlds as well. I have my PI life and I have Owen and my friends. I'd love to say I'm able to keep those worlds separate and distinct from each other. But that's not even remotely accurate. So where did Kimmie's life end and Nóirín's begin? Where did they overlap? Or were they one and the same?

With my feet up on the glider's foot stool I feel my body sink into a rhythm, the calming glide back and forth, my hips and back comforted with cushioned lumbar support. I don't know how long it takes for me to settle in, but I gaze at the wall opposite me. And more specifically, at the bricks in the wall. And mortar. Red against white. And the little chips, cracks, and grooves in between them.

I stop rocking. With my lens, I focus high on the wall. Upper left corner, about a foot from the ceiling. I zoom in again, again, then again, until I can see the grains. That one individual brick slightly… just slightly… juts out from the surface. My readout shows 0.23 millimeters.

Probably normal wear and tear. Probably.

But I can't stop staring at it. I go to the wall and look up, then down at the hardwood floor. Flecks of white dust. I kneel, press my gloved fingertip so the dust sticks to it. I focus with my lens. Looks like mortar flakes.

I find a multi-level folding ladder, bring it out and set it up near the wall. I'm only five-foot-four, so I need to get up on my tiptoes. I'm still barely able to reach the brick. I poke at it with my finger. Nothing. I poke again. Nothing. I remove a leather kit from my jacket. Manipulating the stainless steel lockpick with serrated edge, I pick at the mortar like a dentist scraping plaque off a tooth.

"Come on," I say, using my lens to enhance the visual. "Give me a little wiggle…"

It moved. Not a lot, but it moved. I keep scraping until micro grains of mortar flake away, drifting to the floor like an early snow. I open my hand into a claw, dig my fingernails in and grip the brick around the edges. I feel the brick loosen. I keep at it, further compressing my fingertips, wriggling the brick until I hear it scrape, then remove it from the wall slot.

I examine the brick. Nothing carved out of it or embedded, no secret hinges I can find. The brick feels solid. Although I can't see that high, I then reach up and into the wall slot, and with my fingertips, snatch what feels like a narrow plastic case.

I extract my prize, let it drop into my other hand. "What the hell are you?"

I climb back down and sit on the small couch, placing the contents on the coffee table. Set of diamond earrings, emerald teardrop pendant affixed to a silver chain, six credit-loaded star drives and… sonuvabitch… Aiko's ID. Why would she…?

Was Kimmie-slash-Nóirín holding Aiko hostage? Or holding them for safe keeping?

I use my phone, lens, and orb to access the star drives. Encrypted. No way for me to know how much money is on them. Assuming it's just money.

My phone buzzes. Bernice. I place the phone on the table, put it on speaker.

"I'm in the field. I just found—"

"I've got Eric! Talk to him. Now!"

I immediately transfer the signal to my lens so I can see what she sees. There he is, caught in the containment field.

"Whistler! What's happening?"

"*Chzz… check…*"—audio is garbled—"*check the grid. More dead systems. Five that I found.*" More garbled audio. "*…fabric of* *spacetime... structural integrity... weaker."*

Whistler fades, sounds more distant, like he's been pulled back into a funnel.

"Bernice! He's—"

"I know!!"

Through my lens I can see the lights in her hidden workshop flicker off and on.

"I'm gonna lose him!"

Whistler's more solid, but still caught behind that wax paper.

"... almozzzt foundz..."—audio is garbled—*"accesszzzzz... found... the trizz... trigzzz... trigger point."*

"What trigger point? Whistler! *What* trigger point? For what?"

"Nodezzzzz... nodes... activated. Izzzzz... three days. You gotzzz... you gotta stop him."

"Stop who? Spiky Hair?"

"Findzzzzzz the ... endy iiive. Chz... check... dzzoug... zzfzziner."

The lights crap out. Power switches off.

"Whistler. Whistler! WHISTLER!"

He's gone.

Bernice flips multiple switches. "Sorry, Angela. It's the best I could do. The orbit's too strong."

"He said that before," I say, almost in a daze. *"Doug Finer.* You know that name? I don't know that name. Bernie. You know that name? Heard it before?"

"Hey," I hear Jasmine say. Her voice is calm. Soothing. "Don't blame yourself. You did the best you could."

Not sure what to do, I rest my head in my gloved hand, pressing my fingertips into my jaw and temple, and shut my eyes. I need to let the noise settle down, let my adrenaline fade. I'd love to say my mind is swirling with ideas, schemes, and clever solutions. But all I see right now is an endless canvas of empty space. Nothing. A void.

I open my eyes again and look around, as if the answers I need are in this room somewhere. If only I knew where else to look, or what I'm looking for.

Unless—I stare down at the contents on the table—I've already found it.

Rattle at the door. I scoop the loot into my jacket pocket,

reach for my gun. I tiptoe to the side of the doorframe. I hear a key in the lock. The knob twists. The door opens slowly. I grab the arm, pull its owner inside. I slam them against the wall. I stick my gun in their face.

"No!" the voice squeals. "Don't!"

CHAPTER 18

"**A**iko. Shit." My heart pounding, I shut the apartment door. "What happened to you? Where did you go?"

Like an injured squirrel hunted by a pack of dogs, Aiko stares at me, eyes wide, breathing fast. Her wrist is red from the scratching, but the symbols aren't raised. Unlike the previous times we've met, she's in a light blue tracksuit and tennis sneakers.

"After he... I saw him drive off. I ran the other way."

"Did you see the car? Make? Model? Color?"

She shakes her head nervously. "No."

Seeing how terrified she is, I ease up. She's been through an ordeal. And I need her to feel safe. Well... safer. "All right. Come on. Sit," I say, sounding like my mother. "I'll get you a cup of tea."

The distraction allows me to regroup. She's on the couch. I hand her a mug of green tea. It's all I could find. She takes the mug. She doesn't drink it.

"Aiko. What are you doing here?"

She drops her eyes, shrugs.

She's good, maybe better than I thought. She's playing the role. A far cry from the tough girl act she gave me at our first meeting. Was that the real Aiko? Or is this?

I drop the flash drives and her ID on the coffee table. "Looking for these?"

Aiko instinctively leans forward but catches herself. She doesn't want to seem too eager. "What are those?"

"Aiko. Stop." I open her ID. Show her picture.

This is it. The moment. Gone is her meek and pouty, slumped-shouldered wallflower body language, replaced with the go-fuck-yourself-and-die-twice stare. Her gaze darts between me and the loot. Behind those steely eyes I can see her running scenarios.

Can she literally take the money and run? And before I can stop her? Can she physically subdue or distract me long enough to get away? Or will she decide it's better to play along? She'll have to make a calculated decision before she…

Oh shit. I realize my mistake. She does, too. Her body shifts, leaning just slightly forward, shoulder tilted. In a lightning-fast move, Aiko tosses the steaming tea at my face. I raise my arm as a shield as she snares the loot and bolts for the door. Thankfully my jacket's adaptable fabric acts like a rain slicker, the scalding liquid cascading off me without a burn.

With her hand on the doorknob, I grab her by the back of the hair. I yank her head back and cross my front foot across hers. I twist her torso, so she's spun halfway toward me, then slam her to the floor. I knock the loot away, produce my taser.

The tip crackles, inches from her face.

"I don't want to hurt you," I say, "but the mood I'm in… I just might. Now *get* up."

Her hair still clutched in my hand, I have her twisted, her head hunched down, until I toss her back onto the couch.

"No more bullshit. No more games. What the *fuck* is going on?" She's snarling, not ready to accept her situation. She thinks there's still a way out, that she can claw her way past me. Who knows? Maybe she can. But not before I get what I need. "That thing on your wrist. Tell me again. Everything that happened at the Love Star. And why does Kimmie-slash-Nóirín have your ID? Don't fuck with me, Aiko. There's a trail of bodies. And they all link back to you."

She's huffing through her nose and pawing at the back of her head where I yanked her hair. "You really wanna know?"

"Yes."

"*Do* you?"

I nod.

"I'm trapped! Don't you get it? I'm fucking *trapped!*"

She explains that she met Kimmie-slash-Nóirín at the Symphony Hotel a few months ago. Among other things, Aiko's a pickpocket. Kimmie-slash-Nóirín spotted her moves, snagging Aiko with a hand in her purse. Aiko had been hooking on the street, on her own, but it was getting too rough. Kimmie-slash-Nóirín offered her a spot with Dante.

"She said if we skimmed a little every night—a few credits here and there—in a year I'd have enough to get out."

"She was helping you?"

"That was the deal. A year with Dante. And she gets me out."

"Out of the frying pan... but into the fire."

"Something like that. Dante got rough with the other girls. He wasn't, like, gentle with me, but he kept his hands off like that. He said I was too precious. But I knew he was playing me."

"While you were playing him."

She nods.

"Did he know you were skimming?" Let's see where she takes this.

"I don't know. Maybe. When he'd get drunk or high—he didn't do that a lot; he said he had to keep a hawk's eye on his bitches—he'd get paranoid. Polish those clock rings like they were jewels. He said everyone was trying to rip him off. Us, the johns, the cops, other pimps. He said he knew it was a jungle out there, but he was the lion. And if we didn't bring it home every night, we'd hear him roar."

"And that's why you're trapped? You were afraid?"

"Of course I was afraid! He was a monster! A john I picked up three weeks ago anally raped me. He spit in my face, then kicked me in the hip. I was all torn up. I could barely walk, but when I made it back to his crib, Dante was in a mood. When I told him what happened, he beat me for not getting paid. He never hit me before that. Kimmie stopped him from getting worse. Told him to go easy. That she'd handle it."

From their perspective, when the nastier johns pay their money, they expect obedience and submission. Degradation of body and soul.

"I'm nothin but a piece of meat," Aiko says. "Whore. Slut. Bitch. That's what they call me because that's how they see me. You know that movie? Where the handsome rich guy falls in love with the gorgeous hooker with a heart of gold. Then it's all happily-ever-after?"

"Seen it."

"That's why it's a *movie*. Cuz it's fucking bullshit. They cum, inside me or on me, with every hole open for business. And if they get a little rough during the party... to them, that's baked into the price. 'Take it, bitch.' That's what they say. 'Take it, bitch. Take it.' And if I get pregnant, a UTI, or an STD? Or I'm bleeding inside? That's my problem."

I'm squirming inside. I was nearly that kind of victim myself. Several times. "I know. I'm sorry."

"You're *sorry*? Well goody *fucking* for you. Tell me how *your* sorry fixes *my* life."

She really is a hustler. At nineteen she's already learned how to pivot away from one bad situation and lead into another. Everything she's told me might be one hundred percent accurate. Then again, maybe not. The last thing I ever want to do is doubt a rape victim or diminish the difficult choices some sex workers face.

But like I said, the bodies keep leading back to her.

"I wish things were easier for you," I say, trying to dial down the temperature. She doesn't exactly relax, although the gnarly glint of rage in her eyes tamps back a tick. "But here's the thing." I grab her wrist again, pull her close so that we're almost nose-to-nose. "These markings... they're the key. And don't give me that bullshit about grabbing that bracelet *after* he dropped dead. You saw something shiny, and you took it. *That's* why he grabbed you. Then his heart exploded. You called Kimmie-slash-Nóirín to clean up your mess and grab his bag. You put her in the crosshairs. That's why Spiky Hair killed her, went after Jasmine, then you. You're the last link in the chain."

Aiko stares at me, locked in a tractor-beam of truth. "I... I didn't..."

"You did. You saw a quick score, so you went for it. It got outta hand. And now you're on the run. Here's what's gonna happen. I'm taking you to a safehouse."

I helped a landlord of self-storage facilities deal with a crooked insurance adjuster who was shaking him down. Instead of paying my usual fee, the landlord gave me access to a small unit he never uses.

"Then we're gonna figure out what the markings are for. And get that thing off you."

"It's a bomb."

White flash before my eyes, whistling in my ears. "It's a what?"

"It's a bomb. That's what he said. He was gonna set off a bomb. A big one."

"The markings. They must be a code, or directions." Fuckety fuck fuck fuck. "Or a trigger." My anxiety heightened, I stare at Aiko, in my mind's eye watching half the realm go up in flames. "He needs *you* to set it off. We're getting out of here. Now."

I pocket the ID and star drives and lead her into the hallway. I make a call. Voicemail. "T. We got a problem. Call me now. I got the girl." I text him as well.

We hustle down the interior staircase and back out into the night. With my hand clutching Aiko's arm, I motion toward the corner to get a cab. But then I get that tingling on the back of my neck. Like there's a stranger in my apartment.

Or we're being watched. I stop us short.

Anxious, Aiko wants to bolt. "What?"

"Shh. Listen." Eying the parked cars on the street, I scan above for drones, study the small hedges and trees lining the apartment building. Nothing I can spot. Nothing obvious.

Then why I am so nervous? What am I picking up I can't see in front of...

I turn on my lens. Night vision gives me a clearer view of the streetscape. Still, I don't see anything to—

There. Three buildings up. Lights from a nearby television flash, reflecting off a surface in the bushes. I zoom in. Rifle scope. Spiky Hair's waiting. Ambush.

I regrip her arm and whisper. "Head toward the park."

"No parks! Not at night."

"Quiet," I whisper. "Keep your voice down." I start turning her the other way. "Easier to get a cab."

Like pulling a terrified toddler to the dentist, Aiko resists me with all her might.

"I'm safer on my own."

"Not an option. Let's—"

Spiky Hair steps out of the shadows. Classic set-up. He planted his rifle scope up ahead in one direction to get us heading the other way—toward him. I walked right into it.

Before I can react, he grabs Aiko, pulls her away from me. With his leg wound secured by a medical wrap, he sidekicks me in the gut, his boot landing right below my solar plexus. The tactical strike drops me to my knees. Aiko tries to pull away from him. I swing my arm and catch his knee with my taser. He buckles but keeps on his feet.

With his free hand he reaches over his shoulder. From behind his back, he draws a half-sword. Black chrome. He raises the blade, swings it toward my head.

I've prepared for this. Spent hours in the gym with Master Neering. Weapons training, and defense, with blocks, pivots, and counterstrikes from all angles. But *studying* Arberian martial arts and actualizing them in real time when a skilled combatant is trying to chop your head off are two entirely different scenarios. You get it wrong in practice, you get a bump on the head. You get it wrong in combat, you lose your head.

It's counter-intuitive to relax when you're being assaulted, but the best way to let instincts take over is to stop thinking. I roll over and duck as Spiky Hair launches a surgical strike toward me. In an arching motion he crosses the blade past my sightline and into a downward motion.

And slices Aiko's arm off just below the elbow.

A couple across the street sees what happens. They scream and run toward the traffic.

Horrified at being suddenly mutilated, Aiko stagger-steps forward. She's in shock from her detached limb on the sidewalk. She's left with a gorged stump. There's exposed muscle, bone, tendon, and tissue where her arm had just been. Blood spurts from the severed artery.

Spiky Hair picks up the limb. "This is all I needed. She's all yours."

He sets off a flash pulse secured to his combat vest, blinding me. I squint as hard as I can, my vision a swirl of black, gray, and purple blobs. By the time my sight recovers, he's gone.

I pull off my jacket. In the pouch sewn into the back I find my MedKit. With a single injection, I pump Aiko with a pain-killer/antibiotic cocktail, apply wound gel on the injury and secure it with a medical compression wrap. I call an ambulance, but between the traffic up ahead and a watermain break to the north, it'll be at least an hour. They just can't get through.

No choice. I make another call.

"Hate me later," I say. "I deserve it. But she doesn't."

Her good arm around my neck, I get Aiko to the corner by the park. Banny pulls up quickly. He'd been working an extra shift to make up for the ones I hijacked from him.

I open the back door, pull Aiko inside.

"Angela! Fuck! She's bleeding in my cab!"

"Then drive!"

Being the mensch that he is, Banny leaves the lectures and drives with abandon, getting us to E-Town General while Aiko still has a pulse.

It's only when we pull up to the ER entrance do I notice blood on the back seat. I follow the source. Aiko's bleeding from her side. Spiky Hair must've stabbed her during the flash. Maybe to keep her quiet. Maybe out of mercy. Either way, the result's the same.

Nini and a team of trauma specialists in protective gear are waiting for us in the ambulance bay. They rush to the cab, put her on a gurney. They stick an IV in her good arm, and franti-cally race her inside and up to surgery.

This is the first time I've seen Nini in almost a year. Since Dolores died on the galaxy cruiser. She sacrificed her life to save ours. It wasn't my fault. Or so I've been told. But Nini hates me for it anyway. I hate myself. Knowing that Nini's heart has been shattered, that she'll never be the person she was before, is enough to make me want to leave this realm and never come back.

"I was thinking about calling you," she says.

I've been desperate to hear those words.

"Then I stopped myself." She raises up her arms, her surgi-cal gloves and gown smeared in Aiko's blood. "I'm an ER nurse, and I'm never covered in more blood than when I'm with you."

"I'm sorry. It was an emergency."

"You're never gonna change, Angela. This is who you are."

Every ounce of me wants to scream, "That's not true!" Because sometimes, like now, it *isn't* true. This was a legit emergency. And Nini's an ER nurse. This is the life. But she still can't see me in any other way. I'm paying for the culmination of past sins, some of which are mine. But not all.

One of the trauma surgeons comes down. She removes her protective goggles. "She didn't make it. The arm was bad. But she was also stabbed in the abdomen. She never had a chance. You need to speak to the police. They'll have to file a report."

"I know," I say, my sad eyes avoiding Nini's. "They're on the way."

CHAPTER 19

Olin spoke to the surgical team and hospital administration, filing Aiko's murder under a special investigation. It'll hold for now.

I call Tarrish and tell him we have a bomb threat, but I don't have any details or leads that might point to the target. And I don't have Aiko, the bracelet, or the code. He orders me to come in. Now. He texts me an address I don't recognize. And he's ordered Olin to bring me in at gunpoint if necessary. If not preferred.

Going on fumes, I gaze up at the sun's golden eye winking itself awake. The city is awash in orange and purple streaks as the night's slumber fades into morning blue.

"I spoke to Nini," Banny says. "I'm with you until the end. But after this case, you and I are done. I'm sorry, Angela." The look on his face is a combination of disappointment, heartbreak, and steely resolve. "It's the way it has to be."

I get into the back of his cab. I don't have the bandwidth to consider his threat. Not because he's lashing out in the moment, but because he might follow through.

Olin enters from the other side, her shoulder in a sling. She can't drive. She gives Banny the address.

He looks at it. "That's an odd place to meet."

"Where is it?" I ask as if nothing's changed between us.

Banny looks through the rearview. "I don't know what to tell you. It's the ICD."

"Hardwicke," Olin says. "You really think there's a bomb?"

I consider the question.

"Yeah," I say. "I do."

She shifts in the seat to take pressure off her shoulder.

"How do we even find this guy?"

Speeding down the avenue, Banny eyes me through the rearview. Because he knows what I know, as much as he doesn't want to. We have to make a detour.

"By leaning into the nightmare," I say to Olin. "And you're coming with me."

"You sure you want to do this?" Jody fastens diodes to my head. "You're coming up on the max."

"I definitely don't want to do this," Olin says from the next pod.

"I need you," I say. "Can't do it alone."

The cables and tubes extending from the generator and into the Dream Pods all hum with energy. Another set of cables sync to a converter above us, connecting the pods. And our dreams. And very possibly, our nightmares.

Jody closes us in. I have no memory of falling asleep, but I'm already deep within the bioluminescent forest. Immediately my head throbs, the *whumming* deeper and louder than before. It's like an engine's turbine building up enough momentum to launch a battleship. This happened a few years ago. The *whumming*. But it affected everyone. Now it's only me, only in *my* head. I'm so confused.

I hear rustling in the leaves, then a distant voice calling out to me below the blistering white light of a full moon.

"Hardwicke," Olin whispers. "I'm lost."

I duck beneath a low-hanging branch with multiple limbs. "Where are you?"

Help me. I'm dying. I need you.

"Olin. Talk to me." I stumble and fall to my knees, the pain in my head like being stabbed with a thousand daggers. Moss soaks through the knees of my jeans. "I can't find you."

"You ain't lookin in the right place."

When I look up, I see Dante before me, taller than I remember, the pock marks on his pasty white face more cavernous than before. His torso casts a long, distorted shadow blocking every bioluminescent glow it touches. His clock rings are shiny and polished. He twirls the face on his left ring finger.

"I told you they was stealin from me. But you ain't listen. Can't trust no bitches. Can't trust no one." He tosses me a bloodcurdling smirk, then kneels so that his face is even with mine. The prong scars on the bottom of his chin are oozing with infection. "Not even yourself. Especially yourself. It's breakin down, Hardwicke. It's *all* breakin down."

Hurry. Please. Before it's too late.

I fight through the blistering pain in my temples, push myself up from the mossy path. I'm simultaneously smaller than Dante, the same size, and bigger than him. The rings on his hands are all ticking... *Tick-tick-tick-tick-tick-tick-tick-tick.* Then he gets a look. That look.

Dante unzips his trousers and produces his fully erect penis. Yes, he's going to kill me. But not before he violates me. I'm naked now, fastened by vines at the wrists and ankles, spread-eagle between two trees. And there's nothing I can do about it.

"I knew you wanted this," he says, nude from the waist down. "You all want this. Cuz you know you can't have it."

He steps forward, his throbbing member approaching my face. All I see now is black. And all I hear is *tick-tick-tick-tick-tick-tick-tick-tick...*

I'm fully clothed again. There are no more clock rings, no more Dante. Instead, the crickets, frogs, and cicadas are chirping and croaking louder louder LOUDER until I can feel them all crawling inside my skull. The echo overwhelms me. Then I see it.

Red, spindly tendrils extend from the darkness. I don't know why I know this, but it's the nerves in my eye. The optic nerve. The trochlear, ophthalmic, and abducens. All leading to the white bulb. I feel the pulse of electrical energy crackle along the nerves like rats skittering on a phone wire. The eye is trying to show me what I need to see, what my subconscious is trying to reveal to me. But the messages are stuck, backed up like rush-hour traffic in a single-lane tunnel.

They're smashing into each other, the kinetic energy bashing against the edges of my eye just bashing and smashing until the *whumming* in my head is so heavy I can barely take anymore. *Bam! Bam! Bam!*

Each impact worse and more debilitating until the nerves are no longer red.

They're blue. Bioluminescent blue. I follow the path, which is no longer inside my eye, but through the forest. There's a forest inside my mind.

Olin whispers louder. "Hardwicke. I know who you are."

"I'm coming," I say, and push past more low-hanging branches. "Don't rush me."

"You're always in a rush."

"No, I'm not."

"You can't escape it. You know what's coming."

"Yes, I can." The branches and vines are coming at me. Grabbing me. Scratching my face.

"You can't escape who you are."

"I'm not what you think." Bioluminescent vines coil around my arms and legs, pulling me up into the trees.

"The more you lie, the tighter they squeeze."

The vines are compressing my throat. Squeezing. Squeezing. Squeezing. "Stah… stop it."

"That's why you're—"

"I'm not!"

I'm not sure how, but I'm free of the vines. In front of me now is Olin. She's the one who is trapped. She's on the mossy ground, her foot caught between two exposed roots. Beetles, flies, wasps, and ants skitter along the glowing moss and fungi.

"You shouldn't be here alone," Olin says.

I free her foot from the roots. "That's why I have you."

"I'm not the one you want. I'm a placeholder. A substitute."

As if the vines are once again squeezing the life force from me, I can barely breathe. "Who am I looking for?"

Blistering pain in my head. I wince, but it doesn't help. It only makes it worse.

I've been calling you. I know you remember. Find me. Please. Before it's too late.

I shout into the dark, dense forest. "Stop blaming me!"

The fog rolls in again, billowing and expanding until I'm surrounded.

Whistler descends upon me. He's crying, a wild ugly cry, his eyes a waterfall of tears. "I'm sorry. I'm sorry I'm sorry I'm *sorry!* I didn't mean to do it. To put you all through this."

He's not saying what he's sorry for, or why, as if it's obvious. But the trap door over my heart opens, unlocking a torrent of regret I've buried for too long.

"I'm sorry, too!" I hug him tight, just bawling until there aren't *his* tears or *my* tears, but *our* tears. Our faces are pressed together, cheek against cheek, until our two cheeks, our two faces, absorb each other. There is no him. There is no me.

We're the same. We're one.

"Nice try," Spiky Hair says. "You can't hide behind him."

I'm me again. Not Whistler/me. Just me.

"I'm not hiding."

"Of course you are." Spiky Hair circles me. Twigs snap beneath his feet. He kneels, offers his hand to the ground. A bioluminescent beetle crawls onto his finger then along his arm. He strokes its tiny back. "Which makes you easy to find."

The beetle's head pops open. Its tiny appendages snap, crackle, and expand until the beetle mutates from an insect into a full-size Aiko. She taunts me, waves at me with the bloody stump where her arm used to be. She holds the decapitated limb in her other hand.

"You think you're looking for this"—she shows me the wrist of the severed hand, red symbols highlighted—"but really you're looking for—"

Olin shoots her in the head. Aiko explodes into bioluminescent slop, covering the forest in glowing blueberry splotches.

"You're running out of time," Olin says. "She's not the one you want."

"Then who is?"

The *whumming* in my head. The pressure is building, inflating between my ears. I press my hands against my temples, trying to keep it all inside. To keep the truth from coming out...

"You left me, Hardy." Dolores is on the ground, back against a tree. She's bleeding from her belly. "I've been calling you. Why haven't you come?"

I know this is just a dream, but it breaks my heart all over again to see this proud and strong woman—my friend—lying in a pool of her own blood. Dream blood.

"There was nothing I could do."

"There's always *something* you can do."

Every word from her is like listening to kittens set on fire.

"I couldn't be two places at once. I had to make a choice."

"I know," Dolores says. "But why do your friends pay the price?"

I'm crying again, my tears bioluminescent blue. They've leaked down my arms and all over my hands. The pressure in my head is mounting. "I have to do my job."

"You don't have to do anything."

"I really do."

Dolores coughs up more blood. "You really don't."

"I do, for fuck's sake! I do I do I DO!"

I scream so loud Dolores starts to tremble, her entire body vibrating and thrashing until she levitates off the forest floor. The bioluminescent power cracks through the surface of her skin. The fissures grow more pronounced, releasing blistering white light and bands of golden energy.

"Dolores! What's happening?"

"You know I'm not Dolores."

"But..." I do know that.

"I've been calling you. Haven't you heard?"

I answer meekly. "Yes."

"Then why haven't you come?"

"I don't know."

"You do."

The forest is gone. Instead of trees, roots, moss, and fungus I'm in the far reaches of space. Stars shimmer in the distance. And debris. Fragments of stars, planets, and moons. Dead systems. And cracks in the fabric of spacetime. The fault lines. They're bleeding.

"Rub this on your hands," not-Dolores says, just a voice. I'm holding a jar of white cream. "It'll stop the pain."

I do what I'm told. The buttery cream has an ultra-soothing and deeply hydrating texture. It soaks into my skin.

"They're dead," not-Dolores says. "It's killing me. I can't hold on. It's too much."

"What's too much?"

"You have the answer."

I don't know what she means. "Where? Tell me. I want to help you. *Please.*"

"Do you?"

"Do I what?"

"Want to help me?"

"Yes!"

"Then why don't you?"

"I don't know where to go!"

"I don't have much time."

"Then tell me where you are!"

"Start again. From the beginning."

"Beginning of what?"

"What were you looking for?"

"I don't know." But I do. "The symbols. On the bracelet."

I study my hand. The symbols from Aiko's hand are scrolling over my palms and wrist. I turn them over, following the scroll. There's a pattern. It repeats. "What do they mean?"

"My location."

"But you're right here! I..." The jar of moisturizer is back in my hand. I scoop some out, rub my palms and fingers together. The cream is thick and waxy like a...

She dream-reads my mind. "Like a what?"

I gaze out into the far reaches of the dead systems, where not-Dolores should be. "Like a balm."

"No," not-Dolores says. "Not a balm."

"No. Not a *balm.*" My eyes go wide. "A *bomb!*" Aiko was right. I wake up, hit the panic button.

Jody opens my pod. Olin next.

"Hardwicke," Olin says. "Who was that? What did she mean?"

I rip the diodes off my face. "It means I need to see my son."

CHAPTER 20

Banny doesn't speak to me the entire trip through the snow-capped Baldamere Mountain range. If there was a better way to get here, I'd take it. But since Eddie deactivated my teleport device, this is the only way I know.

The Patch Institute isn't an easy place to find, much less get to, unless you know exactly where you're going. Banny maneuvers the cab upward around the windy, gravel road, the Institute sequestered deep within the mountain like a hidden military base.

Olin and I step out of the cab into the crisp mountain air. The Andromeda Galaxy swirls above us. Purple around the edges, the galaxy's inner swirls fade into magenta, spiraling into its black center—a funnel into the Cosmos. I can feel the pulse of the white-peaked mountains, and the low rumble of that hypnotic Andromeda swirl, like stone gears grinding against each other.

His breath is visible. "Damn, it's cold."

"Banny." I reach out my hand to rest it on the door frame where he's rolled down the window. But I retract my hand. My access to the Institute isn't the only one that's been revoked. "Thanks for the lift."

"Say hi to Owen. I'm gonna miss him."

"Yeah." The snow crunches beneath my sneakers. "He's gonna miss you, too."

Banny rolls up the window, does a k-turn, and without a sentimental lookback or pause in the road, drives around the snowy bend, disappearing into the night. He has every right to feel like I've burned too many bridges with him. I hope when this is all over there will be at least one left to find our way back.

Olin blows hot breath into her cupped hand. The other dangles from the sling. "What are we doing here? How does it work?"

I know I've been cut off, but I follow the old protocol Eddie gave me. I press my open palm against the gray mountain. The surface should ripple like fluctuations on an elastic sheet, revealing the digital grid beneath the holographic image. An optical scanner should appear, read my retinal nerve, and give me access. But not now.

"Hardwicke, fuck." Olin stomps her feet in the snow. "Are we stuck out here?"

"It's why I brought this." I produce the sheath I'd left at my mother's house, slip it on my finger. "It's a skeleton key. It can open any lock. Even this one."

Or so I tell myself. I activate the sheath, press it against the mountainside. I've never used it on this kind of tech. I reach out my hand. No ripple. Just solid mountain. I blow dust off the skeleton key, like cleaning out a USB port. I try again. Same result.

"What about the teleport device?"

I look at her quizzically. "What do you mean?"

"The skeleton key should open any lock?"

"In theory."

"The device has a lock on it. Digital, but still a lock. Right?"

With the swirl of the Andromeda Galaxy above us, I'm feeling smaller and stupider than ever. I never thought to try that. I press the sheath against the device.

"Wait!" Olin grabs my arm. "Don't leave me out here."

I press the button on the teleportation...

And we're inside the Institute's main hangar. Eddie and a small crew of Patches are having an animated conversation... with Tarrish.

"Angela? How'd you get in here?" I show Eddie the teleportation device he gave me. "That shouldn't work."

"You have your toys. I have mine."

There's palpable tension here. Dozens of Patch techs scramble among hissing steam pipes and hydraulic lifts. Others load interstellar transport ships, scrapers, and haulers.

"Not a good time, Anj. We're still on lockdown."

"That's why you cut me off."

"It wasn't just you." Eddie looks at Tarrish, then back to me. "It was everyone."

That it wasn't directed at me shouldn't make me feel better, but it does.

"Wait," I say. "Where's Owen?"

"He's in the junior lab. He's fine."

Tarrish steps closer. "You shouldn't be here."

"We're past that, T. What's—?"

Tarrish shows me his phone. "This the guy?"

Black. Square jaw. Spiky brown hair. "That's him, yeah. Who is he?"

"Ilya Burri," Eddie says. "He used to work here."

My eyes go wide. "He what?"

Eddie's gaze goes to the floor, then back up to me. "He trained here. He was a Patch."

"And you didn't tell me?"

"We didn't know it was him," Tarrish says. "We just got the image from the security drone. He pulled his mask off after the attack in Sinner's Row. It confirms what we thought."

"What do you mean... *confirms?*"

"Angela," Eddie says. "Come with me."

Eddie and Tarrish lead me and Olin down a corridor into a quiet room overlooking the dock heading out into the Cosmos. Before us is an interstellar graveyard. Eleven of the fourteen planets and moons in the Kidasha System are in various stages of destruction. Blown apart and broken away from their original orbits.

My mouth hangs open. "What the...?"

Fragments and dust collide among the pockets of gas and radiation. "That was a test run," Eddie says. "The death count is incalculable. He's a mass murderer now. We think this was a failed detonation or an intentional distraction. Whichever, it'll take months to clean up. Maybe years."

Tarrish looks up from his phone. "I've got every available agent looking for this guy. The Patches are helping."

"But why is he doing this? What's he after?"

"You know what happened?" Eddie says. "With the fault lines. That part is true." He looks to Tarrish, who nods. Eddie continues. "But there's more."

There always is.

"Ilya was in the engineering corps, high marks. But he was too smart for his own good. Too arrogant. He thought he was better than everyone else, like he knew things the rest of us didn't. Not because they weren't knowable, but because we were too stupid to understand or too lazy to learn. He was more interested in researching anomalies than repairing the fabric of spacetime. He couldn't accept having to answer to anyone or justify his decisions. Rules and restrictions were for other people. He demanded free reign to do as he pleased, when he pleased, how he pleased, without accountability, oversight, or consequence."

"A Patch with an ego," I say with an edge I hadn't intended. "Never seen that."

Eddie ignores the jab. "About ten years ago he accessed the archives. Files about the fault lines. There was anecdotal evidence to support the theory. But Ilya... he was a believer. He'd come across a few systems showing microfractures in spacetime. We took his report seriously. We ran every test we had. There was no detectable cause, natural or otherwise, so we chalked up the microfractures to normal wear and tear. It happens. But he was convinced it was worse. Early warning signs."

"Like tingling in the extremities," Olin says, "can indicate a stroke."

"Exactly like that. Ilya said spacetime was alerting us to an oncoming disaster. But we'd heard it all before."

"What do you mean *before?*" I ask. "He wasn't the first?"

He's not telling me the whole story. I need to get out of here. To follow what I saw in the Dreamscape. Patches have insight into the fabric of spacetime the rest of us don't. But they don't know it all. And I can't explain to them what I need to do—or why.

"Every now and then we get a Patch that goes rogue," Eddie says. "They get tempted by the myth. It leads to nothing but dead ends."

A chunk of debris the size of a small city collides with a quarter moon literally crumbling before us. There's a knocking on the door. "Eddie! It's Jill. We need you. Now!"

We rush back into the main hangar. Several repair crafts are already rocketing toward the Kidasha System, their blue-white propulsion plumes radiating behind them. Taking up half the wall adjacent to us is a viewscreen taller than my apartment building.

Debris from the destroyed system is smashing into each other, the damage scattered far and wide. Some of the pummeled planets and moons have been reduced to dust and shards. But other fragments are being drawn to each other.

"The Kidasha System is iron-and-nickel rich. It contains tetrataenite particles," Eddie says, explaining they're highly magnetic. Radioactive decay heats up the interiors of planets, moons, and certain asteroids. Pressure imposed from the detonation was great enough on the molten metal cores to reach convection. "It generates a magnetic field."

"Does it matter? The damage is already done."

"Jill!" Eddie shouts and points toward the southeast corner. "Tell Kamari to load panel four!" He grabs me by the shoulders and shoves me aside. "No! Panel four! Tell her I said so!"

"This was a mistake," I say. "I shouldn't be here. We should go."

"If we can't demagnetize the fragments or neutralize them, they'll keep amassing density. They'll drift through the galaxy and damage other systems."

"Mommy!" I hear someone yell above the shouting, electronics, and mechanicals. Dozens of Patches frantically power up tools and climb into huge machines. Two giant mechanical claws extend from the scraper. On the next pad, a giant spider-like craft stands on the tips of its eight mechanical legs. Like cold spider eyes, a half dozen icy blue scanners above the cockpit probe everything around it.

"Mommy!"

I rush toward the voice.

"They're doing it wrong!"

Owen grabs my hand. He pulls me toward the viewscreen.

Opposite us, four Patches climb into ten-foot mechanical exoskeletons, secured within a bubble dome, and armed with scrapers, picks, and blowtorches.

"Look, Mommy! They're doing it wrong!" He points at the exoskeletons. "They have the wrong—"

"What are you doing here, baby? It's not a good time."

"No, Mommy. Listen! It won't work. They're—"

"Owen!" Eddie says. "You can't be here now."

"Daddy! The gel! It's not enough."

Alarms blare.

Olin ducks in response to the mechanical chaos. "Hardwicke! What the hell? Let's get outta here!"

"Mommy!" Owen grabs my hand. "MOMMY!"

"Eddie! What does that mean? About the gel?"

"Mommy, I can do it!"

"What baby?"

"I can fix it! I can fix the—"

Eddie picks up Owen, grimacing as he does. "You know you can't be here."

"But Daddy!"

"Not now, Owen. I'm sorry. I'll find you later." He puts Owen down. "Jill! Can you get him back to class? I can't deal with this now."

She hustles over, takes Owen by the hand. He pulls away.

"It's not *fair*! They're doing it wrong. I can *fix* it."

"I'm sure you can," she says. "But let them do it. It's their job."

"Eddie. What did he mean? About the gel?"

Eddie sighs, frustrated. Too much happening at once. He leads us back outside the hangar.

"There were two other Patches before Ilya got on the scent. They saw it, too. The pattern. They theorized that if they set off a single detonation along one of the fault lines, it would prove their theory. They stole a freighter and set off a single bomb in a distant, uninhabited region of spacetime. Except the detonation reverberated farther than they calculated. It damaged the ship. One fatality, the other on life support."

"So they were right?"

"Ultimately... maybe. But we didn't know that then. All they proved was that *testing* for fault lines was more dangerous than the fault lines themselves. Which were not confirmed. So we shut down the investigation. We buried the files."

"Until Ilya got onto it."

"He wouldn't let it go. He said the previous team was closer than we thought. Nobody else saw it, but he was certain he was right. He petitioned the Institute to reopen the case."

"Did they?"

"Not at first. But he was relentless. He said even the fabric of spacetime changes throughout the eons. What we understood about it yesterday wasn't a guarantee we'd understand the same thing tomorrow. The Council couldn't deny that spacetime is an organic tapestry even we don't entirely understand. Ilya put in for a small team and resources. He argued Zeno's Paradox."

"What's that?"

"It's an Earth concept. Zeno's Paradox. It posits the only way to reach a physical or conceptual endpoint is to travel in a succession of halves. Each half smaller than the last—fifty percent, twenty-five percent, twelve-and-a-half, and so on. But no matter how small the halves, and the closer you get to the endpoint, more questions arise, resetting the gap. Eventually, you accept you'll never get to the end or know everything, but you know enough to make a decision."

"So," I say, "close enough is close enough?"

"More or less... yes. Ilya said there was enough to go on, and if he couldn't find the fault lines within two years, he'd let it go. But if he *did* find them, he wanted to slather them with the interstellar healing gel we use to treat smaller rips and tears in spacetime. The theory was solid. It was based on our core practices. The Council relented. They gave him resources and two Patches to work on his team."

"It also kept him pacified," I theorize.

"It did. And the Council had a particle of doubt, so..."

"They covered their asses," Olin says. "If they denied him and it turned out he was right, they'd point fingers at each other or find a scapegoat. I see it on the force. The suits pull this shit all the time."

She looks at Tarrish who, as usual, betrays nothing.

Eddie explains that with Ilya leading his team, they scoured the Cosmos for the fault lines. But while exploring untested sections of spacetime, they also stumbled across other obscure and unexpected anomalies.

And trouble they hadn't anticipated, including pirates, assassins, gun runners, smugglers, bounty hunters, and warring factions causing or exploiting those anomalies. The Guild.

"That was a job for law enforcement," he says. "It fell outside our skillset and jurisdiction. We called the ICD."

Naturally. *That's* why Tarrish is here.

Two freighters launch from the adjacent hangar and cross our path. The freighters follow side by side, and in a blink, disappear into the far reaches of the Cosmos.

"See that mess out there? That's how we got the Wednesday Five."

Icy shock waves crackle throughout my entire body. My face is hot. My skin pulls taut. Caught in that elliptical orbit, Whistler kept saying what sounded like *Eddie hive. Eddie hive.*

But not Eddie hive.

I stare out into the cosmos. Unfolding before me is what Ilya feared all along. One fault line implodes, sends shock waves across spacetime until the vibrations hit another. Imploding the next fault line, a chain reaction unleashing more shock waves, creating more dead systems, until they shatter the entirety of spacetime.

The end of everything.

I take a deep breath, consider the ramifications of these critical fault lines, and ask the only question that seems pertinent to me right now.

"Who the fuck are the Wednesday Five?"

PART III:

THE WEDNESDAY FIVE

CHAPTER 21

Wreckage seems to be my life's defining theme. With the cases I take—and the people who know me.

Eddie and Tarrish explain that Ilya and his small team of Patches didn't have the skills, training, equipment, or experience to deal with the criminal element they encountered while hunting down fault lines. And the ICD didn't have the skills, training, equipment, or experience to handle the damage to the fabric of spacetime.

"So you merged," I say. "Patches and ICD. Together, as one crew."

Tarrish verifies my suspicion. Three Patches, two ICD agents. Ilya as team leader.

Patches trained the ICD agents to handle increasingly complicated repairs to the fabric of spacetime. The ICD agents trained the Patches in combat, espionage, and counterterrorism.

"Ilya was okay with this?"

"He was," Eddie says. "As long as the Institute, the ICD, and his team all clearly understood *his* primary mission was to find the fault lines. They were given a budget, supplies, and a highly advanced ship, *The Specter*. They had significant latitude."

On the viewscreen, chunks of planets, moons, and asteroids collide, altering the trajectory of the drift. Eight Patches in mechanical exoskeletons, each enclosed in a bubble dome to protect them from the elements, launch into the wreckage left behind where an entire star system had just been.

Two Patches attach themselves to a larger asteroid and extend the mechanical arms. With concentrated flames firing from the mounted blowtorches, they surgically carve the chunk into smaller, less dangerous pieces of rocks and minerals, and let them float away.

That's how Eddie got his start as a Patch, demolition of stray asteroids. Will Owen be doing that next?

Or will he end up as part of a rogue squadron like the Wednesday Five?

"Hold on," I say. "Who did they report to?"

Eddie and Tarrish eye each other.

"It was a commission," Tarrish says finally. "The Institute and ICD had joint, operational oversight. Their berth was wide. Oversight was not."

Three of the exoskeleton Patches launch small, tactical missiles from shoulder mounts. They destroy a braid-shaped piece of moon hurtling toward a hunk of planet dangling from its core. The first explosion breaks the moon braid into large fragments. The second missile splits into smaller guided projectiles, destroying the fragments. Like treating kidney stones that won't pass, the third missile emits an ultrasonic pulse to further break the smallest fragments into dust.

"The Wednesday Five were approved as a borderline off-book squad despite my strenuous and repeated objections," Tarrish says. "We compromised."

It was determined that Ilya would lead the Wednesday Five as long as *he* understood the investigations would take them wherever they led. And that his fault line mission would take a back seat, whenever needed, so the Five could neutralize, apprehend, interrogate, or, in cases of life or death, exterminate the rogue factions they encountered.

Olin reaches for her injured shoulder. "Sounds like a marriage consummated in Hell."

"It does," I say. "If Ilya's the egomaniac you describe, why put him in charge? What he wanted and what the ICD wanted were totally different."

"Squeaky wheel gets the grease," Olin says. "It shut him up."

"There was some friction," Eddie admits, "but they made it work."

I see where this is going. "Until it didn't."

Tarrish concurs. "Until it didn't."

With significant portions of debris broken into more

manageable pieces, the eight Patches fan out equidistant from one another. Utilizing hover controls, they plant small devices amid the debris. The Patches fan out even farther. From their mechanical arms they shoot energy beams at the devices. Upon contact, the devices activate a pulse-layered net, which captures the debris.

"I don't understand." The headaches are back, the *whumming* in my temples. "How come I never heard of the Wednesday Five?"

Tarrish rolls his eyes. "It must really burn you that the great Angela Hardwicke isn't in the know. It's almost hard to believe."

Eddie looks away sheepishly. "That was meant for me."

"I know," Tarrish says. "But your ex, who is under my jurisdiction for thinking she knows better than everyone else, is once again in the dark, because she thinks she knows more than everyone else."

"But why the Wednesday Five?" Olin asks. "I get the *Five* part. But why *Wednesday?*"

Eddie shrugs. "We asked. They never said."

I gaze out as the exoskeleton Patches collect debris in the pulse net. My mind is doing the same. Scooping up fragments of intel, hoping they form a whole.

"If Ilya is part of the Wednesday Five… as the team leader, where's the team?"

Tarrish and Eddie are locked in a conspiratorial stare, as if wordlessly debating how much to tell me. I don't have time for this.

"Don't give me any classified bullshit," I say, even as I hold back information from them. "The Five are involved. I wanna know how."

Tarrish goes to the long window. He rests his arm high up on the glass, leans into it. The Patches neutralize what is now, essentially, a newly netted asteroid. They'll repeat the cycle until the debris is cleared away. The repair crew will fix or replace the damaged portion of spacetime.

"It's how we discovered the Guild," he says. "Their team stumbled onto a small ship using radiation clusters as cover. The ship was linked to an assassination on Shequesohn Four.

The Five brought the assassins in for questioning. They were tough to break, but we got serious intel. That bought the Five some good will."

"But that's not why Ilya led the Five," Eddie says. "They'd been at it for a year when he took some R and R. Mandatory on a rotational basis to prevent burnout. But the truth is, he was becoming disillusioned with the Five. They cared more about the Guild than the fault lines. It's hard to chase a ghost when you know demons are real."

Ilya came back to the Institute for what he said was a friendly visit. It wasn't the real reason.

"He'd cobbled notes together from before the Five... and during. Somewhere along the line, he'd gotten wind of a map that contained specific cosmologic coordinates. It was supposedly buried withing the archives. We'd already scoured them looking for the map, on the off chance it was real. We ran simulations with thousands of symbols and keywords. We inspected every individual file. Three times each. We never found it."

"Because there was nothing to find?" I ask. "Or because you didn't know where to look?"

Jill rushes back out. "Eddie." Her eyes are wide and distant. I know that gaze. Not good.

Eddie sighs through his nose, his way of trying to contain the stress. "Another?"

Jill nods. "The Bierné System."

Eddie looks as if his head is about to explode in horror. "What? No! How? That's... six, maybe six-and-a-half trillion light years away from the Kidasha system."

I've never seen Eddie rattle under pressure. But his knees buckle and his chest inverts. His breaths go tight. The scale and magnitude of destruction is beyond even his experience.

Anticipating their rush back into the main hangar, I start ahead of them. Jill pulls me back.

"They've got all they can handle," she says. "Come. This way."

She leads us down the corridor in the opposite direction, around one corner then another, through a security checkpoint, and into another hangar. Twice as many Patches are scrambling around enough machines, equipment, hydraulic lifts, wires, tubes, and piping to power a space station.

"Jace," Eddie says, having regained his composure. "Report."

Dark-skinned with a square jaw and nearly glowing green eyes, Jace speaks with a nearly monotone voice. "Eighty-nine point six four one percent destruction."

Eddie purses his lips. His way of concentrating on a problem he'd rather ignore. There were seventeen life-supporting planets in the system, with nine billion citizens. "Survivors?"

Jace's tone doesn't change. "None."

"The fault lines," Tarrish says. "It's started."

Nine repair and removal crawlers power up while another two dozen Patches climb inside the exoskeletons. The fleet of Patches launch into the minefield of destruction where the Bierné System used to be.

"I just don't see how the fault lines can travel that far that fast," Eddie says. "It defies every law of physics we understand."

I probe further. "Could there be other systems? Others you haven't found yet? Connective tissue?"

Eddie looks to Jill. She nods affirmatively.

"We're getting reports," she says, staring at her handheld device. "The Winslow and Denvi Systems. Both unpopulated, thankfully."

"T," I say to Tarrish. "What are you...?"

He's walking away, phone pressed to his ear.

"Eddie, what aren't you telling me? The map. It's real... or it's not."

The second cluster of exoskeleton Patches launch into space.

"I don't know," he says. "I've never seen it. But yes, I think it's real. Before he left the Institute again to rejoin the Five, Ilya visited the private quarters of the Patches who'd been looking for it, too. It had been years since they occupied the quarters, and we didn't know he'd stopped in there until after he left. There was a loose tile in the floorboards beneath one of the beds. We found it with a scanner drone. There was nothing beneath the tile. Which means there was nothing to find. Or if there was...

Olin completes the thought. "He took it with him."

The stress lines on Eddie's face betray the weight of responsibility pummeling him like those planetary fragments into a dead moon.

"We know that now. What we also know is that before rejoining the Five, he chartered a private shuttle to the Lid'la System. Nothing but asteroids and dead moons. He set off a single detonation along a potential fault line, to test his theory. Which, technically, fell under his purview. We examined the site later and found heavy traces of the Perselus Effect."

I should never be surprised when the Institute or ICD holds out on me. Yet here I am again. "The what?"

"When spacetime sustains an abrupt, traumatic injury that exceeds its protective threshold, it can produce cosmologic discharge consisting of a protein-rich fluid teeming with dead regenerative cells. It's the equivalent to *liquor puris* in the human body. It accumulates at an infection site."

"Pus?" I ask. "You're telling me the Perselus Effect is space pus?"

"Essentially, yes. If you have the proper shielding, it's harmless."

"And if not?"

Eddie stares at me. "It causes cellular degeneration and hallucinations. It can alter brain chemistry."

"So you're telling me that Ilya, who was already an arrogant conspiracy nut—who thinks attacking the fabric of spacetime is the way to save it, and is convinced he's doing the right thing—has been exposed to a mind-altering discharge that could enhance his paranoia?"

Eddie considers my question before answering. "Yes. That's what I'm saying."

Fuckety fuck fuck fuck.

Tarrish returns. "It's a full-court press. If he's still on-realm, we'll find him. There's only so many places he can hide."

"Wait," I say. "If he's with the Five, where the hell are *they*?"

Like an oncologist reluctant to share the news of your stage-five cancer, there's a palpable, weighty silence.

"That's the other problem," Eddie says finally. "We don't know. We lost contact."

"You what? Your super-secret squad are just... gone?"

Neither Tarrish nor Eddie answer. Which gets me thinking again. And then I realize...

"Whistler. *That's* what you had him doing. He was looking for the Wednesday Five. You had him..." Something doesn't add up. "You had *Whistler* looking for them, but not me. Whistler. Not me." I lock eyes with Tarrish. "I'm already under your thumb. I'm more experienced, have better contacts, and know the Institute and ICD better than he does. So why...?"

My chest seizes. My body rages with heat and sweat. Daggers in my brain. I'm swirling, unable to center myself. But I don't have the luxury of panic. Not here. Not now. I let my body and mind unclench. I exhale. I was the better choice to search for the Wednesday Five. The more logical choice. I was better suited for the job in every way, except...

Except. Damn.

In my mind's eye, he's right there.

"Owen. You were afraid I might not make it back. And Whistler is more"—I look to Eddie, to Tarrish, to Olin, then back to Eddie and Tarrish together—"expendable."

"It was my decision," Tarrish says. "You were too much of a risk. You don't play well in the sandbox. And the kid's not completely useless. You trained him well enough. And he's eager to prove himself—to me—in a way you're not anymore. That he's as good as you."

Eddie interjects. "Don't listen to him. He wanted it to be you. But I... I couldn't put Owen through that. Not if it meant losing you. I just couldn't. I'm sorry, Anj, but Owen needs his mother more than you need your partner."

I'm so angry I could cry. Not because I'm fuming at Eddie and Tarrish both. Which I am. But because I put Whistler in a position to be manipulated and exposed by them.

Again, Whistler's in trouble. And again, it's my fault.

I was so busy falling down the rabbit hole then crawling back out, I saw only what *I* needed, what *I* wanted. In my attempts to play well in that sandbox, which, clearly, is pretty far from my wheelhouse, I allowed other people, these two men, to decide my fate. And who risks their lives for them, including Whistler. And who doesn't.

"Jo," I say. "We're leaving."

"Fuck, yes. Where to?"

"Eddie. Activate my device. And don't fuck with me. Whistler's still trapped. I'm bringing him home."

"No. I'm sorry, Angela. I can't let you do that."

"I'm not asking. And you don't *let* me do anything. Look at the mess out there. A bit late to worry about me. Activate my device. *Now.*"

He does. Olin grabs onto me.

"But before I go," I say, "both of you can go fuck yourselves."

CHAPTER 22

Out of pure instinct I teleport Olin and me back to my office.

I step inside the bathroom. I stare at my reflection in the mirror. Water cascades down my face. Am I, as Tarrish said, like Ilya? Is he like me? Doing what I want, how and when I want, damn the consequences?

I don't want to answer that. No matter how hard I scrub, the grime never seems to entirely wash off.

She rubs her bad shoulder. "I don't know how you do this. The Institute, the ICD. This is your life?"

"Pretty much."

My vision is blurred, the headache worse. Pounding inside my temples. I try to control my breaths, to minimize the discomfort. I know this pain. I've had it before. It's a distinct and specific pain, from a distinct and specific source. No amount of painkillers, liquor, or sex can numb it away.

There's only one cure, one way to end it.

I recheck my gear. "I know it's a long shot but go back to Kimmie-slash-Nóirín's apartment. See if you can find anything that might tip us off about the final fault line. If not, try Dante's apartment and the Love Star again. Check the lobby, the room. And get up to the roof. It's possible I missed something. I was up there at night. Daylight might be your friend."

"Where are you going? To find Whistler?"

"Yes." I re-holster my gun. "But not yet."

I open the door to my office, let Olin walk ahead. My hand on the doorknob, I pull the door closed behind us. I hear the rattle of the glass pane, the click of the lock. If this is going to be the last time I leave this office—*my* office—I want it to be on my terms.

We're back out on the street. Four half-moons today ghosted through a hazy afternoon sky. Are they actually moons? Or cosmic debris finding its way on-realm?

Olin adjusts her arm in the sling. "Then where are you going?"

I turn up my collar. "To visit a sick friend."

Frankie the Brush is a general contractor, construction specialist, and house painter who works both sides of the street—commercial and residential. He also does galaxy renovation and polishing. So he's got every reason to know people from all walks of life. He's also the only person I know who's been through this before.

He's helped me put down a dozen cases over the years and gives me tips and intel about the real estate and construction business. I push business his way when I can. He's also been there for me when I've needed him most. He's never asked for anything in return.

The monorail takes me all the way to the Downtown waterfront district. About five years ago, a chemical fire destroyed half the neighborhood.

The marina was recently redeveloped, financed by several private investors and tax abatements from the City. Now populating the coastal neighborhood are luxury residential towers, mixed-use properties, a realm-class park, an amphitheater with rolling green space and a glassed-in, interdimensional botanical garden and atrium, new hotels, several restaurants and cafes, and a music, sports, and arts arena with a food hall, and a cosmic viewing station with a window into alternate realities.

Multiple security drones fly overhead in rotation. Always watching.

Bald head, mini-dad gut, Frankie's on one of the smaller pedestrian piers overlooking the harbor. He's cutting a two-by-four on a table saw. In the near distance is The Tee, a hotel set on an artificial island and connected to the mainland by a private bridge. Had a case there a while back. It didn't go too well.

Frankie sees me. With sausage fingers he powers down the

saw. "Hey, Angela. You don't look so good."

"Don't feel so good." I look at him, the years of friend-ship conveying to him all he needs to know. "The headaches, Frankie." Painfully, I glance skyward, then back at him. "They're back. They're worse."

Frankie gazes at the thousands of pedestrians occupying the marina, at the gentle current, then back to me. "I heard there's a problem. A big one."

"Yeah." I squint hard as a blister of pain pierces my left tem-ple. "Could use your help."

"I gotta finish the job."

"I hear ya, Frankie. But if this thing goes to shit—and it's nearly there—there won't be any more jobs to finish. It's her. She back. And she needs our help."

Contractors signed to do any kind of repair work on the Cosmos are given job-specific access to intergalactic travel gates. Frankie keeps me on his employment roster for times like this. We climb inside his van and drive back along the Rubiyat Highway, snak-ing along the Chabaqua River. From here I can see the tip of the psych center where Olin and I met just a few days ago, though it feels like it was from a completely different lifetime.

The pain from the headache, the *whum... whum... whum...* is like a kind of sonar, a persistent, repeating wave of dense energy disrupting my equilibrium. I'm nauseated.

All energy has a source. I know what this source is. I just have to find it. Have to find her.

The perimeter fencing secures one of E-Town's intergalactic travel gate stations and fleet of shuttlecrafts. They're designated for engineers and other licensed technicians subcontracted to do installation, maintenance, and repair work throughout the Cosmos.

We approach the chain-link fence fortified with an electric current and topped with barbed-wire coils. There's a security booth on the end.

Frankie rolls down his window.

"Anj," he says. "Let me handle this." He addresses the guard. "You're Jimmy, right?"

"Yeah," he says a bit suspiciously, even though his nametag says Jimmy.

"Your sister is"—Frankie searches his memory banks—"Kaitlin, right? She has a house in Bayerton Village? I built a deck a few summers ago. You were grilling sausages. Long links."

"Oh, shit! That was you? Yeah... yeah! I remember. You got a couple'a kids. All girls."

"Five."

"Five? Dude! When do you sleep?"

Frankie chuckles. "Any chance I get."

"Ha-ha, I hear that."

"Tight security tonight."

"Yeah. You know how it is."

Frankie chuckles. "That I do. He hands the guard his ID.

"Hey. It checks out." Jimmy has Frankie put his eye up to the infrared retinal scanner. It does its thing. "Good to go."

"Thanks," Frankie says. "And say hi to your sister."

I'm so nauseated I can barely keep my eyes open. Parked inside the shuttlecraft's small hangar, Frankie's van is a beat-up rig with more scars, dings, and dents than my soul. It's crammed with so many tools and parts it's a miracle the gear doesn't bust through the rear double doors. I forget sometimes the kind of jobs he takes.

"Angela. Which system? Where we headed?"

Stomach acid shoots up my esophagus and into my mouth, singeing my tongue and gums. I rinse with a bottle of water, spitting into a disposal tube next to my door. "Not sure."

"That's gonna make this trip a bit more difficult."

"I know, I..."

I lean back in the seat, toolbox next to my knee. I close my eyes and concentrate, focusing on my dreams. Of the bioluminescent forest. And the calls for help. My eyes still shut, I whisper to Frankie, tell him to guide my hands to the control panel. He does. I don't know if I'm back in the Dreamscape or just remembering my time there, but it feels as real and amorphous as it did through the Dream Pods.

I have no idea if I'm surrounded by croaking crickets, frogs, or cicadas. All I hear is the deafening *whum-whum-whum*, like a cosmic base drum, pounding and pounding inside my head. But underneath those base tones, barely audible, are cries for help.

Dolores, who is not Dolores, is up against the tree, bleeding from her stomach. But it's not blood, exactly. It's… power. Energy.

"You'd better hurry," she says. "I don't have much time."

"I know. But I don't know where to find you."

"Yes, you do. Isolate the signal. I've been telling you the whole time."

"Telling me… ah"—I press both palms against my temples—"telling me what?"

"Not *tell*," says Dolores, who is not Dolores. "*Time*."

I can't take much more of the pounding in my head. Bioluminescent roots and vines curl around my arms, legs, and torso, squeezing me, compressing my chest. It's hard to breathe. I dig deep within myself, trying to wiggle free, to push the pain aside long enough for me to…

No.

I'm doing this all wrong. I can't fight the pain. Can't squirm my way out. I have to embrace it. Let the bioluminescence absorb into my skin, communicate with me through my very cells, if not my soul. I have to let it dominate me, overpower me, and hope it sets me free.

I fall to my knees, wrapped in organic, bioluminescent chains. The mist returns, followed by the white fog. Swarming me like a tornado of ghosts are sins of my past. The cases I've taken, the friends I've lost. Or betrayed.

My sister who died of cancer. My parents who were broken by it. Aiko. Dolores. Nini. Whistler.

"What do you want?" I shout. "What can I do? Tell me where you are!"

"All in good time," their combined voices whisper.

Tears leak down my face. "When? What time? What *time*?"

"Come on, now, gingerbread. There's always time." It's Dad. He's younger, like from my childhood. He's healthy. Strong. "Don't be in such a rush. Check the time."

"What does that mean, Daddy? What does that *mean*?"

"It means what it always means," Whistler says. He's replaced Dad, but I've never seen this version of him before. Whistler looks just like always except... different. Poised. Wiser. Calm. "It's what you always tell me. Ignore the time. Go back to the beginning. Start again."

"I *did* start again. I went back!"

"Not far enough."

"Far enough to *what?*"

"I toldja," Dante says. "Can't trust nothin these bitches say. Always in riddles and rhymes. You can tell 'em day and night, but it ain't matter. Sooner or later, they find a way out. One way or another." Dante curls his hand into a chunky fist, his clock rings covered in blood. He pulls his arm back, snarls. "It's just a matter of time." Then thrusts his fist into my face.

My eyes snap open. The forest is quiet. Released from the vines, I get up from my knees. The ghosts are gone, even Dolores, who is not Dolores. At the base of the tree, where she'd just been, is a mossy stump. The bioluminescence is glowing blue, leading me to it, like a landing strip. I see something shiny beneath the moss. I scrape it away. Exposed now are Dante's rings.

Showing me the time.

But the clock faces are designating different times. They're not the same. They're...

Not the time. No. Not the *time*. The *location*. They're coordinates.

Without realizing it, I punch them into Frankie's nav system. I open my eyes.

"Angela," Frankie says worriedly. "You okay? You were gone a long time."

The nausea is gone. So is the headache, and the *whumming*.

"You know where this is?"

He studies the coordinates, pulls up an interstellar map. "It's pretty far out."

I drink more water, wipe tears and sweat from my face. "It's space, Frankie. Everything's far out."

Aboard a shuttlecraft we rocket toward the nearest stable wormhole, then blink into the Cosmos. We arrive in the Soto sector within minutes.

As much as I don't love spacewalks, there's no getting around it. In the back of the shuttle, we step beneath specialized sprinkler heads, activate the device. It sprays us with a protective layer of viscous fluid. We're encased in clear, comet-coated bodysuits, as thin as tissue paper, yet wonderfully malleable. The suits permit full tactility, sensitivity, and dexterity, and with the integrity to withstand the force and pressure of up to six black holes.

The shuttle bay door opens. I walk down the platform, the nearest star system beyond our sightline. Frankie backs his van out of the shuttlecraft and onto a support landing. He exits the van, then presses a button on the side. A panel unfolds like a tray. On it is a keyboard and monitor. He enters a few commands.

On the van's roof is a raised square panel. The panel opens. Four mechanical arms extend then expand, producing a latticework of platforms and support beams. Covered in the body suits, we walk for what seems like miles until we see it.

Against the black of space is a membrane miles-long and wide. I reach out my hand, make contact with the surface. The membrane has a rubberish quality, but also squishy. Like globules from a lava lamp, a patch of glowing yellow emerges where I pressed my hand. Another *whum* in my head. And a cry for help.

"Frank," I say. "You hear that?"

"No. Hear what?"

I'm not going mad. The signal is just for me. Again, I press my hand against the membrane. The yellow globule morphs into odd shapes and configurations, spreading farther and wider than before. I hear it again. The cry for help.

In the vastness of space, I gently place one open palm flat against the membrane, then the other. But I don't push. Not yet. I'm settling in, letting the membrane know I understand. That I'm here to help.

I take a deep breath, exhale. Again. I don't know why it's happening now, but in the drift of my mind I'm back at my parents' house. Dad slumped in his wheelchair, staring absently at the golf simulator. Mom in the kitchen, drinking wine. Alone.

Crying. One daughter dead from cancer, the other taunting her own grave.

It's only now I'm seeing them, not as my parents but as two adults, growing older, lonely, with no better understanding of how and why their life unfolded as it has, powerless to prevent or change the pain they've suffered. The losses they've endured.

Blaming themselves for their inability to better protect their children, to shield them from the indiscriminate cruelties embedded within the contract of life. The Earth philosopher Friedrich Nietzsche said, *"to live is to suffer, to survive is to find some meaning in the suffering."* I understand suffering. The suffering I've endured. The suffering I've caused.

But is there meaning? To any of it?

Does the Cosmos care if we bleed? If our bones break? If our spirits are crushed? Did the Minders of the Universe will the Cosmos into being so that the innumerable lives that've come before, are here now, and will someday arrive, could join the grand experiment? Did the Minders even consider the ramifications of that experiment?

Were we even a consideration? Is a state of being—any state of being—collateral damage from the creation of all? An unintended consequence? Or maybe the *search* for meaning *is* the meaning. That how we conduct ourselves, regardless of circumstance, is all that matters.

Or is meaning an empty pursuit? Do the stars care if they burn or extinguish? Do planets care if they orbit the sun?

Yes. I think they do. Maybe that's wishful thinking on my part. Maybe it's delusional. But if there's no purpose to our endeavors, no significance to our existence, then why exist at all? Why put ourselves through the sheer brutality of survival if surviving is the only point?

People matter. Lives matter. It all matters.

But what if, in the final analysis, it doesn't? If it's all for nothing?

Then fuck it. I'd rather spend the time I do have battling the indignities of the Cosmos than waiting for answers that may never come. I don't know if my life has meaning. But even if it doesn't, I'm going to act like it does.

I'm not sure what's happening, but I feel the entirety of myself relax. The globules engulf both my hands, pulling me partially through the squidgy membrane. Up to my wrists. Then up to the elbows, so my face and chest are flush against the surface.

"Frankie," I say. "Grab my waist. Hold on."

The yellow globules warble up my arms, to the shoulders, pull us deeper through the membrane. It swallows us whole. Covered in globule mucous, I feel the *whum*, the radiating energy throughout. Even covered in the viscous bodysuit, I've got goosebumps all over. We emerge on the other side of the membrane.

There, wounded, in pain, with a peppering of stars in the distance, is my friend.

Dolores, who is not Dolores.

And she's about to die.

CHAPTER 23

"You poor thing," I say. "I'm sorry I'm late."

I never thought I'd see her again. Couldn't think of a reason I would. It's overwhelming to be in the presence of such a stupendous creature. A DNA helix of the Universe hovers before us. Its twisted ladder formation is at least two miles long. She glows with blue bioluminescent strands of tubing fifty feet in circumference, while golden energy bands circulate through the entirety of the Helix, making that persistent *whum... whum... whum...*

Compared with this gargantuan interchange of pure energy, we are microscopic, the size of an eyelash on the underside of a whale.

With his handheld device Frankie extends the platform, one plate after another. It allows us to walk beneath one segment of the double twist. Frankie and I met the Helix before, years ago. The Helix itself is like an organic computer with complex circuitry, code, pathways, and internal commands, mapping a blueprint for Existence.

She'd been injured, and called to me psychically through her vibrations, an S.O.S. across Existence. It gave me debilitating headaches, drawing me into the reaches of space. At the puncture site, where the wound had been inflicted, we found new striations and microvessels, as if the Helix were trying to heal itself. Protecting the essence of its internal infrastructure, its identity. Fighting for her survival. And by extension, the Cosmos.

We bonded then. It breaks my heart to see her suffer. She'd been calling to me all this time. At first, I didn't make the connection. And then, I wasn't sure if it was really her or if I was losing my mind. The last year or so, I've been accused of worse. Of some, I was guilty. The rest of it, well, it comes with the territory. I get blamed often and aggressively for all sorts of transgressions because I dare to shine a light where darkness is preferred.

I put my hand against the twist. The Helix responds with a surge of golden energy and a guttural hum, as soothing as a cat's purr. I'd forgotten what this is like. The outer casing is firm yet pliable, with enough give that the contours of my hand sync with the Helix.

She's in far worse pain now than last time. She's struggling to stay alive.

"What happened to you?" I rub my open palm against her skin. "Why are you so sad?"

"Angela," Frankie says. "Leave your hand there. Let her remember you. Let her speak."

I put my other open palm on her skin as well. Like being plugged into one of Bernice's servers, energy grabs hold and courses through my soul. The entirety of who and what I am is swallowed up and disappears down what feels like a digital grid vortex. One that spirals through the fabric of spacetime until, finally, its structural integrity starts coming apart in digital bricks and fragments.

The all-consuming energy seeps and crackles within my essence, hers synching with mine. The longer I'm connected to her the more I lose sense of myself. It's as if my skin and bones, blood and organs, down to the marrow in my cells and the atoms within the marrow, have merged with hers. I have no sense of shape or form.

I've been obliterated into a blend of digital and organic sand, funneling into and through the next layer of cosmic membrane and into a lake of darkness. I'm overtaken by a stark and brutal awakening, the horror of knowing, all at once, all that exists, everywhere, past, present, and future.

I'm a radiant *whum*, an unquantifiable compression of knowledge, experience, and energy pulsing through spacetime. Hers is a language of vibrations and tremors. Thoughts without words. Music without song. I see what she sees. I feel what she feels. Because there is no *her*, there is no *me*.

We are *we*. We are one.

On the verge of death, clinging to life.

Another surge courses through me, whatever I am right now. I'm consumed by the building blocks of the Universe's DNA—radiation, baryonic matter, dark matter, dark energy, and forces of vitality and intelligence beyond human comprehension. I'm now the living embodiment of a lightning bolt, my skeletal frame electrified in an iridescent glow of cosmic blue and white.

"Ah! Fuck! Frankie." I grab my temples. "How far... how far can you extend the floor?"

"Angela!" I hear Frankie's voice, but I can't see him. "Angela! What's wrong?"

"The floor, Frankie! How *far*?"

"Pretty far. Why?"

"Because we need..." A trillion trillion trillion bits of information consume me, as if I've been organically plugged into the mainframe of the Cosmos. Without my eyes, I see the creation of the Universe. I see its destruction. Its rebirth. Stars coming to life. Going supernova. Black holes swallowing light. Nebulas pulsing with cosmologic gases and radiation. Sentient beings of every form bursting with life, rebelling against death and decay.

And clinging to hope amongst the infinite cosmologic terrain.

"We need to help her," I say, "before it's too late. For all of us. Before we—"

I scream.

The Helix knows my organic body and mind cannot comprehend or withstand the sheer magnitude of what it's trying to share with me. It removes me from my physical form, releasing my very essence.

That essence melts and reforms like molten lava of the soul. Its immeasurable heat flash-boils my spirit, causing it to bubble and steam, catching fire, like pressing flesh against searing stovetop coils. Flesh peels away in chunks and layers, then reduced to charcoal.

The process repeats. Electrifying me. Melting me. Reducing me to black ash.

Over and over again as I cling to the memory of my physical body.

Until it knows I can tolerate no more.

Back in solid, human form, I collapse on the walkway beneath the DNA twist. Steam and electricity hiss off my skin.

Frankie kneels close, reaches out, but retracts his hand. He's afraid to touch me. "Angela. What happened?"

Every inch of me throbs with blistering waves of pain.

"She's not gonna make it, Frankie. It's Ilya. It's all because of him."

"Ilya?" Frankie finally takes my hand. "He attacked the Helix? But why?"

I struggle as Frankie helps me back up onto my feet.

"He was trying to save her," I say. "But he got it all wrong."

Frankie utilizes the hydraulic-controlled platform. He raises us up and beyond this section of twist, along the seemingly endless contours of the Helix until, finally, as if we'd scaled the side of a coastal mountain range, we're on top. Frankie retracts the flooring behind us so that it disappears in folds beneath itself, then lowers the platform along the other side.

We follow the helical pitch for more than a mile. Floating around us are clusters of tiny blue and red bubbles. Like cosmic fireflies, they drift and swirl, the clusters growing denser and more concentrated the farther we travel along the twist.

Then I realize. They're not bubbles. They're fragments of the wounded Helix. Pairs of DNA sequences broken off into globules.

I gasp.

Along the ribs of the Helix is an open wound, a gash as large and wide as the mouth of the Chabaqua River. Flowing from it is a surge of her blood and plasma, dissipating into the Cosmos. We practically swim through the current of infected discharge to reach the wound site.

"I'm sorry," I say to her. "I'm so sorry."

Cautiously, I reach my hand to an undamaged section of the

twist. Her entire self grumbles, a reaction to the sensitivity of the wound. Then she settles down, allowing me to reunite with her. I can't heal her, can't save her. Maybe she can save us.

"I've got some new equipment," Frankie says. "A more direct interface."

He produces a diagnostic tool, attached to what looks like a monitoring pad on the end of an EKG sensor. He secures the pad against the Helix's contour, the pad connected wirelessly to Frankie's laptop.

"*What happened?*" Frankie types, then taps ENTER.

A readout appears on his screen. "*Cracks.*"

Frankie types again. "*What cracks?*"

"*Pain. Coming. Bad.*"

"Frankie," I say. "Can I...?" He steps aside.

I type into the keyboard. "*Where's your brother? Your twin?*"

When we first encountered the Helix, she'd been cut off from her twin brother. The injury she'd suffered then was the result of a failed attempt to reconnect with him. Another Helix.

"*Twin. Brother. Yes.*"

"*Where is he?*"

The cursor on my screen blinks over and over. Her golden waves of energy glow bright, then increasingly dim, like the color of stale honey. Rather than a purr, I feel the Helix shudder. A sigh of heartbreak.

"*Alone.*"

"*Your brother? He's alone? Where?*"

Another sigh. A sad hum of grief, as if she's crying.

"*Alone.*"

"*He's alone or...?*" Damn. She's talking about herself. "*Is he dead?*"

There's a silence now, a cold and dreadful loneliness. The cursor blinks.

"*Dead.*"

The Helix unleashes her grief. The vibrations are so loud and intense they rattle the fabric of spacetime we're occupying, nearly tossing us off the platform.

"*The detonations?*" I type. "*Did they hurt your brother?*"

"*The bad man. The good man.*"

"Two men?"

"Same."

"The good man is the bad man?"

"Same."

"What did he do?"

"Heal. Hurt."

"The good man who is the bad man? He tried to heal spacetime? But broke it instead?"

"Pain."

"The fault lines? Are they real?"

"Stop cracks."

"I'm trying. But how?"

"Stop cracks. Twin. Brother."

"Your brother tried to stop him?"

"Twin. Brother. Stop cracks. Too late."

"The good man who is the bad man. He detonated a fault line? Destroyed a system? Is that what happened to your brother? Killed? By debris?"

"Crushed."

If I didn't know any better, I'd say the Helix is sobbing.

"Slow death. Couldn't help. Love. Hurt."

I feel the diminution of her remarkable lifeforce, the Helix's interstellar plasma spewing from the mammoth wounds, and flow into the Cosmos.

Much like Dolores did, she's bleeding out.

"Is that what happened to you? Injured?"

"Searched for twin. Brother."

"Did you find him?"

"Too far. Can't move. Dying."

I get it now.

"That's why you called me. In the dreamscape."

"Find you."

"You did. But why as Dolores?"

The wounded Helix *whums* with another band of golden energy.

"Love."

"You loved her?"

"Love. Buried."

"Whose love is buried?"

The cursor blinks. And blinks. And blinks.

"Yours."

Standing in the shadow of this beautiful creature, I'm reminded there's no end to the layers of brutality we, as the inhabitants of this Universe, are unwilling to mine. No bottom to the well of indignities, subjugations, and humiliations we endure and inflict upon one another, often for no better reason than thinking we're right. Or to do it, just to see if we can.

And then in moments like this, when I'm right there, when I'm so close to eating my gun because I can't take even one more setback, abuse, or debasement, not one more brush with evil, I understand she's right. I think of the ones I love. The love I bury within me so it can't be used against me.

The life I live, the cases I take, puts me in a position where, from time to time, my friends end up in danger. Some of them are gone now. Because of me.

One friend is dead. Another's cut me off. One more about to drop me, and a partner gone missing, collateral damage from a battle of wills Whistler knew nothing about until he was in too deep to get out.

But this is where I live. Here, in darkness and shadow, in the distant reaches of the Cosmos—this is where I shine. I stop killers and madmen. Search for runaways no one else cares about. Submit to the folds in spacetime. Take a beating. Take another.

Some love me for what I do. Others hate me, some fear me. Even more will never know that I live this life, a life I chose as much as it chose me, because I believe, delusional or not, that it's my purpose to help those who feel they have nowhere else to turn, on-realm or off.

And to do it as well as I can, as often as I can, for as long as I can. Because one day, maybe soon, maybe today, maybe even right here, right now, my time in this life will end. The story of Angela Hardwicke will have closed its final chapter.

So yeah. As much as I don't like to talk about it, as much as I bury that love, don't say the words out loud because once you do you can't ever take them back... I live the life I do and take the cases I choose, absorb the pain, navigate the madness, so others don't have to.

I didn't go to sleep one night as one person then wake up another. This Angela Hardwicke? I earned this me. Fought for it. Paid in ways I can barely endure.

I know I'm damaged and imperfect and on the edge of my own demise. But for however much longer my tenure will last, I'm going to keep being this Angela Hardwicke. This is who I am. I'm not gonna stop.

"The good man who is the bad man. He tried to heal the fault lines?"

"Blind. Mistake. Fire."

"Frankie. What does that mean? *Blind? Fire?* I don't…"

He looks at me. "I got it." Frankie types. *"The good man who is the bad man. He's blind to his own mistake?"*

"Consumed."

Frankie looks to me again. "He thinks the detonations will seal the fault lines. But instead of a topical healing agent, the gel is acting like napalm. And the worse he makes the problem…"

"The more he doubles down. He's got the sickness. He can't stop."

The cursor blinks. *"More."*

I take back the keyboard. *"More… fault lines? They're coming?"*

"Soon."

The Helix shudders again. A wave of golden energy surges along the entirety of itself.

"Where?"

"Stop."

"How? The good man who is the bad man. Where do I find him? Where is he?"

"Angela," Frankie says. "Ask her about the damage."

I do.

"Fix. Heal."

"We can stop the fault lines? We can heal it?"

"Trust. Listen. Heal."

"I do trust you. I am listening. I am trying to heal it. But how?"

Another shudder of golden energy, weaker, dimmer. She's dying. The cursor blinks on the screen. And blinks. And blinks. And blinks. And then:

"Good boy."
"Good boy?"
"Good boy."
"Eric? You mean Whistler?"
The cursor blinks. And blinks.
"Trapped. Stuck. Find."
"I know he's stuck. But where? Where is he?"
"Ship. Five."
"Ship?" I ask aloud. "What ship? What...?" The Five. The Wednesday Five. An elite squad with advanced tech.
"The Wednesday Five? They have a ship. Whistler's on the ship?"
"Trapped."
"I know! But where? Where is he trapped? How do I find him?"
In synchronicity, the blink of the cursor and the wave of golden energy circulates slower... slower... slower. Powering down.

I walk away from the keyboard, put my hand against the Helix. "I'm sorry." I pet her tenderly. "I'm sorry for your pain. I'm sorry for your grief. But most of all, I'm sorry I didn't listen. I know I shouldn't carry the blame for mistakes that aren't mine, but I can't always tell the difference. In my dreams and with the headaches... I thought you were *warning* me. I didn't realize you *needed* me. I'm sorry I got it wrong. But I'm here now. If it's not too late."

Her membrane nearly ashen now, the great Helix lets out a final moan, a siren song of heartbreak and hope. Of love and death.

To her brother.
To the Cosmos.
To me.

With one last surge, a fading wave of golden energy hums through the Helix. The twists darken. Lighten. Darken again.
Whum...... whum......
Whum.
Until its lifeforce is no more.

"What do I do, Frank? Where do I go from here?"
Frankie looks upon me with his dad eyes, through a soul only a parent understands. That to love your children means

to live in fear, every nanosecond, that the worst possible outcome may unfold even as you ignore history, ignore reality, and hope for the best. And grab hold of whatever joy you can along the way.

"She left you something," he says. "Here. On the screen. Look."

The great beast drifts lifeless before me. Its twists are devoid of energy. Yet on the screen, next to the blinking cursor, is one final message. One last clue I'd been told to follow all along but didn't understand. Until now:

Dante.

CHAPTER 24

I go back to the beginning. Not Kimmie-slash-Nóirín the beginning. My first meeting with Dante.

The Helix was telling me in my dreams.

The warmth of the forest. *June.*

The bugs that crawled over me. *Junebug.*

Dante said *coffee. Junebug's Diner.*

Ideally, I'd be back here at dawn, to recreate the environment from my earlier meeting. I don't have time to wait. It's almost 630 p.m., an orange sun in its steady shimmering drift toward the horizon. I count twenty-seven people here, eighteen customers, the rest cooks, waitstaff, dishwasher, busboy, manager, and a greeter.

The greeter, a young woman with a chrome left leg, greets me. "Hi, how can I—?"

"I'm gonna sit there." Without her consultation, I take my place in the same spot, in the same booth I was in with Dante. "Gimme a bacon cheeseburger, will ya? Cheddar. Well done. Bacon extra crispy. Fries extra crispy. And a beer. Hell yes. I'm dying for a beer."

"Uh," she says, "ohhh... kay. I'll tell your waitress."

I sit back in the booth. I start over. I run the drill. The same drill I drilled with Whistler so many times he was ready to punch me in the face. Which is how I know I drilled the right amount.

The silver bell activates—*bing bing.* From the kitchen counter a skinny waiter stacks his arms with a plate of fried chicken and mashed potatoes, a bowl of split pea soup, and a pastrami and rye bread stacked so thick it could choke a hippo.

Diners talk. Plates clack. Utensils clatter. Kitchen crew bark orders at each other.

A patron from outside opens the front glass door, letting in a whoosh of night air and thrum from the streets. Table for three.

I study the layout. Follow the seams in the ceiling and the embedded high-hat lights. The dozens of June bug paintings, sketches, and neon signs mounted on the walls. I carefully study the flow of activity. Waiters and the busboy pushing in and out of the swinging double doors leading into and out of the kitchen. Three customers eat at the counter. A waitress refills their drinks.

It's not long before my food hits the table when I realize it's dark outside now, the interior and exterior lights sharper against the contrast of night.

A customer walks by, accesses the restroom in the alcove a dozen feet behind me. Which signals to me I'm being too rigid. I sit on the opposite side of the booth to switch my perspective, giving me a different vantage point. Next to the restroom alcove is a side entrance with a revolving door, leading back out onto the sidewalk.

A boy about five years old rushes over to the revolving door next to the restrooms.

"D'tal!" His father shouts. "Don't!"

D'tal slips inside one of the three cylindrical enclosures. The divisions hang on a central shaft above and rotate around a vertical axis. With his little hands, D'tal pushes on the tinted glass, giggling as she spins.

His dad waits for the opening. He shoves his arm between divisions, his shoulder pinned against the mechanism.

"D'tal!" he shouts, and with his foot, holds the door in place.

D'tal giggles. "More, Daddy! More!"

His dad sighs, reaches for his shoulder, grimaces. "It's not a toy!"

"But it's fun!"

"I'm sure it is. But it's late and you need a bath."

"Aww," D'tal laments.

"I know," his dad says, the vein in his neck throbbing. The joys of parenthood. "We'll get a cookie."

My mind immediately goes to Owen, who used to pull the

same kind of things on me. He still does. Probably always will.

Safety restored, I watch them leave, the dad firmly gripping D'tal's hand.

They exit through the revolving door. At least, I think that's what happens. The panes of glass in the revolving door are tinted such that once they spun through, they seemed to just... disappear.

I follow inside the cylindrical enclosure. It's a tight fit and moving continuously, with little room to maneuver or time to investigate. The glass panes are solid. Nothing odd or suspicious here. I exit onto the sidewalk and the hustle-bustle of the city at night.

Headlights blind me. I shield my eyes, turn one way, then another, looking for D'tal and his dad. I don't see them anywhere. They couldn't have gone far. But there's so many people, so much activity it's easy to fold into the crowd. Still, they must be... there they are. I see them hustle across the street, then turn the next corner.

I don't know what I thought I was going to find. I head back through the revolving door, and into the diner. I sit back in my booth, facing the revolving door. I eat the rest of my burger and fries, looking for a clue, anything that'll tip me off, that'll lead me to...

This is where Dante was sitting. Where he was studying me. But also giving him a view of the streetscape behind me, gazing through the window near the revolving door. There's a mirror mounted on the wall. Reflected at me, I see the rest of the diner behind and over my shoulder. Just like Dante could.

That's why he was sitting here. Classic surveillance technique. From this one spot he could see ahead, and the action reflected behind him without having to move. No one could sneak up on him.

I take another sip of beer. As I do, staring at the revolving door mechanism, my gut cinches. Flutter in my chest. I get up again, look around, to see if anyone's paying attention to me. Doesn't seem so.

I produce my scout orb, let it hover within one of the revolving door's three cylindrical divisions. I push it one rotation forward, then get inside the division behind it, separated by the tinted glass pane. The orb hovers up and down, examining the inside of the division in front of me, sending a signal to my lens. I see what it sees. Nothing of value.

On the next rotation, I exit the enclosure back inside the diner. I push it around, then stop it to scoop up my orb. I repeat the process, one division ahead, examining the next enclosure. Again, nothing of value.

Back out on the sidewalk, a nearby billboard's neon red and blue lights reflect off a passing cab's windshield. It's probably pointless, but I repeat the experiment one more time, placing the orb inside the division ahead of me, the last one, as I follow one behind.

As I suspected, there's nothing of value. Nothing I can find. Except...

In the corner of my eye is a tiny fluctuation, like the spike of a Geiger counter. This happens often, my lens picking up stray radiation or power readings. It's probably nothing. Probably—

I manually stop the door's revolution and step inside the division with my orb. Even in the tight space, I run the tips of my fingers along the tinted glass pane. Up to the lid above me, down along the seams. I scrunch and twist, crouch and squirm, to run my fingers along the edges in the floor. I don't find anything. No nubs or protrusions. No latches. Just a revolving door.

I don't know what I'm looking for, what I'm supposed to find.

Think, Angela. Think.

What am I missing? What don't I see? What did he say?

The Wednesday Five.

Check with Doug Finer. Check with...

Staring at the themed decorations on the walls, the colored insects, my mouth hangs open. My mind flooded in a tidal wave of realization. He was telling me the whole time.

Check with Doug Finer.

Check with Doug Finer.

No. Not Doug Finer.

The diner.

Junebug Diner.

I immediately slip back into one of the revolving door divisions, but grip the divider's edge, barely catching my hand. Before the revolution closes me in, I drop the scout orb in the division behind me, not in front. Giving me a new perspective. I push through, thinking of D'tal as he spun round and round. I do the same. Rather than exit onto the sidewalk, I let the door spin on its axis, picking up momentum.

It happens fast. Someone else exits the revolving door mechanism ahead of me, out onto the sidewalk. Walking briskly away. I can only see her from behind, but it's a woman, about my height, with straight, dirty blonde hair. Just like mine.

Wearing an olive-green utility jacket. Just like mine.

Blue jeans. Just like mine.

And black sneakers. Just like mine.

I think it's me.

I push again until the door revolves all the way around and exit onto the sidewalk. I chase after me, who can't be me but who, from behind, looks exactly like me.

My lens. The energy spike. It's stronger now, with multiple peaks.

I run up behind her, pushing through sidewalk traffic. "Hey! You! Angela! Hold on!"

I extend my hand to grab the back of her shoulder. To grab me who can't be me. I'm just about there, my fingers about to…

She's gone.

I stop, frantically turning this way and that. How could I have lost her?

She was right there, in front of me, then she vanished. I run to the nearest corner, look in all directions. Street traffic. Pedestrians. Shops and billboards. Monorail in the distance on an elevated track.

I send my scout orb to scour the area, to follow her image and trajectory I recorded through my lens. I crisscross the street, so that I'm staring at the diner. Through the storefront windows I see multiple customers, the manager, the waitstaff. But not her. The me who couldn't be me.

My orb circles back, with no trace of her.

I know it's easy to lose someone in a crowd. But how do you

lose someone from beneath your fingertips unless...

I rush back to the revolving door, insert myself into one of the divisions. I push forward, so the mechanism is rotating on its axis again. And remember what Bernice gave me. From inside the hidden seam in my jacket I remove the signal booster. I secure it to the orb.

I'm working through the spin at its normal velocity. My lens records a power spike, picking up the source. The orb sends more data through my lens. The me who couldn't have been me.

Because it wasn't me.

It was a hologram.

Holy shit. The power source. It's under my feet. It's right below...

CHAPTER 25

The floor vanishes.

In a *whoosh*, I'm slurped through a long and circuitous pneumatic tube system with several twists and curls. From darkness it drops me onto a foam pad, which absorbs my energy.

At least fifty feet below street level, I'm in a stone cavern. There's a waterway a dozen feet up ahead, shimmering against gray walls. I find a glow stick in an open crate of supplies. Activated, the glow stick fills this secret underground space with fluorescent blue. I round the corner, walking along the water, when I come upon another passageway leading to a second alcove. I turn into it and—

"Whistler!"

Hovering off the ground, he's trapped inside an energy bubble. The surface morphs in shape and color so that Whistler, though stationary, drifts in and out of my sightline. And behind him is a craft. This is it.

The Wednesday Five.

That's *The Specter*. This is their base.

Various computer terminals, glass pods, equipment, workstations, tools, and tech I've never seen are scattered about.

I rush over to the energy bubble, Whistler phasing in and out of focus as the surface continues to morph. "Whistler! Can you hear me? Are you okay?"

"Mazzche. Getzzzz me outtzzz."

"How?"

"Zzzjj… zzzjjj… ship. Inside the szzjhip. Turn it offzz!"

Supported by pneumatic hinges, *The Specter*'s entry ramp is open. I go inside. Immediately to my right is the cockpit, with two pilot bucket seats up front near the control panel. Basic power is on, a low hum emanating throughout the ship.

Engines, communications, weapons, life support, medical bay, gravity matrix, defensive shields, cloaking device, telepod, docking thrusters, and a multitude of other systems.

To my left is the ship's interior, the walls lined with equipment, control panels, and storage slots. I don't know my way around, don't know how to turn off the stasis bubble.

Extending from the walls are individual transport pods, two on one side, three on the other. The pods are lying flat, each with a glass dome. The first pod is empty. The undersides of the other domes are covered in frost crystals and condensation.

There are people inside.

If I had to guess, the rest of the Wednesday Five. Life support panels on the sides of each pod monitor their heart rates, body temperature, oxygen, metabolic levels, and neural activity. If I'm reading this correctly, they're in hibernation for long-term travel. Or unscheduled prison time.

I activate the diagnostic scanner in my lens to read various instruments within *The Specter*. I don't want to mess with the hibernation pods and risk injuring or killing any of the Wednesday Five. My lens analyzes the energy coming from the stasis bubble Whistler's trapped in. My gaze follows the path throughout the underside of the ship and to one of the control panels in the cockpit.

My lens digitally traces the power dial, highlighting it with a green digital glow. I need to turn it down to zero, then turn off the three switches above the elliptical coordinates, in the proper sequence.

"Whistler!" I shout, hopefully loud enough so that he can hear me through the bubble.

"*Whatzz?*"

"I'm gonna get you out. Hold on!"

"*Holdzz onto whatzz?*"

"I don't know! But get ready!"

I reduce the intensity of the statis bubble. The *whum* of power grows softer and weaker, until it's completely off. I skitter halfway down the ramp to see if it's working.

The energy bubble is gone, but he's still trapped in place.

"Mache! Get me out! Turn it off!"

No more interference. That's progress.

"Mache! It hurts! Turn it off!"

I dash back inside. "Here we go." In sequence I deactivate the first switch, the second, the third.

"Ow shit!"

I rush back out and down the ramp. Whistler has collapsed onto the ground. I kneel beside him, take his head in my lap. "Hey... hey." I pet his face, then lean over, and kiss his forehead, press my lips there. I hold him close to me.

"You," he rasps, his voice weak and breathy, "you found it. The revolving door."

"That hologram's a good trick. It fooled me."

"Well"—Whistler grimaces, supports himself on his elbows, then takes my hand until he's back up on his feet—"you've always been thick. Stick with me, kid. I'll show you the ropes."

I smile, place my hand on his cheek. Hold it there. "I know you will."

Dressed in black cargo pants, black pullover, and black sneakers, he eases away from me, shuffles over to one of the glass-pod rooms. He retrieves some sort of red vitamin water out of a minifridge.

"Found this earlier." He sips from it. "Ooh!" His eyes jolt open. "I don't know what's in this, but it's good shit." He sips until he's chugging, the entirety of the liquid disappearing down his throat. He exhales heartily, wipes his mouth on his sleeve. "The statis field kept my vitals in check. But, man... I needed that."

He steps over a mechanical box on the floor, stretching his right leg over the top. With his foot about to land, his eyes flutter and fall back into his head. He loses his balance, falls to the side. His shoulder bangs into a glass partition. He sinks onto his knees.

"Whoa! Easy." I go to him. "You okay?"

His head drops, chin to his chest, then bobbles back up. He looks at me groggily. "Mache. The Wednesday Five. They tried to stop Ilya. But he got to them first." He squints, holds it, then tries to paw his way back up to his feet. "And me."

I take Whistler by the elbow and shoulder. Upright, he walks gingerly to a workstation. I ease him into a rolling chair. Shimmering water projects onto the walls behind him.

"Whistler, what the hell happened?"

He explains that, under Tarrish's direction, he was tracking down a lead the ICD had gotten from the Guild member in custody. The plan was to put The Wednesday Five on it, but they were becoming less and less accountable. The Institute and ICD were in constant gridlock about who should have final supervision over the Five and what they investigated, allowing them to fall off the grid. Nobody knew what they were up to.

"Tarrish had me investigate them. He doesn't trust the Institute. He acknowledges the need for Patches. But he doesn't like that what they do, and how they do it, is beyond his purview."

"Sounds like the Tarrish I know. And he was right."

"He was," Whistler says, "and he wasn't." I hand him another vitamin drink. He sips from it. "I heard GGZ had been hired for a hit job on-realm. I followed him to the diner."

The pieces start coming together. I produce my phone, pull up a photo of Dante.

"With him?"

"N-no," Whistler says. "Not him. He was with a woman."

"What woman? Who?"

"Don't know. Never saw her before. She was in sweats, with a hoodie and a baseball cap. No makeup. GGZ said he needed stress release before pulling a big job. But... hang on." He takes my phone, studies it more carefully. He's up on his feet, pacing. "The clock rings. Mache. I've seen this guy. Yeah." Whistler looks up from my phone. "I've seen him. He was... oh shit. He was two booths behind GGZ. He was..."

"A pimp. A nasty one."

"A pimp?" Whistler finishes the vitamin water. "But what's he got to do with—?"

"He's dead. Ilya did it."

I explain about the attack at Dante's crib, the bag, Aiko, her missing hand, the bracelet, and the final coordinates.

"That's how I found this place," Whistler says, his energy

returning. "I was onto GGZ. He went out through the revolving door. I followed him onto the sidewalk. He was fifteen, maybe twenty feet ahead and just—"

"Vanished."

"No. He rounded the corner. I was about to follow him. But then I saw—"

"Saw what?" I interrupt, nervous with anticipation.

"I spotted Ilya. He went into the diner. No way that was a coincidence. I sent my scout orb to follow him. He entered through the double doors in front, went to the counter, ordered a coffee to go, then exited through the revolving door. Once he was back on the sidewalk, I followed him, too. Then about twenty feet away, *he* vanished. Just... gone."

"Then how'd you find him?"

Whistler flicks his eyebrows at me. "Of all things... a police drone. One flew overhead. I used some tech Tarrish gave me and piggybacked on the signal. I reviewed the video. The security drone sent a signal sweep down at street level... and cut Ilya's legs off. It was clearly a hologram. Which made no sense. Unless it was there to throw me off the scent. I traced it back to the revolving door, then down here."

I'm still trying to understand how I never saw the diner before. I realize I can't know every greasy spoon in E-Town, but I would've remembered a place like this. Wouldn't I? Or is that just the way things go? Hiding in plain sight?

"Did you find Ilya? What did you do? What did he...?"

"I found the others. The Wednesday Five. The other four. Ilya took 'em out."

"He what?"

Whistler leads me back onto *The Specter*.

"Her." He gestures to the third pod. "With the cut under her chin." We can see her through the dome. Oval eyes, ebony skin. "Ojore. I heard one of them call her that before passing out." Whistler says she was in bad shape, but the only one still conscious. He didn't know how long it would take to get medical attention, so he put her in stasis, then left the ship to get a signal. To call for help. "I stepped on a booby trap. It was right outside the onramp. Caught me in the orbit. I was there the whole time. I couldn't get out. And had no signal."

We're going to have to do something I don't want to do. I study Ojore's face. The beauty and the pain. It's like looking at Nini, so much like Nini, I almost can't tell them apart.

"We have to wake her up."

"No, Mache. It could kill her."

"I know." I run my fingertips over the pod's control panel. "But there's no choice."

We activate the various controls to bring her out of stasis. An I.V. tube inserts into her arm, pumping her with vitamins and stimulant. The pod dome slides open. Like a hospital bed, the back of the support bench she's lying on raises up forty-five degrees.

"Ojore," Whistler whispers. "Ojore."

Her eyes flutter, then open. "Where am I?"

"You're in a stasis pod. On the ship. You're injured. I'm sorry to do this, but we're out of time."

"Ojore. I'm Hardwicke. He's Whistler. What happened here? Where's Ilya?"

She struggles to answer. "He... attacked us. Where's—?"

"They're in the other pods," Whistler says.

"Alive?"

"Barely. We have to hurry."

Ojore's breathing strengthens and weakens. Blood soaks through medical bandages on her torso, both legs, and one arm.

"Ojore," I say. "Ilya found the fault line files at the Institute, didn't he? He broke the encryption. He followed the coordinates."

"Y...yes. He detonated a charge in an uninhabited suh...system. After all those years... he finally found it."

I lean a little closer. "Did he tell the Institute? The ICD?"

She swallows weakly. "No. The shock waves from the charge. It changed him. It messed with his mind. It disrupted his biorhythms. It drove him mad."

"Like there's a *whumming* in your head no one else can hear."

"Ilya complained about the noise. He was too close to the blast. When he ruptured the fabric of spacetime, it triggered PPD—Paranoid Personality Disorder. By the time we figured it out, he was too far gone."

I swallow hard. Has that been happening to me? The *whum-ming* in my head from the Helix. Did it make me paranoid? Amplify my fears? If so, can I trust my own thoughts? My instincts? Or am I chasing a ghost? So I ask, unsure if I want the answer. Because what if it happens to me?

"He got worse, didn't he?"

"Ilya set the charge without telling us. He"—she coughs painfully, blood thickening the gauze pads on her chest—"he said he could fix the fault lines. He needed to coat them with gel. From the Institute."

"So he did it again."

"Two more systems to prove his theory. But the gel didn't work."

"Let me guess. It only intensified his conviction. Every *no* got him closer to a *yes*."

"He was obsessed," Ojore says. "He barely ate or slept. He worked round the clock. The last system he destroyed was heavily populated. He said he wasn't using enough gel. But if he kept at it, he'd find the right formulation, on the right coordinates, along the right fault lines. He said that system was a critical link in the chain."

"Eddie," I say aloud. "Damn."

"Eddie?" Whistler asks. "What did *he* do?"

"I was at the Institute. I saw the damage, the dead systems. They knew all along."

Ojore's pulse is holding. "I don't know. Maybe, maybe not. We wanted to report back to the Institute. Let them handle the fault lines. This was guh—" She seizes. Her eyes roll back into her head. Warning light flashes. Frantic distress beeps.

"Mache! What do we do?"

"Hold her steady! I need to check her lines."

Whistler grabs her with both hands as I run my fingers through the medical bed.

"Here it is." Her I.V. came loose. I reinsert it. She stabilizes. Her heartbeat slows. "Hey... You with us?"

Ojore's eyes flutter, then open half-way. "What... what happened?"

"You're okay," I say, relieved. "You're okay."

Whistler grabs my arm, pulls me aside. "Mache. You can't. She's won't make it."

I look at Ojore. She's weak. In pain. But I don't see Ojore. I see Nini staring back at me. I see Dolores. I see Aiko. I see Dante. Everyone who hasn't made it back because they drifted into my orbit. Or got pulled into it.

"She might not," I say. "But we don't know enough. And we're out of time." I return to Ojore. "I know you're tired, but this is important. You wanted to tell the Institute about the fault lines."

"Ilya... he wouldn't let us."

"What?" Whistler says. "Why? That's insane. He founded the Wednesday Five for that very reason. Why wouldn't he...?

Ojore is fighting to stay lucid. "He said... he said... it had to be him. He understood what the Cosmos was going through. No one else could do it. He said he could hear this... call... that *whum* you said. He was fuh... following it to the source. I don't know what that means."

"I have a pretty good idea," I say. "Then what?"

Ojore's slipping in and out of focus. From the best we can tell, she says Ilya admitted to his plan. He hired Guild members they'd encountered to set off a round of explosives along various fault lines. Ilya surmised the detonations didn't resolve the problem because he was setting them off one at a time. He's convinced that if he sets off a *series* of detonations, with the healing gel layered on specific coordinates, it'll heal the entirety of spacetime.

"He's trying"—Ojore struggles to remain conscious—"to save everyone. But he's gonna kill them instead."

"He snapped," I say. "The rest of you tried to stop him."

Ojore wheezes. "The way he saw it, *we* betrayed *him*. He knew our systems, how we fight. He used it against us."

"Then how'd you end up in the pods?"

"He just needed us out of the way. He put the others in stasis. Except for me. I'd gotten off a shot, clipped him in the arm. After that... I blacked out."

"I found her out there," Whistler says. "I got her inside the pod, then went back outside to call Tarrish. But like I said, I never made the call. I got trapped in the orbit."

"You'd... better hurry." Ojore's eyes sink beneath her lids. "He's gonna set another charge. He found the trigger point. Somewhu... somewhere on-realm. He does that... it'll take us all out."

CHAPTER 26

The final rock to be thrown on the ice. Seventeen star systems, scattered across trillions of light years. No previously known connections to each other. Now splintering across the fault lines of Existence, eroding the infrastructure of spacetime. Destroying planets. Wiping out civilizations. And next, the entirety of the Cosmos.

The great purge.

I call Tarrish, explain the situation. He's sending extraction and medical teams to see if they can save the Wednesday Five and, if possible, collect any evidence that might be useful in finding out where Ilya is headed next. The trigger point.

"He's en route," I say. "Wants to debrief."

Whistler stares at the waterway beneath the city. "I don't know what else I can tell him."

"You didn't see anything, hear anything?"

"No. Like I said. I found my way down here, found them, then got caught in…" He studies the canal, the glow stick's blue light giving the water a shimmery effect. "Hey. You see that?" He kneels, points. "Mache. Look. My lens is picking it up. I've resynched to yours. There's something down there."

I kneel beside him, focus through my own lens. "You're right. What the hell is that?"

"Could be anything. Could be nothing."

"Or," I say, "could be something."

I scramble around the Wednesday Five bunker. I find a gripper in a pile of tools. I stick the claw end into the water, manipulate the gripping action from the handle. It takes me a few tries, but I slowly pull up whatever it is until it's completely exposed.

I let it dangle above the surface, water dripping off it.

Whistler cringes. "What the...?"

It's Aiko's severed arm. I lay it out on a workbench, wipe it down with a towel. I slip on surgical gloves, turn the wrist over. "See this here? These raised marks beneath the skin? They're coordinates. That's where Ilya's going. To set the final charge."

"All right! Let's go! Where?"

"That's just it." I look around again, for a clue, a signal. Something. "I don't know."

"What do you mean *you don't know*? You just said they're the—"

"I know *what* they are. I don't know *where* they are."

"*He* obviously does."

"I know! But Ilya must have..." It's coming to me. "You were trapped. The Five already immobilized. But he came back here anyway. He came back *here*. *With* the arm. Why did he come back here? What was he...?"

"Hold on. Ilya sent the coordinates to GGZ. *Before* he came back here. That means Ilya already knew them. He didn't need to confirm. Unless"—Whistler looks around, then back to me—"this place. Down here. It was his escape route. He was gonna set the charge on a timer, then bolt. He was prepping *The Specter*."

"Yeah." I nod, though I'm unconvinced. "Could be. Maybe. But... no. I don't think so."

"Then what are you thinking?"

"Let's play it out. If he sets the final charge and it works, he fixes spacetime. He stabilizes the structure and integrity of the Cosmos. Not a bad day's work. Even Patches can't do that. He'd want the credit. And bask in the glory. But if it *doesn't* work... if he destroys the realm, the ship, the fucking Cosmos..."

Whistler nods. "There won't be anywhere to go because there won't be anywhere left. Okay. Then why *did* he come back?"

I feel it, then I hear it. The click of the safety being switched off.

"I wanted to make sure they were okay." In full gear, but without his mask, Ilya points a Taylor Five Eight handgun at us, pulse rifle slung over his shoulder. "We lived together, we served together. They were my team. But they lost focus. To them, it was an assignment. To me, it was *everything*. They lost faith in me because I lost faith in them. I'm great with theory, not leadership. I work better on my own."

"Don't do this. It won't work. It *doesn't* work. Every bomb you set off... every system you target... the damage is worse."

"I couldn't wrap my head around it." Ilya steps closer to us, in short paces. "Until I saw how big it really was, yet how simple it all works." He gestures his gun at Whistler. "You. On your knees."

"I just got out."

"I can put you back in."

Whistler bristles, clenches his fists. Goes down on one knee, then the other.

"Hands behind your head."

Ilya takes one of Whistler's hands, loops his wrist with a zip tie. He pulls Whistler's arm down and behind his back, then does the same to the other wrist.

"It's an old shipping lane down here. It leads right out to the river, beneath half the city. I got an alert. Security breach. I figured it was you."

With Whistler neutralized, Ilya shuffles over to me. He presses the mouth of the gun against my temple with enough force to convince me he'll pull the trigger if need be. He reaches inside my jacket, removes my gun, slips it behind his waist.

"You're gonna kill everyone," I say. "You're literally going to implode the Cosmos. Every planet, every star system, every civilization. Every living thing. All of Existence. Destroyed. All because of you. The damage you caused already? It'll be like a grain of pollen in a hurricane. Too small to matter."

"I know you think I'm crazy. They all do. But I know what's wrong now. I see the mistake."

Whistler pushes back. "How many people you kill so far? Two billion? Three? All to prove a theory?"

"To prove I was *right*!"

"Mass murder is right?"

"My *theory* was right. My *plan* was right. The *execution* was wrong. As a Patch, we analyze the fabric of spacetime.

We study its elements. The texture, its configurations. It's a vast and elegant system. It's also imperfect. Conceptually. Structurally. Physically. Susceptible to its own demise. That's why I formed the Wednesday Five. To find cracks in the system. With fault lines... and trigger points. And use them to rebuild. And reform. So it never happens again. No more patchwork. A permanent fix."

"Patches don't do this," Whistler says. "They fix. Not destroy."

"I *was* a Patch. But not anymore. For that very reason."

"Because you want to break things?"

"Because their minds are too small! Being a Patch isn't just a job. We can feel vibrations the rest of you can't. Tremors of energy, ripples of pain. We're more like doctors than construction workers. If you know that, you also know that severing a gangrenous limb isn't barbaric. It's to save the patient. It's putting what's best ahead of what's pleasant or preferred. It's having the conviction to do what's needed when the rest of you won't."

The Whistler I met five years ago wouldn't have been able to handle Ilya the way he is now.

"Or maybe you *like* the pain. Genocide wrapped in self-righteousness."

Ilya cranes his neck, his eyes pulled into an insulted, bemused stare. "Who, exactly, is self-righteous? Do you weep for a star that goes supernova? Of course you don't. You don't even know when it happens. But I do. I feel that pain. I experience that loss. The galaxies surrounding those stars become lifeless thereafter. It drops me to my knees. Yet you weep for the death of strangers and tell me I'm the one who's heartless."

Whistler still isn't having it. "You just described every zealot in history."

Ilya ignores the pushback. "I didn't want to hurt those people. I had nothing against them. It was a matter of calculus and perspective. Billions to save trillions. I learned. Every detonation taught me something new, got me closer to the solution. My mistake was setting them off one at a time. The theory *was* right. The *scale* was wrong. I need to set the charges. All at once."

"Plans are just mistakes you haven't made yet. And in your case, the more your plans fail, the more you double down. The scale isn't the problem." Whistler narrows his gaze. "You are."

"That's what they said." Ilya gestures to *The Specter*, pulling the gun from my forehead. "But they knew I was right. And hated themselves for it. That's the thing about honor. It's easier to keep when there's no threat to lose it."

A Patch first, soldier second, Ilya's inadvertently exposed himself. Putting my years of combat training ahead of his, I pull out my taser, swing it at his exposed knee. But he learned from last time. He raises that knee, cracking my nose. Knocks my taser aside.

Starbursts shoot across the black of my vision. My face is all scrunched, timing and balance fucked up. My eyes fill with water. I reach for my face. Blood leaks from my nose, spilling into my cupped hands.

"I know you're trying to help," Ilya says. "But you're out of your depth."

"No," Whistler says, "you are."

Arms ziptied behind his back, he charges like a bull, shoulders hunched forward. Headfirst, he smashes into Ilya, knocking them both into the water.

Ilya drops his gun. I pick it up with my bloody hands, wipe it down for a better grip.

"Whistler!" He's thrashing in the water. "Whistler!"

Through my lens I see Ilya dive in and swim away. His shadow shimmers on the surface. I point the gun. Squint with my left eye. Focus with my right.

I breathe in, then out. Find my center.

I squeeze off a round, then another, and another. Bullets whiz below the surface. I miss with the first two shots. But within the water now I see a cloud of dark red blood disperse like smog. Ilya disappears around the bend.

Hurriedly I pull off my jacket and sneakers and dive into the water. Whistler's frantically kicking his legs, hands still clasped behind his back. I struggle to keep my eyes open, stung by the water, blood leaking from my nose.

I clutch for him. I snatch an ear, clamped between my thumb

and forefinger. I squeeze as hard as I can to keep my grip. Aided by the water's buoyancy, I lift him up just enough that I grab the back of his shirt with my other hand.

Whistler's taller than me. Because I can't lift his hands, I'm struggling to get his head above the surface. I push his torso against the concrete edge, grab hold of it with my free hand. I breathe quickly to oxygenate myself, then in one motion sling my other hand away from his shirt and up to his shoulders, lifting him just enough so his face is pinned against the edge.

I pull myself out of the water, then pull him out. He's not breathing.

With my boot knife, I clip his hands free, lay him flat on his back, then clear his airway. I take a deep breath. As droplets of blood leak from my nose and onto his cheek, I squeeze his nostrils closed and press my mouth to his. I force air into his lungs, pull my mouth away, watch his chest inflate, then deflate.

I resecure my lips around his, force more air into him.

Before I can do chest compressions he spasms and kicks his feet. Water shoots up through his mouth and down the sides of his face. He coughs roughly, his shoulders spun to the side.

I lean on my back, soaked, exhausted, reclaiming my own breath.

"Did you...?" Whistler huffs, the air flow starting to normalize, "did you have to yank my ear?"

I lift myself up. "That's what you want to talk about?"

"It hurt."

"I'll remember that for next time."

"What do we... what do we do now?" Whistler asks. "We still have the arm. You think the ICD... the Institute... think they can decrypt the bracelet? If it still works?"

"I don't know. Maybe. If we had enough time. But we don't."

"Then what do we do?"

"I don't know. I don't..." My mouth stretches into a sneaky smile. "What do I always do when I'm stuck on tech?"

Whistler chuckles, squishing the excess water from his pockets. "Bernice. Booyah."

"You can say that again."

"Booyah."

I give him a look. "You didn't actually have to say it."

"I know," he says. "But it's my thing."

I ping Bernice through my lens. No response. I try again. Nothing.

"Whistler, did she give you an access code?"

"Yeah. Why?"

"Try her."

He does. "No answer."

I text, call, text again, then send her the emergency code through my lens. Still nothing.

"You think it's *The Specter*?" Whistler says. "Or any of the tech down here? It's hard to get a signal out."

"It's possible, but I don't think so. She gave us a custom frequency. At this range, the signal should bypass most blockers and go right to her."

A wave of dread washes over me. My mind locks onto an image of her face. The side of her face. With the cybernetic implant.

I scroll through images on my phone. "From the diner. When you trailed GGZ. He was with a woman. You said sweatpants and a baseball cap. This her?"

Whistler looks. "Yeah. She's all made up, but yeah. That's her."

"You didn't think to mention the cybernetic implant? Important detail, no?"

"Why? You know who she is?"

Fuckety fuck fuck fuck.

"Yeah," I say. "I do."

We don't have time to make our way across the city. I look for a shortcut.

"Come with me." I lead Whistler back inside *The Specter*. He grabs Aiko's severed arm, bags it, shoves it in his front thigh pocket, half in, half out.

We do a quick check to ensure the crew are still preserved safely in the stasis pods as the system continues to pump them with fluids, antibiotics, and oxygen.

Whistler stares at them through the bubble domes. "They gonna make it?"

"If we don't stop Ilya, no one's gonna make it." Back in the cockpit, I scan the control panels again, then reach inside my jacket. I produce the teleport device. "Eddie said this was only for Institute access. I bet it can do more."

I continue scanning for an access port.

"Here. Let me." Whistler takes the teleport device from me, studies it closely. He presses a button on the ship's control panel, turning the button from white to red. It glows. So does my device. "There we go. Synched."

I take the teleport device back from him. I want to be impressed. But I'm also suspicious. "How'd you know how to do that?"

"Tarrish trained me on some tech."

"Wait. What? He? Lionel? Tarrish? Lieutenant Tarrish. With the ICD. Angry. Grumbly. Thinks you suck. *He* trained *you*?"

"Well, not him personally. His guys did. To chase after the Guild, I needed tech to match theirs. The ICD has some cool shit. If you played nicer, they might've trained you, too."

I'm thinking real hard about tossing him back in the canal with his hands tied. Maybe later. Instead, I grab him. By the ear.

"Ow fuck! What the—?" We teleport to inside Bernice's bunker.

And face a whole different problem.

CHAPTER 27

Bernice's primary workstation is unoccupied. Weapons drawn, Whistler and I fan out. We circle around the various other workbenches, littered with tools, wires, monitors. We meet on the other side of the equipment. The retractable brick wall is open, exposing the hidden room.

The consoles, experimental tech, and machinery are activated, including multi-directional cameras mounted on overhead lattices, projecting 3-D holograms over the platform. One image is the entirety of the Cosmos. Set against a black background are innumerable galaxies. They appear as specks of glowing dust, and amorphous pockets of bioluminescent gases.

Fault lines are threaded like arteries along the fabric of spacetime. The sinuous blue-white lightning bolts irradiate from distant points in the Cosmos. At the source of each bolt is a glowing blue-white dot.

Trigger points.

The lightning bolts all lead to one destination.

The second hologram is Eternity. Our realm. Focused on E-Town. Regardless of the points of origin, the fault lines converge toward the realm. Like a tactical strike from an enemy combatant. Attacked from multiple directions.

Bernice is in her hoverchair. Her implant flashes red-red-yellow. Red-red-yellow. *Distress.*

No shit.

"Hey," she says, her chrome arms by her side.

"Hey," I say.

Jasmine's at one of the workstations, finger on a switch. She's wearing a gray, long-sleeve lounge top, matching pants, and sandals. Then it hits me.

"That cut on your foot," I say. "It was a tracker, wasn't it? That thin piece of wire."

"It dislodged from the bracelet. I stepped on it by mistake. It was sharper than I thought."

"You're a great liar. I'll give you that. I shouldn't be surprised."

"No," Bernice says. "You shouldn't. But I rarely surprise myself. I permitted delusion to circumvent experience. I indulged in the most foolish of all endeavors—convincing myself I could save someone from the depths of their pain. As if I could control the outcome. As if this bunker could serve as our sanctuary, if not our salvation."

I nod, my lens scanning the bunker for any advantage I can find. But my gaze goes right to the console. And the switch Jasmine controls. "That what I think it is?"

"Cybernetic calibration. She can overload my implant."

Whistler shuffles forward a step. "That'll kill you."

Bernice concurs. "It most certainly would."

"That's quite a display." I scan the holograms, hoping to pinpoint the exact location of the final trigger point. "How did you crack the encryption for the...?"

Bernice.

Chrome limbs.

Hoverchair.

Cybernetic implant.

Trigger points in my mind.

In quick succession I get flashes. Moments, details, fragments of conversations that seemed disparate and unconnected at the time. I can now see they all led to one conclusion.

"It was you, wasn't it?" I say to Bernice. The certitude of my realization overwhelms me. "Back when you were a Patch. *You* tracked the fault lines. You experimented with a solve. *That's* how you got injured."

I close my eyes, absorb it all. Her suicidal depression was triggered by far more than her physical injuries. The isolation. The loss of self, which is its own kind of death. The destruction she invited, if not caused. Her relentlessness blinded her to the risks she was taking—and asking others to take on her behalf, whether she appreciated the danger or not. She was as obsessed as Ilya with finding the fault lines. I open my eyes again.

"Your partner got killed chasing your theory," I say. "Only one of you died. But you both got buried. Him in a grave. And you... down here."

I've known Bernice a long time. But how well do I actually know her? How completely, intricately can you ever know anyone?

"I was reckless," she says finally. "I was smarter than them. Better. And I knew it. The fault lines were real. They wouldn't listen. Same as Ilya."

"So you broke away from the pack to do it on your own," Whistler says. "You were less concerned with being right than with them being wrong."

Bernice's implant flashes again. Blue-blue-pink. Pink-pink-blue. *Relief.*

"You always heard me, Eric. Even when you weren't listening."

"Yeah," he says. "Maybe I was."

And so was I. Only now do I understand what she's been holding back.

"You've been helping them," I say. "The Institute. The ICD. You've been tracking the fault lines." The life of a private investigator, especially the cases I take, can be a festering pool of lies, half-truths, and deceptions. Yet my heart tumbles down a bottomless pit of rejection. Because this one stings most of all. "Bernice. Why didn't *you*, of all people, tell *me*?"

She stares at me. Her eyes fill with water. Her cranial implant flashes red-red-yellow. Red-red-yellow. *Shame.*

"I couldn't, Angela. I couldn't tell anyone. The discharge from the fault lines. It... changed me. Infected me. The only way to survive was to cut myself off. The Institute enlisted my help. I wouldn't give it. Not because of apathy or indifference, but because I don't trust them. I don't trust anyone. I barely trust myself."

"But why didn't they tell me? I could have..."

I already know, but she says it anyway. "Because they don't trust *you*."

And there it is. For all the good I've tried to do, the cases I've solved, my ledger still leans in the wrong direction. The collateral damage I've inflicted has come at a cost. I understand the ICD keeping me at arm's length. Tarrish is a master at manipulating me, enlisting my help when I think I'm the one defying him. But how could Eddie do this? Especially now. Knowing I have a relationship with Bernice and that I can...

They played me. They fucking played me.

Eddie and Tarrish. Together.

They put Whistler onto it first, because they considered him expendable. Only after he went missing, and I got onto the fault lines, they let me inside. They allowed me to see just enough to chase down leads in the ways that I do. But they didn't tell me about Bernice because...

"They used *me* to get to *you*," I say "They let me think it was my idea. But I wouldn't betray you. I would never turn on you like..."

Bernice. Of all people. Is being held hostage. In her own bunker.

I was worried about Olin. That Tarrish might have flipped her for being on Dante's leash. I'm such an idiot. There *was* a long con. Turns out, I was worried about the wrong woman.

"Jasmine. You don't have to do this."

"You're right. I don't. I'd been out there on my own, had other pimps. Dante was a brute. But he taught me something important. When it comes to sex work, go all in—or get out. Anything in between and you'll get eaten alive. That's what happened to Aiko. Kimmie, too. She wanted to protect us *from* the life while being *in* the life. But she had a life on the outside. Some girls have more control over their bodies and their business. There's no violence. They take the clients they want. They keep everything they earn. That's not how it is for me. That's why I got the implant. A way to set me apart. And it did. In all the worst ways."

The clock's ticking and there's no time to waste. But the longer I keep her talking the better our chances of getting her off that switch.

"You think you've seen it all," Bernice says, knowing that just the flick of Jasmine's finger will fry her mind. "Then you wake up one day and realize that beneath all the chrome, the implants, and synthetic organs... all the circuitry in your body..."

Oh, no. I see what she's doing. What's she about to do.

"Bernice," I plead. "Don't—"

"Loneliness has a way of soaking into your DNA," she says. "You think it's your only friend, your companion. Your lover. It *knows* you because it *is* you." She smiles. Sad. Wistful. "And then a pretty face shows up after so many years alone, and you think about the mistakes you've made, the life you lost." Bernice grazes her cranial implant. "I thought she understood me, that she was my way back. And like the fool I seem to be, I let my guard down. Because no matter what I tell myself, I'm still human after all. I let myself think about life outside the bunker. About possibilities. About the future. What could be."

"That's what I sell," Jasmine says. "Fantasy. My body is just the vessel. And when this is done, I'll be well paid. To afford any life I want. Kimmie had Dante twisted around her finger. But I had her twisted around mine."

"You can't actually believe that," I say. "Ilya doesn't care about money."

"I know he doesn't. But I do. He already gave me the down payment. And there's lots more to come. All I have to do is keep her occupied."

"You're making the wrong choice."

"Right after I got my implant, a client booked a suite. The Chenault Hotel. Fancy. Gorgeous. Champagne on ice. But it wasn't fancy and it sure wasn't gorgeous. He had a cybernet fetish. And another one. He had me dress up like a cow. Made me wear cow horns, strapped an udder to me, made me wear a butt plug with a cow's tail on the end. He forced me onto my knees and told me to moo. 'Like the cunty cow you are.' That's what he said."

I've heard these stories before. I've walked in on worse. And each time another little piece of me crawls away into a dank corner and dies.

"Then he unzipped his pants and urinated into a champagne flute. He told me I could wear it... or drink it. And he wouldn't let me leave until I chose. I won't tell you which choice I made.

That's between me and the cow fucker. A few months later, Dante stumbled onto GGZ." `

GGZ had a thing for prostitutes. Dante saw a long con with him. The girls roped him in. Led to his score. Then ripped him off. Or tried to.

"Our play brought Ilya into my life. He presented me with a new choice. To do what I do best. Seduce, disarm... and listen. Which was a whole lot better than the choices I'd had before."

"I'm sorry that happened. But Ilya... he's gonna get us all killed."

"Then there won't be anything to argue about. You might as well get comfortable. We'll be here for a while."

This is why Nini won't talk to me, wants nothing more to do with me. It doesn't matter that I'm fighting for our survival. I didn't set Ilya on this suicide mission, didn't cause the fault lines in the fabric of spacetime. But somehow I'm in the middle of madness again, with the people I care about most paying the price.

"You." Jasmine gestures to Whistler. "The arm sticking out of your pocket. Aiko's. Toss it here."

"Eric," Bernice says. "We share a bond, do we not?"

Slow to respond, Whistler places his hand on the bagged arm. "We do."

"Then honor that bond. Don't do it."

"She'll kill you if I don't."

"She won't," I say. "It's the only leverage she has."

Jasmine's implant flashes. "That's where you're mistaken. No Bernice, no code. No code, no coordinates. Pretty soon, it won't matter anyway. The job will be done. And I'll get paid."

"You flip that switch"—I cup my scout orb into my palm—"same goes for you. You'll never get paid again."

Jasmine chortles. "You won't be gassing me. Not like at Dante's apartment. Yes. Bernice told me about that. It wasn't hard to figure out how to deactivate the gas from here. So you won't be gassing me. You won't be gassing anyone."

"Mache," Whistler says, "are you thinking what I'm thinking?"

"Absolutely."

Jasmine inquires: "And what scheme is that?"

"Back to basics," I say. "I'm gonna punch you in the face."

"From there? I don't see how."

"You won't see it at all."

Bernice activates her implant, which flashes red-red-red. *Terror.*

Jasmine screams. She reaches for her head, pulling her hand away from the control panel. I toss my hand forward, thrusting the scout orb. With a signal from my lens, I direct the orb to operate outside its standard operating procedure.

With maximum thrust it smashes into Jasmine's forehead, knocking her flat on her back. Knocking her out cold.

I rush to her. She's alive.

"Bernice, you were going to sacrifice yourself for—"

"Save it," she says, her implant flashing. "Eric, bring me the arm."

Whistler does, unbags it. Bernice places the arm perpendicular on a rotating chrome stand in the center of a white tabletop scanning box. Red lasers from 360 degrees scan the wrist until the symbols reappear. The symbols are transferred to Bernice's computer terminal.

"Can you decrypt the code? Is there enough time to—"

Bernice looks at me—*really* looks at me. Her gaze drills into my soul, her cranial implant flashing in various patterns. She's right. I can't decrypt the code without her. And she can't decrypt the code any faster than her abilities will allow.

Not because I'm impatient. Because I'm still an addict.

Clues, answers, mysteries, cases. That's what I use to fill the holes in my soul. Pressuring my friends to bend the laws of time and physics because the stakes are just that high. And they are.

But that doesn't change anything.

Bernice knows how serious this is. She knows better than anyone. Yet here I am again. No matter how closely I look at myself, I never see what's...

A long-buried truth comes rushing into the forefront of my mind. My hands tremble. A single tear wells up. I'm sick in my gut.

"Mache," Whistler says. "What's wrong? What's happening to...?"

The lasers complete their scan. Code scrolls across Bernice's screen.

"Angela," she says. "Look at this."

I was right.

"Whistler," I say. "Call Banny. We need a ride."

"Did that already. He's waiting outside."

"He is? How did you...?" I chuff at myself. "Because you know me better than I ever give you credit for. Bernice, get me the Institute."

"Line's open."

It buzzes once.

"Eddie! We found the fault line. And the trigger point. Send everyone. Send 'em *now*."

"We just broke the encryption," he says. "We have the coordinates. We're on our way."

"We'll meet you there when—"

"Angela."

His voice is level. Serious. And worried. There's something else.

My heart pounds in my ears. I can barely breathe. I don't know how I know, but I know what he's going to say. I almost vomit on myself as I utter the words. "Is it...?"

"It's Owen, Angela. He's—"

I open my mouth again to speak. Nothing but the wispy heartbreak of a grieving mother tumbles out. Clenched jaw, throat like sandpaper. I'm so dizzy I'm about to pass out. "Is he...?"

"He's missing, Angela. We lost him in the chaos. I don't know where he is."

CHAPTER 28

I've never believed in destiny or fate. That our thoughts, our actions, the course of our lives, are predetermined. That we're just bit actors in a play that's already been written. But it's getting increasingly difficult for me to ignore the interconnectedness we share. The links that run deep.

Jung, whose theories about dreams and nightmares still rattle around in my mind, also believed in that very interconnectedness. He contended that in all moments in time and space we are exactly where we're supposed to be, doing exactly what we're supposed to be doing. And the reason he knew that whatever happened was meant to happen, was that it *did* happen. And if something else was meant to have happened, it would have.

Maybe that's a slightly more nuanced way of saying that everything happens for a reason. And maybe that's true. Maybe it's not. Yet here I am. Again. And now that I *am* here, right now, in this moment in time and space, I feel in my bones it's the place I'm supposed to be. That it was inevitable. I just hope I live long enough to find out why.

In the center of E-Town, separating East from West, Breoniki Park is flush with people. Some strolling easily, others sitting, either alone or in groups, some drawing on vape pens. Others relax on communal saucers. The concave pads glide and rotate, mimicking the ebb and flow of lily pads on a pond.

Projected from the center of E-Town we see the proximal glow of blinking lights and 3-D holograms. The digital billboards and hovercrafts. Interior lights from apartment buildings and office towers and the elevated tracks of the city-wide monorail. All combining into an acrobatic blur of relentless energy. Five milky-white moons glow above us. I feel a distant rumble, a vibration from above.

"Mache," Whistler says. "You think he'll know? That they're Patches and ICD agents?"

"Assume he does. And that he's ready for them."

I text Eddie through my lens.

"Where's Owen? You find him?"

Scrolling dots... scrolling dots. And then: *"No. Not yet."*

"How, Eddie? How could this happen?"

More scrolling dots. *"I don't have a good answer."*

Which brings me full circle. Five years ago, Owen had been missing. Taken as a toddler.

On my instructions. For his own protection.

I was coming out of such a bad place that, in my drug-addled state of mind, I didn't know what I'd done, or what I'd set in motion.

And then a madman from Earth came to this very spot, where the old Anna Pavilion used to be. His narcissistic delusions of grandeur in full force, he said that with the realm's attention focused on him, we'd finally see what he meant. What horrors lurked beneath the surface of the Cosmos. And in the depths of our souls.

Maybe Jung was right. About being where we're supposed to be.

Because here, on this very site, we're all shadows beneath the new centerpiece, the Eye of Time. As if it willed itself into existence. As though the fabric of spacetime called out to the engineers, architects, and designers to ensure it was constructed here, on this very spot.

The final trigger point. For the final fault line.

The eyeball crackles with interdimensional energy, its iris morphing between shades and colors. And its black pupil, with the golden hue behind it.

Stare into the Eye and it reveals a truth to you and you alone, never again to be revealed to anyone, ever, in precisely the same manner. I don't know if I can handle any more truth. I don't know if I can afford not to.

Surrounded by a hundred and fifty agents at least, I let them vanish from my consciousness. I think of Owen. Of everything he means to me. Will always mean to me.

In my mind, his smile lights up. Full of life. Of curiosity. Of compassion. I see him. As an infant. A toddler. A young boy.

My baby.

My Owen.

My son.

I'm terrified to see what the Eye will reveal to me. But my fear is irrelevant. Truths don't change based on the way we feel. Only our interpretations.

It's time, Angela. Open your fucking eyes.

I do.

"Hardwicke!" It's Tarrish. "You're blocking the snipers."

With my lens I spot at least two dozen perched in the trees, behind boulders, and prone in the grass. Their weapons are propped up, hidden in darkness and shadow.

I feel like I'm radiating energy, the power of the Eye tapping deep into my essence. It's got a grip on me. It won't let go. Trapping me between worlds. "Whu… what?"

Tarrish grabs me by the elbow and hustles me away from the Eye. But just because I'm not looking into it right now doesn't mean it isn't looking into me.

"I'm focused," I say, not entirely focused. "I'm okay."

"Hardwicke." He sighs. "Angela. I'm sorry about Owen. If you need to go… go. We've got the site locked down. If Ilya's here, we'll find him."

"Thanks. I'm okay. We can—"

"Mache," Whistler says. "You feel that? The vibration? The buzzing?" He surveys Breoniki Park. "Oh shit. Mache!"

I turn back to the Eye of Time. It penetrates the dimensions of my soul. There's a flash in my mind. Of the bioluminescent forest. Of the great Helix. Of Whistler caught in the elliptical orbit powered by *The Specter* and…

The Eye releases me.

Coming out of the daze, I study the Patches and ICD agents in civilian gear, huddled on the lily pads.

"They're connected," I whisper. Then louder, "They're *connected*. T! Get 'em off! The agents! Get 'em down now! It's an ambush! He led us here. Get 'em off the…"

In quick succession, the agents are encased in bubbles of energy, caught in artificial orbits. Cut off from us. Trapped.

"Snipers!" Tarrish commands. "Target close! Lock on!"

Infrared target beams from multiple vantage points cross-hatch and cover the grounds.

"Don't!" Whistler shouts. "He can track the sensors!"

"Yes," a voice says, a gun shoved in my back. "I can."

With his free hand, Ilya presses a small device. The orbits trapping the Patches and ICD agents extend across Breoniki Park, enveloping all the snipers. It's the second time Ilya's literally sneaked up behind me. He reaches around, removes, and tosses away my taser. He already took my gun. He pushes me forward.

"So, you're Lieutenant Tarrish." Ilya points his gun at him, gesturing for Tarrish to give up his. "Wasn't sure we'd ever meet."

Tarrish slowly reaches into his shoulder holster. He removes his gun, hands it handle-first to Ilya. "I was sure we would."

"The Institute had the right idea about artificial orbits. They just couldn't stabilize them. We figured it out. The Guild steals experimental tech. We steal it from them. Then make it better. You shouldn't fight me. We want the same the thing."

I feel that rumble again, that vibration from above. "Storm's coming."

Ilya corrects me. "That's not a storm."

Whistler points skyward. The five moons are all dimmer somehow, losing their brilliant white luster. "It's happening. Debris from the other systems. They're following the fault lines. They're gonna take us all out."

"Not if I set the charge," Ilya says. "The Eye of Time. It sees what I see. What needs to happen. What will happen. It's sitting atop the fault line. The great blast is coming. No matter who sets the charge."

In the far distance we see crackling blue-white lightning bolts. Getting closer. And pieces of debris colliding, crumbling into dust.

"The gel doesn't work," I say. "Look what you've done."

"I've run the calculations. The formulation is right. It'll work."
He's convinced that setting off the charges at once will excite the gel with enough intensity and propulsive force to radiate throughout the Cosmos. Logic can't penetrate his delusion. Maybe honesty will.

"You hurt a lot of people. You didn't mean to. You didn't want to." The Eye's energy is still coursing through me. In my mind I see various moments of my life, individually, and all at once. "But sometimes, when the threat is too great, you have to step outside the lines. Even if that means hurting people you love."

Ilya offers a glint of validation. "That's right."

"The problem, Ilya"—I send Whistler an eye-text, from my lens to his—"is you tried to make your case, but your ego took over."

His faces contorts. His breathing tightens. "It's a good plan," he says, his frustration leaking out. "It'll work."

"Look around," I say with a forced laugh. "If this is how you succeed, I'd hate to see you fail."

"I didn't fail. *They* failed. I was right."

He's getting more visibly upset. I antagonize him further. "Right? About *what*? It's a total shit-show."

"About the fault lines! About the trigger points!"

"You weren't."

"I was!"

"And that's where you failed. You had all this intel…."

I eye-text Whistler again. *"Get ready."*

And keep pushing Ilya. "You had all this proof…"

"It's right there!"

"You go high."

"You still couldn't sell it."

"They wouldn't listen!"

"I go low."

"Your blood was boiling."

"They wouldn't hear me!"

"Now!"

In a coordinated strike, with my front foot I side-swipe Ilya's knee that buckled last time we battled, while Whistler throws a right-left combination to his jaw. Our timing is impeccable.

We're still too late.

Ilya swings his rifle butt at Whistler's hands, deflecting his attacks. My strike hits Ilya's leg, but my foot recoils. He's covered his leg in a combat pad. The impact is so intense a ligament pops in my right knee, dropping me to the ground.

Tarrish makes his own move, with a right jab to the face. Anticipating the attack, Ilya counterstrikes. He knocks away Tarrish's arm, presses a combat knife to his throat.

"I can read your eye-texts," Ilya says. "Your tech is good." He checks the digital readout on his wristband. "Mine's better."

He's neutralized all three of us. On the ground, I shimmy out of my jacket. From the back pouch I remove the MedKit, wrap my knee in a flexible brace. It fills with impact gel. I pick myself up, hobble awkwardly toward him.

"Okay," I say as the blue-white lightning bolts, the cracks in the galactic ice, are spreading closer to the realm. "You've got my attention. I'm listening."

"I know you are. We're almost lined up. Then I detonate. The fault lines will heal. After that, it won't matter what happens to me. Or you. It'll all be worth it."

"Bullshit. That's why we're here. You need more. It's not enough to be right. You need an audience."

That catches him. "So what if I do? No one will forget my name. Ever."

"Ilya." Trying to convince a zealot to change their mind is like asking the ocean to remove its own salt. But what choice do I have? "You were right about the fault lines. You were right about the trigger points. But the gel doesn't work. Not like you think. How do you not see that?"

"Mache. You see *that*? There. From the debris. One piece. It's..."

I scan the sky, the black of night turning ashen. Then I see it. One element emerges from the debris. With a blue-white plume behind it.

"Is that...?"

"It's a thruster," Tarrish says. "And it's changing course. That's..."

"Mache! Holy shit. Look!"

I sharpen my lens to maximum range and clarity. My heart pounds.

Whistler steps forward. "It's Owen."

Ripping through the night sky, my baby boy is encased in an exoskeleton with bubble dome shielding. From the mechanical arms, he's firing concentrated plasma blasts, breaking the larger fragments into dust.

"No!" Ilya checks his wrist guard. "It's too soon!"

With the butt of the knife, Ilya smashes Tarrish in the nose, which explodes with blood. He then knocks me down and tosses Whistler out of the way. From his wrist guard, Ilya sprays us with a sticky gel, like trapping flies in amber. He mounts the rifle against his right shoulder, presses his eye against the scope.

"No! He's just a boy!"

"Like you said"—Ilya manipulates the targeting dial on the rifle to pinpoint his target—"when the threat is too great, you step outside the lines. And your son knows what I know. There's only one way to save spacetime. Nothing can stop it now."

He breathes intentionally, curls his finger around the trigger.

To assassinate my son.

The *blam!* is deafening.

My heart ruptures in a river of agony.

And I'm covered in gore.

Because Ilya no longer has a face. His skull and brains are now chunky splatter.

"I don't care *what* you believe," Olin says to Ilya's headless body. She rolls his torso with the bottom of her shoe. "You need to go."

Smoke drifts off the end of her gun. She holsters it, reaches down with her good hand to help me out of the goo.

"Reach inside my jacket. Inside seam. Press the snap."

Olin does, releasing a dissolvent in the adaptable fabric. It takes a few minutes to get it all, but it neutralizes the gel, cleans the muck off me. She gives me her arm. I take it. She pulls me up.

"Didn't think you'd come."

"Like I said," she says. "I always make good."

"Mommy!" Shed of his exoskeleton, Owen rushes toward me. "I told you I could fly it!"

He jumps into my arms. My bad knee buckles. I don't care.

"You did. And you can. Whistler, let's get the agents down. T... you okay?"

Tarrish leans against a boulder. His head is tipped back. He pinches his bloody nose. "Fucking great."

"Hey. The kid. Language."

"Mom," Owen says. "You say way worse things."

I laugh. "You're making it very difficult for me to argue with you."

"Mache, we still have a problem. What about that?"

Whistler gestures to the blue-white lightning bolts crackling against the black of night. The fabric of spacetime. It's still eroding. My phone buzzes. It's Eddie.

"Mommy," Owen says, and squirms out of my arms.

"Hang on, baby." Then to Eddie. "I've got Owen. He's okay."

Eddie sighs in relief. "He stole an exoskeleton."

"You don't say."

"Where are you?"

I tell him.

He mumbles. "He followed the fault line."

"Looks that way. He came from..." I look to Owen, to the exoskeleton, then into the night. "Eddie. Hold on. He *followed*? From where?"

"He's been halfway across the Cosmos."

"He's been *where*?"

"The fault lines."

"I know. You said that."

"No, Angela. He's been following *all* the fault lines."

"Why?"

"I don't know. The damage is done. But the fault lines can't reach the realm. Not without the final charge. There's nothing to connect them. We'll have to restrict off-realm travel. For now, at least. We're neutralizing the debris."

"I told you, Mommy! I can fix it."

"Owen. Buddy. Let me talk to your dad." To Eddie: "So we stand down."

"Yes," he says. "Stand down. It's over."

"But Mommm. I can fix it!"

"Owen," I say, blood rushing to my ears. "You can't just rush off like—"

As if propelled by a slingshot, he scampers away from me— and toward the Eye of Time.

"Owen! No!"

He runs as fast as his little feet will carry him, my eight-year-old son rushing toward an eyeball a hundred times his size, with the power to read his very essence. Owen stops before the giant orb. He stares directly into it. From his jacket, Owen pulls out several pads. With his foot, he depresses the concrete slab on the ground. The slab opens on a hinge, providing access to the underground mechanisms.

I rush after him on my bad leg. "Owen!" Each stride puts pressure on my knee, aching even with the support brace. "Owen!"

I'm too late. He disappears down into the opening. Beneath the Eye of Time.

I nearly stop in my tracks.

The Eye of Time crackles with energy. I ignore it, refuse to get pulled into its visions. I get down on my stomach, gripping the slab's edges, my head over the access port. I call down.

"Owen. Owen! OWEN!"

I switch my lens to infrared. All I can see are mechanicals chugging and shifting. I scan the bowels of the apparatus. I can see various access ports.

"OWEN!"

"Hi, Mommy!"

"Owen! Where...?" I hear giggles, then turn my head, look over my left shoulder. Owen's standing behind me with Whistler.

"It'll work, Mommy. My healing pads. They'll work."

"Your what?"

"The healing pads. The ones I made. At the institute. I told you, Mommy. They were doing it wrong. I put pads on the other fault lines. It'll work."

"Work? What do you mean work?"

Owen looks into the sky, the blue-white lightning bolts

exposing the fault lines. "Gotta go!" He charges away.

"Owen! What are you doing?"

"I told you!" he shouts back and rushes to the exoskeleton. "I'm gonna fix it!"

Olin and I chase after him.

"No! Owen! Where are you going?"

He secures himself inside the exoskeleton. He fires up the thrusters, hovers above me. "To the final trigger point, Mommy! To set the charge!"

CHAPTER 29

"Eddie. Where's the fault line? The trigger point?" The message is garbled. "Eddie. Eddie!"

I frantically search for an answer. There's no need. That access point is already lording over me. I hang up and walk over to the Eye of Time. I stand before the massive white orb, feel its energy encapsulate me. I breath in, exhale. Then again.

I stare into the Eye. The Eye stares into me. "Okay," I say. "Show me."

I don't know if my physical body is still in Breoniki Park or I've been distilled to my pure essence, but I feel myself hurtling into the iris of the Eye, caught in this interdimensional vortex.

Or Helix.

At an incomprehensible velocity, I soar with the golden, thrumming vitality the great beast had shared with me before its demise. Imbued with bioluminescent force, it's as if I've been swallowed by the Universe itself, hurtling through the expanse, rocketing beyond the boundaries of time, space, and dimension. Beyond life or death. Beyond consciousness.

There it is. Hovering in the great expanse.

Dolores. If it's even Dolores.

"You don't need to save me."

My heart crumbles just the same.

"I left you there. Alone."

"You did. But not alone."

"Where are you? What is this place?"

"Come on, Hardy. You know where you are. We're in the dreamscape. Your dreamscape."

I'm shaking.

"Why?"

"Because I don't need saving."

"Then who does? Please. Tell me. I need to know."

"Hardy," she says. *"You already do."*

I'm snatched in the clutches of the blue-white electrical energy. What I perceive as my body crackles. Dolores shows me what I need to see. I'm absorbed back into myself. I gasp.

"Whistler! Come on. Let's go."

"Where?"

"Jo. You'll want to see this."

"Hardwicke!" Tarrish shouts. "Where the hell are you going?"

"To save my kid. Unless he saves us first."

Tarrish interjects. "You're not going anywhere. We have to control the—"

"Sorry, T." I rush off. "My time has been served."

Banny's on the avenue. Motor's running. I put Whistler in front, me and Olin in back.

"I wasn't sure you'd wait," I say.

"I told you." Banny throws his cab into gear. "I'm in it until the end."

"We're twenty minutes out," Olin says. "If you hit every light."

Banny smiles devilishly, eyes us through the rearview. "I'll make it in ten."

Breaking every traffic law on the books, Banny gets us back on the Rubiyat Highway, across from the Manuela Projects, then finally to the access road leading to the abandoned Hurling-Aberdeen Psychiatric Center lying dormant on the river's edge.

The night sky is still ashen and littered with debris from the destroyed systems that drifted outside the realm. No shuttle-rafts rocketing in the near distance. Except for one.

We follow the plume of Owen's exoskeleton as it soars over the river. The waves grow rough and angry. A portent of things to come. The plume disappears around the bend.

"Banny!" I point through the window. "There!"

"I see it!"

We pass a thick stretch of bushes and trees along the coastline.

"Mache! We're not gonna make it."

That draws Banny's ire. "The fuck we won't."

We go careening inside the cab as he plows us through a thicket of growth. Banny stunt-maneuvers around trees, snapping branches like toothpicks. Moments later, he steers us out from the brush and onto a dirt path dangerously hugging the river's edge. We rattle up and down, the path uneven beneath us. He makes a sharp right, up an embankment, and onto the unkept roadway on the Saiwyn Peninsula.

Owen's exoskeleton is perched by the dock. I point through the partition. "Banny! There!"

He parks his battered cab next to the exoskeleton. Before last week I'd never been out here, yet again I find myself in the shadow of the old, abandoned brick-and-sandstone tower. Connected by a series of arched corridors, the gothic campus and administrative tower and pavilions are too extensive to cover in the little time we have left.

"Fan out," I say. "He's gotta be close."

"Owen!" Whistler shouts. "Owen!"

I call again to Owen. "Buddy! Owen. Come on. Where are you?"

My mommy brain is overloaded, my heart swelling with fear and anxiety. I'm acting like the victim. I need to switch that off. Because I'm not the victim. I'm the perpetrator.

My entire life has led to this moment. When the totality of choices I've made, much like the fault lines in the fabric of space-time, have exposed the weaknesses. Revealed the cracks in the system. The microfractures that can't be repaired. Interstitial fibers that need to be ripped out. Replaced.

Which means, right here, right now... I need to be me.

Not mommy me. Private investigator me.

My footsteps crunch the gravel as I approach the exoskeleton. I kneel. Footprints. Heavier on the toe, lighter on the heel. Definitely Owen.

With my lens I track the footprints. They lead beneath a brown-brick alcove.

Whistler calls out from the foot of the administrative building. "You got something?"

"Footprints."

"Me, too."

"Here," Banny says, kneeling four alcoves away.

"Owen," I whisper, sprayed with mist from the river's crashing waves. "Owen?"

Her left arm still in a sling, Olin creeps up the adjacent brick staircase and leading to a set of double doors. She presses against one of the doors. It opens. She steps inside. Whether by its own heft, by Olin, or other forces, the door slams shut behind her.

"Mache! Look there! It's Owen!"

My heart jumps, scrambling to follow Whistler's sightline. "Where?"

"Up there! In the tower. He just ran past the window."

In the opposite direction of Olin. I know I should, but I can't worry about her right now. I call Eddie. No signal goes through. I look up into the dusty night sky. I call Tarrish. Same again.

"Whistler! You get a call out?"

He checks. "No! It's blocked! It's..."

I already know. Owen. From the exoskeleton. Signal dampeners.

Whistler rushes over to me. "Mache," he says worriedly. "He's not really gonna...?"

I don't have to answer, but I do. "He thinks he's right."

Whistler sighs in exhaustion. He thinks on it, squints. "You think he is?"

"Don't know. He might be."

"Yeah."

"But he might be wrong," I say. "And if he is..."

Whistler nods again. "Yeah..."

No more time for *maybe, might,* or *could be.* "Whistler, follow Olin. I'm going after Owen. Banny, stay here."

He gazes at the abandoned psych center. "Sold!"

Through the arch I rush up to the south tower, Whistler to the north. We check our lenses. Still no signal out, but we're connected to each other.

I ascend an old brick staircase, push open the double doors leading into a wide, unlit foyer. Stray beams of moonlight are my only illumination.

I don't believe in ghosts. Never did. But as I call out to

Owen, I whisper. Afraid to disturb lingering spirits with unfinished business.

"Owen," I whisper again. Then a bit louder, "Owen." I pass the abandoned front desk. The hallway is littered with broken chairs, stray papers, and cobwebs. A staircase leads up. I follow. "Owen. Where are...?"

I don't see it, but I feel a surge of activity. A vibration. A *whumming* energy like from the great Helix. I take the stairs to the next landing. Another long hallway. I can see open doors and entranceways stretching in both directions.

Unsure which way to go, I feel for the vibrations, turn right. Stained-glass window at the end of the long corridor. The nameplate fastened beneath it says, *The Shadow of Life*. I feel the pull, that cosmic *whumming* force. But I can't find the source. The sensor grid in the corner of my eye fluctuates. On the hardwood floor, like directional arrows, blue-white lightning bolts appear.

"Whistler," I eye-text. *"I found the fault line."*

"Me, too. It's leading me down a corridor."

"Same."

"You find Olin?"

"No. Owen?"

"No."

I follow the path, one cautious step at a time. My weapon out, I pass what looks like an old dormitory-style guest quarters. Twenty-four metallic bed frames with beat-up mattresses. But no fault line. I turn back. Out of the corner of my eye I see... something.

A person? A shadow?

"Owen?"

No. Too big for Owen. Eyes up, but following the fault line, I pass a long, horizontal mirror on the wall. My reflection stares back at me. So does the reflection of me, behind the reflection of me. A second me.

I open and close my eyes to clear my vision. The second me is gone.

Then she's back. Only it's not me.

It's Olin.

"Fuck, you scared me." I turn around to face her. "Don't

sneak up on me like…" Olin isn't blinking. I can barely see her breathe. Her dark skin has nearly gone white. "Jo. You okay?"

Olin's staring at me.

Beyond me.

Into the mirror.

Through my lens, in the iris of her eye, is a reflection. Not mine. Not hers.

Her voice is flat. "The Eye of Time. It showed me the truth. I know why she did it. Why she killed herself. Now that I'm here, I can't see anything else."

I turn to face the mirror. No reflection. Not mine. Not her aunt's. Not hers. No one. I turn back to face her. Only now I'm staring down the barrel of her gun.

"I'm sorry." Her voice is breathy, haunting. "I can't let him do it."

My chest tightens. Fear jolts through my soul. I can barely get the words out. "Do what?"

"My aunt felt the fault lines. She tried to warn us. To tell us what was coming. They said she suffered from paranoid delusions. Hallucinations. They gave her electroshocks. Anesthetized her. Told her she was crazy." Olin coils her finger around the trigger. "She saw the end of the realm. The end of everything. All because of him. Because of Owen. She jumped out that window. They covered it with stained glass."

"Mache, what the fuck?" Whistler races down the hallway. He points his weapon at Olin. "Put it down. Whatever you're doing… don't. Just put it down, Olin. Put it down."

"I can't let him do it."

The life I choose. The choices I make. They all led me to this moment. Here. Now.

"Shooting me won't stop my son. And it won't save you."

"There's no other way."

"There's always a way."

"Mache," Whistler says.

Olin's caught in traumas of the past, trying to prevent trauma of the present.

"We just need to find Owen. He'll listen to me. I'm his mother."

"*Mache*," Whistler says, louder, through gritted teeth.

"He won't listen," Olin says. "*Because* you're his mother."

"Mache!"

"WHAT?"

Whistler head-gestures down the hallway. We all look.

It's Owen.

"Hi, Mommy. I set all the pads. It's time to go." Small object in his hand.

Olin fires a shot. An hour ago, she saved Owen's life. Now she wants to end it. The bullet misses him by a few feet, shattering the stained-glass window behind him. I elbow her bad arm. She winces, drops her shoulder. Whistler grabs her gun.

"You can't!" she cries. "You can't let him do it."

"Baby," I say to Owen, my voice quaking. "Where did you get that?" It's a detonator.

"I took it from the man with spiky brown hair. When he had hair. No head now."

"She was right!" Olin is sobbing. Sad, defeated tears roll down her cheeks. "My aunt was right. The sins of the son will be the sins of us all."

My hands are shaking. "Don't do it, baby. Whatever you're gonna do... please. Don't. Just don't."

"Don't worry, Mommy. I told you. I can fix it."

The fault lines glow more intensely, radiating like the bioluminescent forest.

"Please. Baby. Owen. I know you mean well. I know you think you're right. But sometimes when we try to fix the problem, we only make it worse."

"I know, Mommy. But I learned it from you. When the threat is too great, you step outside the lines. Even if that means hurting people you love."

He smiles at me, a smile I've never seen before. Loving. Confident. And layered with regret. Because some decisions, once put into motion, can never be undone.

"No!" Olin runs full bore toward my son, about to push them both out the stained-glass window. The same window her aunt leapt from a half century ago.

Whistler and I raise our guns. We can't fire. If we miss, we might kill my son. Which might save us all.

But it doesn't matter. Because Owen extends his hand. He's holding the detonator.

"Owen." My voice is shakier than my hand. "I love you."

"I know, Mommy. I love you, too."

Olin lunges at Owen. His right thumb, on the trigger, bends at the knuckle.

Whistler takes my hand. Our fingers interlace.

The totality of my entire life—everything I've seen, everywhere I've been, everyone I've known—it all rushes through me. Owen looks right at me.

Goodbye, baby. I love. Mommy loves you.

Click.

CHAPTER 30

The Cosmos is a weird fucking place. If it's a place at all.

What is space? Is it an endless landscape of empty terrain stretching in all directions, with no discernable beginning or end? With no boundaries, across countless dimensions? Is space a waterless ocean? Is it a figment of our imagination? Or are we the figment?

I don't have those answers. Not sure I want them. Not sure it matters.

Whether my existence is real or conjured from the will of the Minders of the Universe, or some other being or force I've never considered, I'm here. I'm alive.

At least... I think I am.

For now, that'll have to do.

Because Owen was right. He could fix it. He did.

The pads he created, from the magic of his own mind, healed the fabric of spacetime. Reset the infrastructure of the Cosmos. Fault lines sealed, fractures closed up.

Owen's back at the Institute with Eddie. But I'll be far more involved going forward. Owen needs me around more than I realized. And I need him. Not to mention the Institute will, as Eddie said, spend months, if not years, cleaning up the mess Ilya left behind.

Speaking of a mess that needs cleaning up, I've got my own to deal with. In particular, my life. Not sure I'm ready to take that case. I start with my office.

Tarrish formally released me from ICD custody, my PI license returned to full standing. My record expunged.

Olin took a leave of absence from the Force. This life isn't for everyone.

I will say, though, that Darren, my kinda-sorta boyfriend, might be a keeper after all. I found a set of his drumsticks in my apartment. So I invited him over. We reconnected. Twice.

But for now, it's about reconnecting here, in my office. It's funny how much significance a physical place can have. Four walls, a door. A window. A box by another name. Yet it grounds me. Reminds me why I'm here, what I'm about.

I sort through a stack of 3-D holocubes on my desk. Cases Whistler hadn't been able to get to while he was pulling double duty, keeping the agency on its feet, and working for Tarrish on the side. I'm even thinking about getting one of those gliders for my office. Turns out, Kimmie-slash-Nóirín had one for the simplest reason of all. It was comfortable.

There's a knock on the door. It opens in. I don't have to look. The smell of her perfume. I know who it is.

"Hey," Nini says. "Mind if I come in?"

"Sure. Just wrapping up. I'm taking Owen to see my mom. The whole weekend."

"Two days with Betty? You're braver than I thought."

I chuckle. "Yeah, well, I figure our problems have been at least a little my fault. Possibly. Maybe. Somewhat."

"How's your dad?"

I take a step closer. "He needs a senior care facility. But my mom, she's got a lotta anger to sort through. She knows it's not fair. It's not his fault. But she blames him anyway. At least a little. It's just her fear and fatigue kicking in. She's not ready to let go. She can't. Not yet."

"I feel that."

"I figured. So... about Dolores..."

Nini lets her purse drop to the floor as we fall into each other's arms. To grieve. To forgive. To move on.

I'm not sure how long we hold our embrace, but my mind goes to my very first case.

I was twenty-three and full of go-fuck-yourself determination. Decked out in a leather motorcycle jacket, lots of chains hanging off it, motorcycle boots, six earrings in each ear, nose ring, my hair shaved down to fuzz on the left side.

Trying way, way, *way* too hard to prove how tough I was. That nobody should mess with me. I could fight even then. I was a nasty brawler, but poor technique. More like a mongoose with a tequila buzz.

My boyfriend at the time, Gregor, rode a big, loud chopper with lots of chrome. The body shop he went to for maintenance and repairs had been robbed. The cops looked into it. Kinda. But not really.

The owner, Bianca, was going to lose her business if she couldn't get her supplies back or get reimbursed by the insurance company. But they would only pay a fraction of what was stolen. They said her security was poor. That it wasn't *their* responsibility to pay for *her* negligence. They had no case, but she couldn't afford to sue.

I told her I'd look into it. She was going to lose her business anyway, so she figured, even if I failed, which was likely, I couldn't make it worse. She was wrong.

The investigation took me out to the Scherzeron Cruise Port. I admit it. The big galaxy cruise ships dazzled me back then. Wondering what it would be like to take a fancy trip on a fancy ship, essentially a luxury hotel, and journey into the far reaches of the Cosmos. To see the wonders that existed far beyond the realm I'd been confined to.

I'd gotten word of a fence who was moving product through the baggage handlers. I asked around. The consensus was, if you wanted to know who was moving what, to whom, and where, there was only one person to ask.

Out on the tarmac, beneath a galaxy cruise ship, a baggage handler was feeding luggage onto a loader, leading up into the belly of the beast. She was a big burly woman who looked like she could crush diamonds in her fists.

"For a PI, that's a lotta metal shit in your face. I thought you were supposed be all sneaky and incognito."

"And I thought you were supposed to be smart. You ripped off my friend."

Twice my size—basically a brick wall with arms and legs—she didn't take that too kindly. But like they say, the bigger they are, the harder they fall. And as I learned, the harder they hit.

She moved in on me, shoved me up against the baggage loader. With the force of her weight on me, it was hard to breathe.

"I ripped off who?"

If she wanted to intimidate me, it worked. But I wasn't about to back down.

"Stolen parts from a motorcycle shop. Corner of McLeeson and Jade. Cleaned her out. Heard you might know about that."

She dug her fist into my shoulder, leaned in until the ligaments near my rotator cuff started to strain. Then she pushed off me.

"I might know a thing. But you challenge my integrity again, the next case you work will be your own. Lots of cruise ships flying to lots of places. On-realm... and off. Bags get lost. A lot. Occasionally... a passenger. When it comes to stowaways? That's a whole other story."

I had to admit, I kinda liked that chick. But I couldn't let it stand. I threw all my weight into a roundhouse kick to her knee. Figured I could topple her like a stack of toy blocks. Boy, was I wrong.

She snatched my leg, then punched me in the head so hard my grandkids will have memory loss. When I came to, she handed me an icepack.

"I checked your ID," she said. "Hardwicke, huh?"

I nodded, pressed the icepack to my head.

"First case?"

I winced. "At this rate, could be my last."

"Trying to prove something?"

"That I'm dumber than I look."

"Mission accomplished."

I chuckled painfully.

"You're looking for a guy named Gregor," she said. "Rides a chopper. You know him?"

If I was hoping to be humiliated, and humiliate myself, I picked the right case.

"I heard of him."

The baggage handler extended her giant hand, helped me up. "I'm Dolores. I kinda run things around here. Unofficially.

You need intel, you got a problem, come to me. But next time... ask a little nicer."

I squinted into the late morning sun, my head throbbing. "Next time?"

"You got big brass lady balls," she said. "Start applying that brain of yours, you might actually have something."

"Thanks. I think." I handed her back the icepack. I looked around at all the galaxy cruisers. It's one thing to see them flying off into the sky. It's another to be close enough to touch one. "You ever been on one of these? Take a cruise to who knows where?"

Dolores inhaled a breath deep into her lungs, held it, craned her neck up to feel the sunshine on her face. Then exhaled.

"Me? Nah. I like my feet on the ground. You leave the realm, go way out there... no telling what kinda shit you'll find. I got enough shit down here."

Nini presses her hands into my back, wipes her eyes on my shoulder. Whistler walks in on us.

"Oh, hey," he says. "Sorry. I can come back if you..."

Nini pulls away from me. She collects her purse. "You guys talk. It's all good."

"Neen," I say. "Drinks? Next week?"

"Any night but Tuesday."

"First round's on me."

"Girl. Please. *All* the rounds are on you."

"Pick the place. I'll meet you there."

Nini leaves us alone. It's the first time Whistler and I have been here, together, in this space, on equal footing.

"How you feeling?" he asks. "You good?"

"Getting there. But, yeah. I'm good. You?"

It's awkward between us. Tension in my chest. Thick. Tight.

Whistler steps to the circular table, brushes his fingertips along various files. "I remember when I first got here. My third week. You were looking for the Cornelius file. You told me to find it, or I was fired."

I chortle. "You ripped this place apart."

"Yeah. Until I realized there *was* no Cornelius file."

"You took it seriously," I say. "That's what I was looking for."

"And watching me squirm."

I smile. "That, too."

We're saying words, but not what we mean.

"So... Mache. I've been thinking. About you and me. The cases we've worked."

My heart is pounding. Slow, heavy, agonizing beats echo in my ears.

"And?"

"It's been tough. And *amazing*. And scary and exhausting and humiliating. And thrilling. I've learned things. I've seen things I didn't even know *were* things. You changed my life, Angela. In ways I'll never forget. So for that, you have my gratitude. You helped me get to this place. To this me. Without you, I'd be... someone else, somewhere else, doing something else. For better or worse."

I don't know what to say. I couldn't if I tried. My words, my breath, are caught in my throat.

"And you were right about something."

I hope my voice is solid, but it comes out shaky. "What's that?"

"It embarrasses me to admit it, but I didn't appreciate what it took for you to build all this. Not really. You turned this agency... yourself... into a force to be reckoned with. And you raised a great kid." He shakes his head in awe. "If he's like this at eight, what'll he be at eighteen?"

I'm caught between a laugh and a cry. "I'm in no hurry to find out."

Whistler laughs. He goes to the bookshelf, leaving his final mark, now running his fingers across the spines of hardbound books I keep around. *The Complete Book of Poisons, Quentin's Manual of Investigative Techniques,* and *The Psychology of Artificial Intelligence.* "You told me some hard truths. I wasn't ready to hear them. But you were right. I wanted a piece of your life I hadn't earned. I had no right. I didn't see it then. I do now." He offers a close-mouthed smile. "I'm sorry."

And here he is, Whistler being Whistler. Growing, learning,

maturing, whether I want him to or not.

"Thanks," I say. "I'm sorry, too."

I know what's coming. Whistler doesn't want to do it, but he knows he needs to. He's not sad, exactly, but I can't tell if he's happy. Then again, this life isn't about joy. It's about having a purpose you can believe in.

"I'm leaving," he says.

It really is the end for us. I'd convinced myself I'd be able to solve the mystery of him and me before this, figure out how we could be the best versions of ourselves, together. As partners. But I knew I wouldn't. Not because I couldn't.

Because I didn't want to.

Maybe that makes me a coward. Maybe it makes me selfish, maybe even a fool. They say the truth can set you free. It can also tear you apart.

So I ask, "Opening your own shop?"

But I'm Angela Hardwicke. I'm a private investigator. I take the kinds of cases you'd think I'd take. Missing persons, arson, extortion, kidnapping, murder, corporate espionage. I also take on cases dealing with time travelers, shapeshifters, and androids. Teleportation pods and intergalactic sex traffickers. Nanobots, alternate timelines, the dreamscape, fault lines in the fabric of spacetime, and a helix of the Universe's DNA.

It's not just what I do. It's who I am.

"No," he says. "Actually... I'm joining the Wednesday Five. I'm taking Ilya's spot."

I'd rather do this job with Whistler. See what we could really be now that he's found his groove. And I've found mine with him. But if not, it'll be just me again, flying solo. Back to basics. Because whether I have a partner or not, the cases will keep on coming.

"Really?" I say. "For how long?"

"Don't know. We leave Wednesday. At five. We'll see how it goes."

The Wednesday Five. Huh. Never saw that coming. But that's Whistler for you. Whenever I think I've got him figured out, he turns the tables on me.

"I want to redo the office anyway. I appreciate you keeping the lights on. But the place could use a little more Angela Hardwicke."

I lead us toward the door. On the frosted glass, my name is stenciled in black letters.

Whistler chuckles. "Scotch in the drawer and gun at your side?"

"Or vice versa." I switch off the lights on my way out. "I'm good either way."

ABOUT THE AUTHOR

Russ colchamiro is author of *Crackle and Fire*, *Fractured Lives*, *Hot Ash*, and *Blunt Force Rising*, the first four novels in his sci-fi thriller series featuring hardboiled private detective Angela Hardwicke. Russ is also the author of the rollicking time travel/space adventure, *Crossline*, the SF/F backpacking comedy series *Finders Keepers: The Definitive Edition*, *Genius de Milo*, and *Astropalooza*, editor of the sci-fi mystery anthology *Love, Murder & Mayhem*, and co-author and -editor of the noir anthology *Murder in Montague Falls*. Russ has also contributed short stories to nearly two dozen other genre fiction anthologies.

A member of The Mystery Writers Association, The Private Eye Writers of America, Horror Writers Association, and author collective Crazy 8 Press, Russ also hosts and produces his *Russ's Rockin' Rollercoaster* podcast, where he interviews a who's who of sci-fi, crime, mystery, thriller, and horror authors.

Russ lives in New Jersey with his wife, twin ninjas, black lab, Jinx, and rambunctious cat, Callie. Follow Russ on social media:

Website: russcolchamiro.com

Instagram and Threads: @AuthorDudeRuss

Blue Sky @AuthorDudeRuss.bsky.social

YouTube: https://www.youtube.com/@authorduderuss/featured

Facebook: https://www.facebook.com/russ.colchamiro

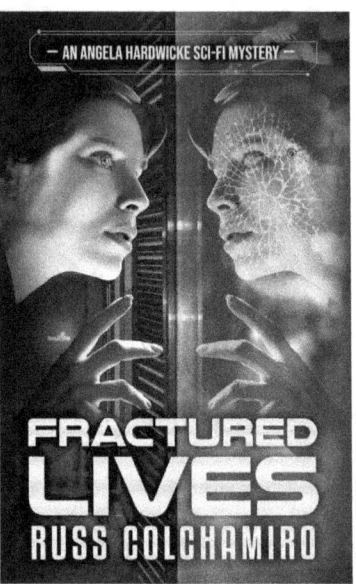

The Watson Chronicles

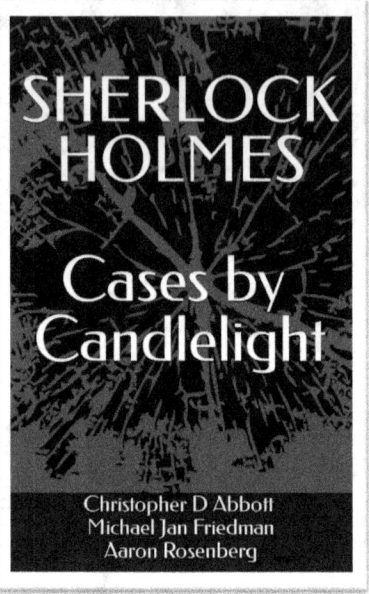

Christopher D. Abbott, Michael Jan Friedman, and Aaron Rosenberg team up to bring you a stunning collection of four new Sherlock Holmes adventures.

From the cobbled streets of smog-filled London to the sweet country air of Scotland and beyond, Sherlock Holmes and his faithful friend Dr. John Watson embark on cases that test the detective's intellectual prowess, as well as his affinity for the unusual and the bizarre.

Pull up a chair and prepare yourself to hear these cases…by candlelight.

www.ingramcontent.com/pod-product-compliance
Lightning Source LLC
Chambersburg PA
CBHW070846250626

47159CB00003B/951